For Ian, my resident football aficionado

A Striking Result

Scottish Island Escapes

Book 8

MARGARET AMATT

Cover designed by Margaret Amatt
Map drawn by Margaret Amatt
ISBN: 978-1-914575-84-6
An eBook is also available: 978-1-914575-85-3

LEANNAN
PRESS
INDEPENDENT PUBLISHER

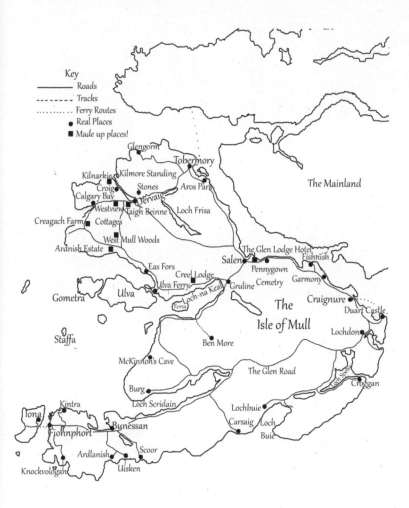

Key
—— Roads
----- Tracks
·········· Ferry Routes
• Real Places
■ Made up places!

Glengorm
Tobermory
The Mainland
Kilnarkie Kilmore Standing
Croig Stones
Calgary Bay Dervaig Aros Park
Westview Taigh Beinne Loch Frisa
Creagach Farm Cottages
Ardnish Estate West Mull Woods
Eas Fors The Glen Lodge Hotel
Creel Lodge Salen Fishnish
Ulva Ferry Pennygown
Gometra Ulva Loch-na Keal Gruline Cemetry Garmony
Eorsa Craignure
The Duart Castle
Staffa Isle of Mull Lochdon
Ben More
McKinnon's Cave
The Glen Road
Burg Old Spew? Croggan
Kintra Loch Scridain
Iona Lochbuie
Fionnphort Bunessan Carsaig Loch
Buie
Ardlanish Scoor
Knockvologan Uisken

Chapter One

Carys

Carys belted out "Heaven is a Place on Earth", repeating the chorus and humming the bits she couldn't remember – which was most of it – as she climbed what had to be the five hundred and eightieth stair. The door of Ronan's flat wasn't getting any closer and the pot plant weighed a ton. She'd grabbed it in the twenty-four-hour Asda after work on a whim but after lugging it across Glasgow it didn't seem like such a great idea anymore. Making a home with Ronan was exciting after the years of living with her chaotic family or with *friends* she'd rather forget.

She passed another landing, resisting the urge to stop, fall flat out and lie rolled in a ball for several minutes while she recovered. Soon, she'd be inside and she could grab a quick cuddle with Ronan before he left. Night shifts in the care home still made her head spin but she couldn't complain. A job was a job.

A door slammed above and footsteps approached, echoing in the cavernous stairwell. A woman spun around the corner, a handbag dangling off her arm, dark hair hanging around her shoulders.

Carys's exhausted brain took a few moments to process her.

'Hi, Jaylee,' Carys said. *What's she doing here this early?*

'Hi.'

For someone who worked in a salon and always posted beautiful pictures of hair and nails on Instagram, Jaylee was oddly dishevelled. Without a second glance, she tottered down the stairs dangerously fast and whipped around the corner into the giddying chasm of railings and concrete steps.

Two flights later, Carys hit the twenty-fourth floor. She balanced the plant, searching for her key. She had a habit of misplacing keys and gave the door an optimistic push. Her hand froze in mid-air as the door swung open. Not locked. Strange.

Carys dumped the plant and her bag beside Ronan's overalls, work boots and rucksack heaped on the floor. She'd find a place for it later, she wanted to see Ronan first. He'd be leaving in half an hour.

A shimmering blueish light emitted from the half-open bedroom door. She poked her head around. The room reminded her of a teenager's, not one she shared with a twenty-six-year-old man. His lava lamp glowed, casting its hazy light onto a pile of his clothes on the floor. He always left the room so untidy. Carys had plans to decorate it and hopefully persuade him to keep it tidier. Mess made her skin crawl.

'Hey,' she said, dipping down to kiss Ronan's forehead.

He leaned against the headboard propped in a half-sitting position, his right arm behind his head, his left hand clamped to his phone. He scrolled, glued to the screen and didn't look up or reply.

'I came back as quick as I could to see you before you left.' She sat on the bed and a waft of scent engulfed her. A pleasant scent, but all wrong. Too feminine. Her heart flickered. Her brain jumped to Jaylee.

Ronan grunted and smacked his phone onto the bed.

'I met Jaylee on the stairs.' Carys's voice was higher than usual and she fiddled with her cuff. 'I don't know what she was doing there at this time in the morning. Doesn't seem like her.'

Ronan flung back the covers and got out the far side of the bed. 'She was here. We've been shagging all night. Lucky you came back early, really.' His words slapped her where it hurt. 'Saves me telling you.'

'Telling me what?'

'We're finished.'

'Why?' She stared at him. Everything was going so well, wasn't it?

'I let you move in here so we could spend time together, then you piss off on night shifts and I never see you. No wonder I'm forced to go elsewhere.'

Heat fired in Carys's cheeks. Was that all he was after? 'But, Ronan, I tried to get back early. And when you're not here I do loads for you.'

'Oh yeah, like tidying my stuff away so I can never find it? And what about the cooking you said you'd do?'

'I always make dinner when I'm not at work.' Her brow furrowed. She couldn't believe her ears. She cooked every day. Left to his own devices, Ronan blew all his wages on beers and pizza.

'No, you make rabbit food. You never make anything I actually like. I'm done with it. I can't live like this.'

Blood pounded in her ears as Ronan whipped past her towards the shower. As it clanked into action, her mind followed. What just happened? She was being dumped for what? Being too healthy. Trying to make the place nicer for them both. Why was the world so screwed up?

And what did she expect? Weren't all relationships the same? Just when things seemed great, the bomb dropped.

She grabbed her rucksack and stuffed her clothes into it. Tears pricked when she saw the pot plant by the front door. She'd have to leave it. So much for her new home. Closing the door behind her, she hit the stairs. At least she wouldn't have to do this trek ever again. She wanted to cry until her core ached but she knew from experience that would only help for a little while, and she needed to be miles from here when the floodgates opened.

Now was the time to phone friends, commiserate, and let them call Ronan every name under the sun, but she didn't dare. Most of her friends had fallen out with her after a previous break-up. Another shitstorm where she'd been nothing more than a pawn. She shuddered at the repercussions. That bastard of an ex might have got what he wanted, but she'd ended up with compromising photographs all over social media and not one person who believed her innocence. She'd cut ties with them all.

If the agency bosses ever saw those pictures her job was up the spout.

What a talent she had for picking the wrong people. *What's wrong with me?*

She clicked her chinstrap and hopped onto her bike, her pride and joy. Now for a ride across Glasgow from Ronan's high-rise in Maryhill to her dad's place in Possil. She stifled a yawn as she kicked off. What would she tell Dad? With him, Kat and the four kids filling every inch of the flat, one more would push them to breaking point but did she have a choice?

Her dad wouldn't turn her away. He'd never have her back on the streets, after saving her from that fate when she was a tiny tot. If he was roused enough, he'd want to go around and kick Ronan's door down. But he probably wouldn't survive the climb to Ronan's apartment without his lungs packing in.

Grim flats in the ugly built-up area towered around. She searched for somewhere to chain her bike. People here could be the salt of the earth, help you out in a pinch and watch your back, but they'd also be the first to nab something this shiny and claim it as their own. She wouldn't put it past some of the neighbours to carry metal cutters.

Her family were in a ground-floor flat and her ears tuned in to the unmistakable sounds of Kat yelling at the kids to get ready for school, their furious protests and a thump like someone had thrown something heavy in disgust.

She knocked on the door. More thumps and shouts followed and a loud yell of 'Someone's at the door.' Carys recognised her half-sister Daisy's voice.

'Answer it then, instead of shouting at me!' Kat bawled in return.

The door flew open and a face peered around. Carys raised her eyebrows. She hadn't seen Daisy for a few weeks and a scary transformation had taken place. The baby-faced twelve year old could suddenly be mistaken for sixteen.

'Hi, Daisy. You look so grown up,' said Carys. An anxious pang assaulted her tummy. Wasn't it a bit much to be dolled up like that for school? Carys remembered doing the same thing not so long ago, trying to be grown up, desperate to prove herself. At least Daisy had a mum to guide her. Since Carys's stepmum, Joanne, had left, she'd had no one. She bit her lip; the punch of emotion that always accompanied thoughts of Joanne swooped through her. Losing Ronan was nothing compared to Joanne. She was the only mum Carys had ever known.

'Hi,' said Daisy, then yelled, 'Dad, it's Carys.'

Kat came out of the living room carrying a half-dressed child, Donny, the youngest. Only four but already a little terror. 'Oh, it's you,' she said.

'Hi, Kat,' said Carys. 'Do you need a hand there?'

'I'm fine,' muttered Kat, slinking into a bedroom.

Carys's dad, Lee McTeague, lounged across the sofa with his feet on one end and the remote control in his hand, flicking through the channels.

'Hey, Dad.'

'What you doing here, lass?' He glanced up, patting his belly. 'Come give your old man a hug.'

Carys leaned over and he pulled her into a giant bear hug that almost broke her back at this funny angle.

'Can I stay for a bit?' said Carys, biting back the tears that threatened with the burst of affection.

'Of course, lass. What's up?'

'Ronan and me… It didn't work out.'

'You've been dumped again,' muttered Daisy, grabbing a book and leaving the room.

Carys nodded at the blank wall. *Yup. Again.*

'You think we've got room here?' said Kat, standing in the doorway with her hands on her hips. 'I need to get the kids to school.'

'Aye, we'll always have room for my big girl.'

Carys took in the trail of devastation left by four children and a dad who didn't lift a finger. 'It won't be for long.' She dropped her rucksack and lifted some dirty dishes from the coffee table, almost invisible under the plates, cups, old food, paper, magazines and toys. 'I'm on nightshift, so I can sleep on someone's bed while they're out. Or the floor. Or anywhere. I just don't want to be out on the street.'

'No, lass. You'll never be out on the street,' said Lee. 'It'll never come to that. I'll not stand for it. But it's high time you got somewhere more stable. Find a better bloke, someone like your old man.'

Carys gave a wry smile as she took the plates into the kitchen. *Holy shit.* She stopped dead. A bomb exploding wouldn't have caused this much damage. Placing her hand to her forehead, she drew in a sigh. Now Kat was off on the school run, she would give the place a quick clean before grabbing some shut-eye. Poor Kat. Lee was protective of his kids but being hands-on had never been his thing – neither had cleaning. No way did Carys want to find a man like him. 'I'd rather not have one at all,' she muttered.

She needed to look into renting a cheap place. She'd spent quite a bit on a new bike and a tablet. Maybe it was stupid. But the bike gave her freedom and the tablet let her collect recipes and write up ideas, and didn't take up as much room as the heaps of notebooks she'd kept previously, that got lost between houses or chucked out by flatmates or exes who didn't bother to find out if they were important or not. In her free moments, she dreamt big and was researching a book on how to change people into healthy beings, one human at a time, but not with faddy diets and crushing exercise regimes; she wanted to free people's souls and help them discover beauty in themselves.

'Get me a bacon roll, lass,' shouted her dad.

Carys set the water running in the sink as she hunted for bacon in the horrendous fridge. What the hell was she supposed to cook it in without starting the great fire of Glasgow? Everything was caked in grease and solidified fat.

'Dad, how would you like me to get some new stuff?' said Carys five minutes later, bacon roll in hand, shoulders sagging in relief that she'd managed it without setting off any smoke alarms, if the flat even had them.

'What new stuff?'

'Avocado toast is delicious.'

Lee roared with laughter. 'Sounds like you want me to eat an ancient bathroom suite. I'll give it a miss.'

'Dad… Maybe—'

'Shh, what's this?' He grabbed the remote and upped the TV volume to deafening.

Carys followed his sight-line. A male newscaster was speaking. In the corner was a photograph of a footballer with his arms in the air like he'd just scored.

'No fucking way.' Lee scraped back his grey hair and pinned it to his scalp, grinning at the TV.

'A report has now confirmed that Scotland international and Celtic striker Troy Copeland sustained serious injuries in a car crash earlier in the week. The driver reportedly walked away with minor injuries. A spokesperson for Mr Copeland said the injuries included a broken femur, a dislocated shoulder and several broken ribs. A medical expert said on this programme earlier, "How and where the femur was broken will be crucial in his recovery." It's understood that Copeland has undergone several surgical procedures and close friends say he's lucky to be alive. It is now clear he'll miss the cup final and possibly the beginning of next season. The spokesperson stated the thirty-year-old footballer, whose glittering career has seen him score over sixty goals in club matches, is now in a stable condition.'

'Excellent,' said Lee.

Carys frowned. 'Why is it excellent? It sounds like that poor guy is badly hurt.'

'That "poor guy" is a bastard of a striker. If he's out of action, that'll help our chances next season. Ya beauty.' Lee punched the air with his thick fist. 'Rangers for the win!'

Carys knew better than to argue. Football was her dad's religion. Sometimes in this city, it seemed like the root of all evil. Carys lifted the remaining dishes from the coffee table and set to work cleaning the kitchen, a far cry from the morning she'd planned.

Chapter Two

Troy

Troy stopped the video playback on his phone, wincing at the pain in his shoulder.

'Can you quit watching every report about yourself?' Pippa Hayes raised her diamanté encrusted sunglasses and pushed them on top of her head, pinning back her platinum blonde hair and squinting into the line of traffic backed up at the lights. On her slender ring finger, a solitaire glinted in the May sunshine. That engagement ring cost a fortune but if it marked Pippa as his, he'd pay it twice over. When they'd met in Giovanni's bar two years ago, she'd caught his eye and several other guys on the team too. But he'd won and here she was, driving his car, wearing his ring and taking him home.

The implications of his injuries and the *what might have beens* made vomit rise in his throat. But he had Pippa. If anyone could help in his recovery, it was her.

'Chris wants me to make a public statement, but what should I say?'

'The truth,' said Pippa, revving the Porsche closer to the traffic lights. The white Georgian buildings in the crescent gleamed in the sun and the full-leafed trees cast dappled shadows over the bay windows. Troy stared at them. Facing the truth meant admitting these injuries might end his career. At thirty, that day was looming ever closer but now… No. He would return. Football was his life. His only life.

'I'm not sure what they want to hear,' he said. 'No one has a crystal ball. I just have to make sure I train hard and—'

'Troy, you can't stand.' Pippa glared at him. 'You're not allowed to drive, you can't walk, you're propped up by crutches and your leg is in that thing. How do you think you're going to train?'

He glowered at the robot-like contraption his leg was strapped into, extending from his hip to a flat-footed boot. Its likeness to a prosthetic leg was humbling. He was lucky to have come out with all his limbs. 'I meant do my physio,' he muttered. Pippa was telling the truth but he hated every damn ugly word that suggested he couldn't do it.

'Do the physio, do whatever,' she said. 'I can't believe this has happened.' Her voice cracked.

Troy glanced over. Was she crying? She never cried. Sometimes she screamed but crying wasn't her. She was tough. 'Hey.' He stretched out his hand, but she pulled away, gripping the steering wheel. 'This isn't easy for either of us,' he said. 'It's not exactly a picnic for me. But I've got you. We can get through this.'

She harumphed but didn't reply. Was she gathering herself? Regrouping? Troy gave her the time. She turned away, clearly not wanting to be caught crying or upset. He stared out the window as the familiar streets of Glasgow passed by. The Anniesland Cross junction sprawled before them and he spotted an aeroplane high overhead. Maybe his parents were aboard. They'd rushed home to ascertain he was still alive, but Pippa had been edgy around them. They'd picked up on the vibe and flown back to Spain rather than accompany him home.

He sighed. They'd never been the most concerned parents but he'd seen them right, buying them their dream Spanish villa. Perfect. Only nothing was perfect any more. These injuries could end the dream. Troy had enough money to live comfortably for a long time, but without football, what was he? Nothing.

Troy held his leg as they rolled along The Switchback Road. He'd had injuries before but this was a whole new level of pain. All the way to Bearsden, he clenched his teeth. Pippa steered into the cul-de-sac of modern houses, gated and sparkling with mono-blocked driveways – clean enough to eat your dinner off – gleaming cars, and gardens of perfect green, smooth-edged lawns and topiary bushes at every door.

They rounded the bend towards his millionaire mansion. 'Fuck's sake.' He threw his good hand in the air. Outside his gate was a clamouring crowd of photographers. 'Seriously?' Couldn't they give him some peace?

'Oh Jesus,' said Pippa.

The Porsche had blackened side windows, but Troy pulled his baseball cap low and kept his head down as he zapped open the gates. Pippa edged through the throng. Troy hit close on the remote as soon as they were in, not checking if the paps had moved. If one of them got crushed, then more fool the idiots for being here. He pressed the garage door button and they waited for it to rise.

Inside the garage was a side entrance to the house. *Thank Christ,* because he didn't want the paps to witness what happened next. A few weeks ago he could run ten laps of the pitch, sprint one hundred metres in under twelve seconds, lift weights and score goals from incredible angles. Now he couldn't even get out of a car.

But he had to try. Opening the door was almost impossible. He nudged it, expecting Pippa to be there any second to get it. 'Damn it,' he growled. Where was she? He shuffled himself around on the seat, frowning. Had she already gone inside? By herself? *Jesus Christ.*

So much for the poster-boy footballer. What was he now? Fumbling with the crutches, he struggled to get one under his bad shoulder. With tremendous effort, he hauled himself towards the side door, lurching and just managing to keep himself upright by leaning on the wall. Nauseating pain overcame him for a moment and his breathing grew ragged. He stood panting. This couldn't get any worse. And his teammates thought he was lucky to be alive. Even the one who'd thought it was a good idea to test his new Ferrari on a country road at 160mph. The same one who'd walked away with a few bruises while Troy had at least six months of recovery time and no guarantees. How to change a life in a few seconds. If only changing it back was that fast.

Troy stalled, allowing his breathing to even out before taking the two steps into the side corridor and limping into the grand hall. Pippa was waiting, tapping her foot on the polished floor. Behind her, the enormous staircase swept around towards the balcony style corridor. His blood ran cold. *Shit.* Why had he turned down the home assessment the hospital had offered him? This house was going to be impossible in his state. It was one nightmare after another.

'Right.' Pippa folded her arms, facing him. 'You're home. Now, I have to go.'

'Go?' He frowned. The effort of standing was getting to him. *Must sit… and soon.*

'Yes, Troy. I know this is bad timing but really, there was never going to be a good time.'

'I don't follow.'

Pippa fiddled with the solitaire, spinning it around a few times, then tugged it off and put it on the ornate oak plant stand by the door. 'I wanted to tell you before the accident.'

'You're breaking up with me?' Hot rage boiled in Troy's gut. 'Now? After everything we've been through?'

'We haven't been through anything,' she snapped. 'You have. And I'm sorry. I'm sorry this happened to you, but I can't do it.'

'Why the hell not?' Raging heat and nausea battled inside him. He needed to know but at the same time, he wanted to curl into a ball and cry. They'd had it all planned. Next year, the wedding, after that, kids. Where had things gone wrong?

'We're just not right together.' She picked at a nail.

'Seriously? That's it?'

'Yes.'

'What about your stuff?'

'I took it when you were in hospital. I thought your parents might have noticed and given you the head's up.'

'What? No… Where will you go?'

She checked her watch. 'I need to leave. I'm getting picked up in five minutes but I don't want to wade through those bloody paps.'

Troy wanted to smash all the glass in the house, then burn the place. How could she do this? His parents had left because of her and now she was leaving him too. But his mind and his body had lost the fight. He hobbled towards the massive glass doors into the living area and barely made it inside before he slumped onto the sofa with a groan. His body ached, his head hurt and his heart shrivelled. Closing his eyes, he hoped he'd never have to open them again.

'Troy,' said Pippa from the door.

'What?' He didn't open his eyes.

'I'm sorry about the timing, but honestly, this is something I should have done a long time ago.'

He opened his eyes and held out his hands. 'No, it isn't. You just can't stand it that I'm not... in one fucking piece anymore.'

'Whatever, Troy. Make up whatever crap you want to hear, that's what you're good at, listening to yourself.'

'You talk a lot of shit.'

'Do I? I don't come out with half the stupid stuff you do.'

'What did you call me?' He glared at her. *Stupid?* The word fired the rage in his belly.

'I have to go,' she said.

'Seriously, you can't leave me like this.'

'I'm not going to be your babysitter,' she said. 'You can hire someone to do that. You should have accepted the help they offered you in hospital, but oh no, you knew best.'

'Because I thought you'd be here. You have to at least help me find someone before you go. Call an agency or something.'

'Do it yourself. Or phone your agent. I'm done slaving for you. You might have been a great footballer but you're also a lazy arsehole.' She strutted out.

Troy's mind was willing to follow and have it out with her but his body wouldn't move. Slaving? Was that how she saw life with him? Lazy? *Bitch.*

He woke his phone and pressed the contacts icon. Chris's photo appeared. He hit it, waiting for the call to connect.

'Hello, Troy. Is that you home?'

'Yes. I'm home.'

'And have you decided what you want to say in your statement?'

'Not yet. I need some other help.'

'Oh yeah, what's up?'

'Pippa's left me.'

'What?' Chris roared. A deadly hush followed. 'That won't look good for either of you. Why did she leave?'

'Who knows. I'm lazy apparently. Can you fucking believe it?'

'Right, well, we might need some damage limitation there. I'll speak to the press officer. You didn't have a fight or any kind of public bust-up, did you?'

'Nope. She just walked out.'

'Ok. Probably the best way. It's bad timing on top of everything else though.'

'You can say that again. In fact, that's why I'm phoning. I need someone to help out.' The word carer jammed in his throat. He didn't want to say it. It made him sound like he was crippled for life.

'You have a cleaner,' said Chris.

'Yeah. But I need someone who can help with everything.'

'What about your parents?'

'They've gone back to Spain. I need someone now.'

'Haven't you got a sister?'

'I do, but she won't want this job.' Troy didn't want that either. They weren't close. Nina had a beautiful suburban Glasgow home and an easy lifestyle courtesy of him and that was the extent of their relationship. Her tear-stained face in the hospital had been the most emotionally connected he'd felt to her in years, but even then, he hadn't known what to say. 'She's too sensitive.'

'Well, I'll investigate some care agencies and send you a list. In the meantime, get thinking about what you want to say to the press. And I'll arrange for the counsellor to get in touch. I think it would be sensible. You've been through a lot.'

'No. I don't want that.'

'It would be a good idea. You've been in football for a long time, you've had a great career. This won't be easy.'

'I'm coming back, ok? Stop talking like it's over. Football is still my career.'

'Yes, Troy. Try not to think too far ahead right now, but consider counselling, especially after what just happened with Pippa.'

No chance. Troy stood his ground. The last thing he needed was someone rummaging about in his empty head. He ended the call and another wave of nausea spilled over him. Chris could send him a list of carers as long as his arm, but what would he do with it? He couldn't read it. He was on his own. The world he knew had slipped away and he was barely treading water. He leaned back on the sofa and screwed up his face, damming the emotions threatening to rupture him. Was Troy Copeland finished?

Chapter Three

Carys

Carys threw her arms in the air, jigging left, then right. As she bent to touch her toes, she let out a laugh. 'Staying Alive' rocked from the sound system.

'Keep bopping, Mrs D.' She clapped as ninety-four-year-old Mrs Dowey did her best Zimmer moves. When the song ended, Carys cheered. 'You guys are the best.'

The elderly residents shuffled back to their seats, getting comfy after their workout. 'I'm fitter than I've ever been,' said Mrs Dowey. 'I wish I'd learned these moves seventy years ago.'

A colleague pushed her head around the door. 'Dana wants to see you.'

Big boss Dana? Carys pursed her lips. What did she want? Had those awful pictures resurfaced? Maybe her temporary contract was being renewed. Or was she being pulled up for introducing Zimmer-Zumba and generally disturbing the peace?

Carys put on the TV for the residents and headed for Dana's office.

Dana was shutting down her computer with her coat over her arm when Carys got there. 'I was just coming to find you. I had a call from the agency earlier. They want to talk to you about another job.'

Carys fiddled with the edge of her tunic. 'Am I not staying on here then?'

Dana closed her bag and looked up. 'I'd love to offer you a permanent contract but I'm at the mercy of the council. See what the agency have to say.'

'Ok, thank you.'

'I'm heading off. Use the phone in here if you like.'

Carys waited until Dana had left before taking the swivel seat behind her desk. She straightened her back as she grasped the phone.

After the pleasantries, the administrator said, 'We have another job on the books if you're interested. It's a six-month contract with no chance of renewal. It's a live-in position. Days off, holidays and free time are to be negotiated.'

Carys bit her lip. Live in for six months? It sounded like someone who was terminally ill. Someone in that situation would desperately need care, but could she handle it? Without meaning to, she always got emotionally involved with clients; how could she say goodbye? It was bad enough when a resident died.

'Er, what's the remit?'

'Ok, we can't divulge much information. If you take on the role, you'll have the opportunity to meet the client and see if the position suits before committing to the contract. You won't have much time to decide though; the client wants an immediate start. What I can tell you is that the client is incapacitated through injury. You're required to provide general care throughout the day, cooking, laundry, general admin, driving to appointments and assistance with physiotherapy.'

'Ok.'

'The only problem is your age.'

'Why is that a problem?'

'The client wants someone older. Twenty-four is too young to be experienced for this kind of role. Unfortunately, we haven't got anybody older willing to live in.'

'What kind of money are we talking about?'

'On top of the wages, you'll be given full board and a private space in the house to use as your own. The wages will be fifteen hundred a week before tax.'

Pound signs lit up in her eyes as she computed how much fifteen hundred pounds a week equated to over six months. She'd never dreamed of so much money.

'The client needs care straightaway and we don't have any other options. This contract is big for us, so make sure you do your best at the meeting. I'm pulling you from your other job immediately and you can come over tomorrow morning and sign the preliminary documents. Then you can meet the client.'

'What if they don't like me?'

'Make sure they do.'

'But I don't know the client's name or the address or anything. I assume it's somewhere in Glasgow? I only have a bike. If it's somewhere else, I'll have to organise transport.'

'The client lives in Glasgow. When you get here and sign the necessary documents, I'll give you the address.'

Why the urgency and secrecy? What if she didn't get it? Would they strike her from the books? Finding an agency to take her on after she'd been let go would be next to impossible. Would they black mark her?

'You won't believe the job offer I just had,' she told Mrs Dowey as she helped her into bed later that evening. 'It doesn't seem real.' She pulled the cover over her and explained.

'Oh goodness, all that money. I'll miss you if you get it. But it sounds like a good move. Money doesn't buy happiness but it definitely helps, especially when you're young. You're like a bright little bird, you need space to fly.'

'I just hope they like me.' She didn't want to think about the alternatives, but one way or another she wouldn't be back.

'I'm sure they will. Just be yourself.'

'Night night, sleep tight.' She patted the old lady's hand and went to check on the next resident.

*

Carys set off for home the next morning. She'd only have time for a quick shower and no sleep.

'Hi,' she said, pushing open the door to the morning pandemonium. She chipped in, helping get the kids ready for school as she waited for her turn in the shower.

'Mum's really annoying me,' Daisy said. 'She thinks I'm too young for a boyfriend.'

'Twelve is quite young,' said Carys. 'And your mum's just looking out for you. Better to have one who drives you mad than not have one at all.'

'Is your mum dead?' asked Donny.

Carys pulled his jumper over his head. 'I don't know where my real mum is. I never met her.'

'Is it true she left you in a bag at the side of the road?' said Iris.

'Yup, it's true,' said Carys.

'In a bag?' said Donny. 'On a road?'

Carys ruffled his hair. 'Sounds like a scary story, doesn't it?'

'So, did Dad find you?' asked Donny.

He had, but not until she was two and he'd learned about her existence. It sounded so much more sensational than the stark reality. 'A man walking his dog found me and called the police.'

'That was lucky,' said Donny.

'Yup. Now, off you go, you don't want to keep your mum waiting or be late for nursery.'

She supposed it was lucky she'd been found. But it didn't answer the question of why she'd been dumped in the first place.

Now, she had to shower, get to the agency and sign the papers.

Twenty minutes later, Jenny handed her a printed document. 'I need you to read and sign this, then I'll give you the address.'

'And do I get to know who the client is?'

'The client will do the introductions once they've met you and decided if you're suitable. And, Carys, you really have to do your best. We can't offer the client anyone else at the present time and we can't afford to lose a contract as big as this.'

'Ok, I'll try.' But her shoulders tightened and she chewed her lip as she read over the confidentiality document. What the hell was all this for?

'Great.' Jenny scanned over the document, then handed Carys a card. 'This is the address.'

7 Redshaw Park, Bearsden

Bearsden? The suburban home of millionaires. No way would she be good enough for someone who lived there.

'If the client is happy with you, then the job will start immediately. If not… Well, let's hope for the best.'

Tingles of panic rippled through Carys as she unlocked her bike. What if she didn't get it? What if the client was horrible? Could she bear it for six months? Maybe if she forced herself to concentrate on the money.

She cruised into the traffic and pedalled towards Bearsden. It was easily five miles from the city centre and was going to take at least thirty minutes. So much for the client being in Glasgow. That was a stretch. Still, this was a good workout. As she got closer, she checked the directions on her phone. High walls and hedges marked the entrance to Redshaw Park. Carys's eyes popped. She couldn't live here. Not even for six months. She had holey jeans and a t-shirt from Primark.

A throng of people gathered at the gate of number seven. Her hands shook as she dismounted.

'Hi.' A man approached her, bold as brass. 'Can I ask you a few questions? Are you visiting Troy Copeland? Perhaps you can tell me about that.'

'Er, no,' said Carys. 'Who?' She scanned around for the entry buzzer but the man stuck to her.

'Are you working for him? Are you the cleaner? Perhaps when you're done, you could give me some insight on how he's feeling.'

Carys pressed the button and waited.

'Yes,' a gruff voice replied.

Carys dipped closer to the mouthpiece, hoping the man wouldn't overhear. 'It's Carys McTeague from Calvert Care Agency.'

'I'll open the gate, the front door's open. Come straight in. Don't let the paps follow.'

'The whats?'

'The reporters.'

'Oh, ok.'

The huge black gates clicked and opened smoothly. Seriously? The pedestrian side gate would have been fine, not these humongous things. She sidled in like an ant entering the land of the giants, wheeling the bike across the perfectly laid mono-blocks and resting it on the house front. Without looking back, she climbed the steps and took a deep breath. Cameras flashed behind as she fumbled with the giant brass door handle. The black door opened and Carys entered the outer porch, then slipped through a set of glass double doors into a vast room with a gleaming wood floor and a wide sweeping staircase. A man limped towards her, propped on a set of crutches, his skin ashen.

Her heart hiccupped so fast it might jump out on the floor and slip him up. This man was too young, too handsome and far too damned hot to be her new employer. There must have been a mistake. Who the hell was he?

Chapter Four

Troy

A vision in ripped jeans and a flimsy white top, with a pink hoody tied round her waist, and navy Converse stood in Troy's hallway. He raised his eyebrow at the black and shocking pink cycle helmet as she unclipped it, revealing wispy strawberry blonde hair that matched her overall appearance of fragility. One breath of wind might knock her over. This was the new carer? Christ on a bike. Had Chris lost his mind agreeing to someone this inexperienced?

'I, eh, I'm Carys.' She slunk forward and put out her hand. Troy balanced on his crutches, stretched out his arm and shook. A pink tinge covered her freckled cheeks, but her grip was strong. Thankfully, he'd extended his good arm because she almost dislocated his wrist. Not as delicate as she looked then. So, when Chris said the agency had found someone younger than his brief, they'd meant several years younger, not two or three.

'Troy,' he said. His head hurt. Everything hurt. Even doped up with painkillers it hurt. He hadn't eaten since yesterday – making food meant too long on his feet. He hadn't slept – sleeping was impossible; there was no position that wasn't painful. 'If you take a seat in the living room, we can… chat.' Though fuck knew what about. He needed someone who knew what to do. He couldn't guide her.

'Yes. Absolutely.' Her eyes roamed around. Troy struggled with his crutches. What was she gawping at? Or more to the point, what did she see? This was what money could buy. A palace fit for a king and his ten kids. But who lived in it? One sad, lonely man.

Carys skirted around the plant stand towards the chaise in the corner and sat. Troy frowned and opened his mouth.

'So.' Carys placed her hands on her knee. 'Did you read my CV? I have all the skills you asked for.'

Troy pulled a side pout. Did he read her CV indeed? Chance would be a fine thing. He could barely read his own name if it turned up somewhere unexpected. And what was she doing there? No one had ever sat there before. That chaise just decorated the minimalist hallway. 'My agent said your CV was cool.' He furrowed his brow. 'Are you ok?'

'Fine. Why?'

'Well, I just wondered why you're sitting there.'

She glanced around, then stood. 'Would you prefer me to stand? Is this your seat? Sorry.'

'No, this is the hallway. I meant for you to go into the living room. It's around here through the doors.'

'It is? Oh... Right.' She moved around the corner and peered through the French doors. 'In here... Oh, I see now. How did I miss it?'

Troy hobbled up behind her, his head whirling, the room spinning. Was he going to keel over? 'Go in, it's easier if you open the door,' he said. This was ridiculous. How could a girl like this do everything he needed her to? Would she simply goggle at the house, then run off and gossip about what she'd seen to all her mates?

She pushed the doors open and gaped around, her mouth hanging wide. 'Oh my god. I mean, can I sit here?' She pointed to a giant plush sofa.

'Anywhere.'

She sank down and placed her cycling helmet next to her. Troy gingerly eased himself into a chair. Jesus, did he need to sit.

'Do you need a hand?' she said.

'No.' He propped his crutches beside him. 'Did you come on a bike?'

'Yes.'

He frowned. 'But can you drive a car?'

'Yes.' She ran her palms over her jeans, smoothing them down.

'Good, because if I give you this job, you'll have to drive me. I'm not allowed to drive yet.'

'I should think not,' said Carys. 'What happened to you?'

'Car accident.'

'Oh no. You definitely won't want to drive for a while then.'

'I wasn't driving. I was a passenger.'

'Even worse.' She pulled a face.

'Why? Are you not an experienced driver?' How could she be? She looked like she might have passed her test about three minutes before she came in.

'Not very experienced, but I passed first time.'

Troy arched an eyebrow; he didn't dare ask if she'd driven at all since passing.

'Well,' said Troy. 'I'd like to... you know...' A woozy sensation washed over him.

'Talk about what the job will entail?' she asked.

'Yeah. You can take notes if you like.' That's what his team manager always said, but Troy didn't, of course. He was notorious for messing around or turning up late – anything to stop them from asking him to write something on the board.

'You're too big a dickhead to write it for yourself,' his teammates would jeer. 'Which minion are you gonna have do it today?' Troy would lob the pen at someone and play along. Once he was on the pitch it was a different story; that was where he was king and his body could do the talking.

He shuffled into a semi-comfortable position – with the bones in his body playing Kerplunk, it was difficult to find any pose that didn't feel like he was about to topple into a splintered pile. Carys stared around wide-eyed and smiley. 'I'll remember,' she said.

'Ok. So, first, everything you see here is confidential, right? One word of anything gets out and your career's over.'

'Er... ok. I signed the papers. I'll not say a thing about... anything.'

'Good. Privacy is important, right?'

'Of course.' She nodded, her eyes wide, her front teeth nipping her lower lip. Crap, that must have sounded completely shitty, but his head was about to burst.

'Well, here's the deal. I can't do squat. Standing for long periods hurts, sitting for long periods hurts. I can't cook; it takes me hours to get up and down stairs; getting dressed is a bloody carry on. But the most important thing is my training. I need help to get through my physio so I can get back to training.'

'What kind of training?' asked Carys.

'My football training.'

Carys gave him a grave nod. 'Ah, I see. You love football, do you? So does my dad. He's a fanatical Rangers supporter.'

Heat rose in his neck and he balled his fists. Either she didn't know who he was or she was messing with him. 'Right.' He needed to call Chris. This was ridiculous. It wasn't going to work. She was even more clueless than him.

'So, doesn't anyone else live here?'

Troy shook his head. *Ow.*

Carys bit her lip like she was trying not to stare or say what was going through her mind.

'Ok. So you like football and that's a big priority,' she said. 'What about your work? Do you have a job I need to take you to or help you with?'

Troy exhaled a little and looked towards the window doors and the view to the long ultra-perfect lawn. Any minute now, he was going to either faint or throw up. 'Football is my job.'

'Oh.' Carys's eyes widened and she leaned forward. 'You're a footballer?'

'Yes. I'm Troy Copeland.' His insides cringed as the words gushed out. *I'm Troy Copeland! Ugh!* What must he sound like?

'Ok,' said Carys. 'Sorry, I don't know much about football.'

'I'm a striker for Celtic, and I was the team captain... until this.' He glared at his leg.

'Celtic?' She rubbed her forehead. 'Oh god. My dad is going to kill me.'

'Er...' Troy threw out his good arm. 'It doesn't sound like this job's for you.'

'Oh, no.' Carys waved her hands. 'It's ok. I can make it ok. What else do I need to know?'

Troy gritted his teeth. Was there any point continuing? How could he get her out? This was Chris's job. Why wasn't he here? In fact, why had none of his teammates come over to see him yet? He'd told them all what happened with Pippa but not one saw fit to check he was ok.

'Technically, I'm still playing for the club, though, obviously, I can't do much right now.' He rubbed his forehead and half closed his eyes. 'I'll need to use the medical and physio rooms and attend training when it starts up again. You'll have to take me. Then you'll have to speak to my physio and work out how to get me back in shape. You need to buy and cook… food and you know?' He closed his eyes and leaned back. Why wasn't Chris doing this? He needed to rest or eat or…

'Troy! Troy!'

His eyes didn't want to open. When they did, he blinked. His head was leaning back and both his feet were rested on a footstool. How? What? His neck hurt as he tried to straighten.

'That's it,' said a gentle voice and a hand took hold of the back of his head, helping him sit forward.

'What happened?'

'You fainted.'

Troy squinted up to see Carys on the arm of the chair, still holding his head. This felt almost as disorientating as waking up after the accident.

'Did I?'

'Here,' she said. 'You should drink this.' She handed him a glass of orange juice. 'And if you can manage, try and eat this.' An energy bar landed in his hand. 'I couldn't find much in the cupboards.'

'My… er… parents were staying.' He sipped the drink. 'They obviously didn't buy stuff for me coming home.' They thought Pippa would do that, just like he had.

'That's all something I can do,' said Carys. 'If I get the job, I mean. Do you have a specific diet? If you have any special requirements, I'm happy to learn.'

'Lots of carbs, preferably unrefined, protein for breakfast, plenty of fruit and veg. There's very little I won't eat. Right now, I'll literally eat anything.'

'Ok, you sit there and eat that. I'll go make you something.'

'But I haven't given you the job yet.'

'It's ok. Even if I don't get it, I'm not going to leave you like this.' She shifted off the sofa and bustled out the door. Troy ate the energy bar and drank the juice as she'd said, then leaned back with a sigh.

Carys may look little more than a college kid but she'd kept her cool and sorted him out. Maybe she'd be ok after all. Did he have a choice? How long would it take to find someone else? Maybe it'd be best to take her on and see how things went.

It felt like ages before she came back, but it wasn't. Time had slowed to almost dead. Sitting around like this was his worst nightmare.

'Here we go.' She laid a tray on the chair next to him with bowls full of pasta, cooked veg and nuts. 'It looks random, but it'll get you some energy.' She sat on the opposite sofa, watching.

'I couldn't bear to cook last night. Well, I can't.' He started to devour the food.

'I get that,' she said. 'Did someone drop out? I mean, shouldn't someone have been here when you got back?'

'Na. Things changed,' Troy muttered through his food.

'Well, I'm trained in basic physio and I'm really interested in dietary planning.' She put up her hands and her pale irises glittered. 'I'm currently developing my own programme for a healthy mind and body and I think it's something that'll work really well with you.'

Troy cocked his head, taking another forkful of pasta. 'You mean I currently have an unhealthy mind?' How could he not say it? It was true. His brain didn't work properly. Here was a girl who looked straight out of school, had little further education, but could develop programmes. He barely knew the meaning of the word let alone how to set one up.

'Absolutely not,' she said. 'But after injuries like you've had, your brain will be under a lot of stress.'

Good answer. She had a point. Hopefully she wouldn't get talking to Chris. The two of them would have him packed off to counselling ASAP.

'I'm doing a lot of reading and research into ways to make the brain happier and healthier and that, in turn, impacts on life as a whole. I think you'd benefit from that.'

'Cool.'

Carys beamed and a little tingle of pleasure crept through his weary bones and aching body. If he agreed to take her on, he could look forward to that sight for the next few months.

'And you know the position is live in because I train long hours. Does that suit?'

'Yes, it's fine.'

Troy finished off his last mouthful. 'That was good, thanks. I feel more like myself now.'

'Great,' she said. 'I'll clear it away.'

Troy breathed slowly and deeply as she tidied around him. She beamed as she lifted the tray.

'Back in a sec. Is there anything else you fancy?' Her cheeks reddened slightly and he looked away.

'No thanks.'

This was it, wasn't it? He should offer her the job. Having strangers about was part and parcel of his life. He was always working with new teammates, physios, trainers, coaches, doctors, but none of them were as up close and personal as she was going to get. She'd be in his house, driving him places, knowing his every move.

She returned to the room and rubbed her hands together. Glancing around, she sat back on the opposite sofa.

'Ok. How about I offer you the job… on a temporary thing to see how you get on and if it suits me… and you?'

'Sounds great,' she said.

'Cool.' He nodded. His legs felt stiff from sitting for so long. 'Would you like to see your bedroom?'

'Yes. Though I'm sure it'll be fine.'

'I might have put you in the basement.'

She gaped for a second, then a smile spread across her face. Troy matched it.

He grabbed his crutch.

'You can stay if you want,' she said. 'If you tell me where, I can look myself.'

'I need to move.'

'Ok.'

'Where did you work before this?' He hauled himself to his feet.

'I've just finished at a care home. Before that, I worked with underprivileged young people in the city centre.'

Troy swallowed as he shifted a crutch under his arm. And now she was about to babysit an overprivileged sport star. Even if he donated a substantial part of his next wage to charity, it didn't come close to helping real people, the people he'd once been part of. Helping his parents and sister was about all he could claim in his favour and he wasn't sure it was a good thing. Now he'd set them up so well he hardly saw them.

Before he grabbed his second crutch, Carys lifted it, took his injured arm and gently but firmly wedged the crutch into place. His instinct was to snarl and tell her not to. He could manage. But fuck it, he couldn't. This was what he would be paying her for. He had to get used to it because it was going to get a whole lot worse. Heat blossomed in his neck as he imagined her dressing or washing him. Whatever happened, she was NOT doing that. Then there would be massages. It was easier to desensitise himself to a forty-plus nurse with a mumsy air than a lithe-bodied twenty-something. Still, Troy Copeland was an iceman when it came to women, he could handle it.

'Up the stairs and turn left.' He pointed when they were back in the hall. 'You'll find a lounge, bedroom and full en suite. A cleaner comes three times a week, so none of that will be in your duties. I won't come up. Once a day on the stairs is more than enough.'

The giant stairs swallowed Carys's tiny figure as she made her way up. Troy hobbled to the chaise where she'd sat on her arrival and lowered himself onto it. This was what he'd become. A man who couldn't stay on his feet for longer than two minutes. He put his face into his hands. Was he doing the right thing? Right now, his need for basic things like food overrode everything else.

Pippa hadn't loved cooking, but she'd ordered meals from specialised caterers. Troy had no idea who they were; he'd always left it to her or cooked for himself from memorised recipes. Now, he couldn't stand in the kitchen for five minutes, let alone attempt food prep. She hadn't even bothered to order food for his return. Now she was gone. *I don't miss her.* He was too angry to think about her without wanting to punch something. What had they ever really had in common? His career came first and she was part of the image, but he'd never really opened up or been himself around her – not that he did with anyone. No one knew the real Troy. Not even himself.

At the sound of footsteps, he glanced up. Carys glided down the staircase, her eyes huge and a dreamy smile on her lips.

'Is it ok?' he asked.

'It's amazing.' She jumped off the bottom step. 'It's bigger than my last flat.'

From the living room, a loud jingle vibrated out. 'That's my phone,' he muttered. 'It might be my agent. He wants to make a statement to the press.'

'They're at the gate,' said Carys.

'I know. They want answers I can't give. Like, when I can play again.'

'Should I get it?'

'Please.'

Carys bustled into the living room and returned with the phone no longer ringing.

'Who was it?'

She woke the screen. 'Shaun Eddery.'

His teammate was never off the blower when he had something to moan or bitch about; he was worse than a girl, but he was the only one who'd bothered to return Troy's voice message. 'I'll call him back in a bit.'

The phone chimed his message tone and Carys held it up to show him. His face opened it and the message displayed the usual jumble of letters that would take him an age to read. Feigning a need to cling to his crutches, he said, 'Read it out, will you?'

'Hi, mate…' Carys began. 'Sorry to bother you, know you're not great, but you have to hear this before you hear it from someone else. Daryl has just told us he's seeing

Pippa. Been doing her behind your back for months. The sleaze is laughing his dick off about it…' Carys's voice trailed off. Seething hot rage surged through Troy's veins. Daryl Woods. That bastard. The same dickhead who'd run his car off the road and landed Troy in this position. *All the while, he's been sleeping with my fiancée!* Maybe he'd crashed on purpose. Troy's knuckles whitened on his crutch.

'Get my agent on there,' he said with barely controlled fury. 'Now.'

Carys tapped the screen. 'What's his name?'

'Chris Charles.'

After Carys started the call, she held the phone in front of Troy. The second it connected, Troy snapped, 'Get me out of the club right now! I am never going back.'

'What the hell?' said Chris.

'I mean it. Daryl has been shagging Pippa. I will never go back there. NEVER! How can I look at him again, play with him? It's not happening. That's no teammate of mine. That's a back-stabbing shithead who for all I know was trying to kill me last month.'

'Hey, calm down,' said Chris.

'No, I bloody won't.' He'd been screwed over once too often. He might never be the brightest button in the box, but he was damned if he'd be made a fool of. 'Find me something else, because I'm done there. Done. You hear me? I'm never going back.'

Carys peered at him as he fumbled at the screen to press the end call button.

'Isn't that a bit hasty?' she murmured.

'Don't you start,' he growled. 'If you're going to be working for me, you can't second-guess me.'

'I wasn't.' She held up her hands. 'I meant for your recovery. If you leave, you won't have access to the physio rooms.'

'I'll pay for somewhere.' His insides burned. He was thirty, he could hardly walk, and now he was leaving the security of a club he'd been with for four years. He had an exit clause in his contract but he never thought he'd have to use it like this. Who the hell would have him now? There was no certainty he'd ever play at the top level again. But he couldn't go back, he just couldn't. He'd be a laughing stock in the lockers like at school when he was the class clown. He wouldn't put up with it anymore. Not now. He paid Chris big bucks to sort out this kind of mess and he could bloody well get on with doing it.

Chapter Five

Carys

Troy lay face down on the massage table wearing nothing but his black boxers. For someone who spent his life outdoors, he was oddly pale except for his left side, which was covered in blue, purple and yellow bruising. His leg was strapped and his shoulder had a clean dressing over his stitches. Carys rubbed her hands together. A twinge of nerves fluttered in her tummy. In basic physio training, the models hadn't been this attractive. Even with the scarring, his body was in incredible shape. Touching it felt sacrilegious.

Placing her hands gently on Troy's shoulders, she applied pressure. His skin was cold and his back barely rising. Was he breathing? A tight knot of tension had balled at his neck, spreading along his shoulders like he was cinching them. Here lay an international footballer. *Oh god.* She sucked her lip; she couldn't make any mistakes. So far she'd got the job for a trial period but if she messed up, she'd be out. If she made things worse, he might sue her.

Her palm ran along his smooth shoulder blades. His head was sideways on the pillow, facing away. His profile was strong, youthful, handsome. He'd be considered attractive even if he wasn't a multi-millionaire, but with that kind of money plus looks... Well, no doubt he had armies of admirers. Carys swallowed. *He's just a person. I have a job to do.*

'Try and relax,' she said, as much to herself as to him. 'I know with the bruising it's difficult.' She gently kneaded the taut flesh.

With what seemed like a forced breath, Troy's shoulders relaxed fractionally. Carys worked along them.

'If this hurts, tell me.'

'No pain, no gain, and all that.' The words sounded like they came through gritted teeth.

She plied him with rhythmical strokes, focusing on the consistency of the movement rather than the pleasurable tingling building in her fingertips. Troy inhaled sharply and Carys eased the pressure a little.

Over my dead body. That would have been her dad's response if she'd told him who she was working for. She'd chickened out, saying it was 'a well-off person in Bearsden.' But the words fitted eerily with the pallor of Troy's skin.

She kneaded over the plains of his back, trying to inject some colour and life back into him. For such a powerfully built body, it seemed to have lost its vigour.

Never in a million years could she have imagined herself living in a house this size. It was well decorated and fashionable but something about it was cold and soulless. Still, it was a far cry from anywhere else she'd lived.

Her mind rolled back to a time years ago when her dad had been with Joanne – the happiest time of her life. She'd had a dad and a mum and they'd given her everything. Joanne had been pregnant at least twice and miscarried. Not long after the last one, she'd said goodbye to Carys and never come back. Her dad had told her Joanne was bitter about not being able to have kids of her own. She'd tried to get at Lee by causing trouble and Lee had gone to all sorts of lengths to keep her away. Then Kat had moved in.

As Carys pressed on Troy's spine, she frowned. Those memories often came back to her. She remembered her mum's – Joanne's – stories. She'd grown up on an island and always promised to take Carys. But it had never happened. Carys had been dumped by another mum, as she had been by her birth mother, just as she had been by two boyfriends… She couldn't afford to be dumped now. This job was important for her future.

Troy groaned and Carys stopped. 'Is everything ok?' she asked.

'No,' he muttered. 'Nothing is fucking ok.'

Carys placed a few drops of arnica oil on her palms. 'That's not strictly true.' How often had she used those words to placate elderly residents in the care homes? 'There's always something to be thankful for.'

'Hmpf,' Troy grunted.

It didn't take a psychotherapist to work out why he was seething. He'd been publicly dumped and now his ex had run off with a teammate – the very teammate who'd crashed into a tree and left Troy in this state. Who wouldn't be furious? If he'd been an octogenarian in a state, Carys was confident she could've talked him down and brought him round, but he was a hotshot footballer with an explosive temper and she wasn't sure she dared try.

Outside the gate, the camp of paparazzi hung around like a rancid smell. It set Carys on edge thinking about it. How could anyone live with that constant scrutiny? Even after Troy's most recent statement, they hadn't given up. Troy had instructed his agent to go public with the news he was leaving a much-loved club not because of poor treatment but because of one teammate who had 'acted in a way not fitting of a team player.' Carys was certain Troy wouldn't have used such delicate language if he'd made the statement himself.

'Do you think…' she tested her luck, 'your club will sack Daryl Woods? I mean, the way he's treated you is awful.'

'Ha.' Troy grunted. 'No, they won't. He's too good a player. He might get a reprimand but no.'

'That's a pity.' She pressed her knuckles into his spine and he groaned again. This time, it sounded less irritated. 'If they'd sacked him, you could have gone back.'

'Maybe.'

Troy's shoulders lifted and he sighed. She pummelled to the bottom of his spine, above the waistband of his boxers. How would it feel to run her fingers over that shapely backside? *Eek, button up those thoughts!* Purple bruises sprouted from the top of the strapping on his thigh.

Last night, she'd perched on the giant bed in her glamorous suite and googled the life out of Troy and the accident.

Reporters liked to make everything sound dramatic, and she knew too well how social media could blow things out of proportion, but several accounts suggested he was lucky not to lose his leg. If it healed enough for him to walk again, that would be a miracle – never mind play international football. She didn't dare ask what he might do if he couldn't play again. Something told her that was an eventuality he wasn't considering. In his mind, he was going to play again and the sooner the better.

He was a young guy, not much older than the boyfriends she'd had and while they were lazing about posting lies on Instagram and sleeping around, he'd been using his talents to make money and build a life for himself. She worked back up the ridge of his spine. What must it be like to have ambition and skill? And then lose it all? *Just awful.* Her heart ached for him.

47

He'd gone to bed insisting he didn't need help with washing or dressing. After almost carrying him up the stairs, she wasn't sure how the hell he'd manage on his own, but part of her was relieved. Online stalking him when he was a few doors away was a lot more comfortable than helping him take a shower and get ready for bed. And it meant she could work on her book. This experience would be invaluable if she could really help him heal but what if she got something wrong? Would she get banged up by the football police if he never got better? Or have her name spread across the front pages as the negligent nurse who ruined his career? How many more people might she lose if something like that got out? No one would employ her after that and she'd be hated by rafts of football fans.

'Right,' she said, bottling those thoughts. 'Let's see if we can get you on your back. I'll help you roll over.'

'No,' he said.

'Why not?'

'Just no. That's enough for now.'

She frowned. That was her job to decide surely, but she didn't have the nerve to press him. 'Ok. We'll leave it there for now, but I have to work on the front too.'

'Later,' he growled.

With a final pummel on his back, she crossed the room and flicked on some music. 'I'll put on some calming sounds and I'd like you to spend ten minutes relaxing. Don't think or worry about anything. Just breathe and exist.'

Troy snorted into the massage pillow.

'Would you like me to guide you through the relaxation or would you prefer to be alone?'

'Alone,' he muttered.

Leaving him to relax – or possibly to stew – Carys took the laundry to the utility room and started the machine. If her dad discovered she was washing Troy Copeland's pants, he'd be round the gate with an army of yobs, assuming he could drag himself off the sofa for long enough.

The alarm buzzed, signalling Troy's ten minutes were up. Carys threw the last towels into the dryer and returned to the huge basement kitted out as a gym, health suite, games room and home cinema. Did he ever use it? Maybe when he'd been fit and with his girlfriend, they'd hosted big parties. Now it was sad, empty and lonely. Just walking around this house gave her a workout. How could one man justify living here? Even with a family, it would be ridiculous – they'd never see each other.

Carys opened the door. 'Time's up.' Troy was still face down on the table. She pursed her lips in surprise. 'I thought you'd have run away.'

'I can't run anywhere,' he muttered.

'True, but I expected an attempt to escape my hippy healing regime.'

His back shook slightly and with an effort, he twisted his neck so he was squinting at her. 'I never thought I'd say this,' he mumbled, one cheek squashed to the pillow, 'but it was quite relaxing.'

'Good. It'll help in the long run.' She approached him, catching his eye. Even in his flattened-to-the-pillow state, his half-smile was disarming. She had to not notice or care. 'Now comes the fun of getting you off this table.'

'Oh, Jesus.'

'You got out of bed yourself,' she said. When she'd knocked that morning to check on him, she'd heard frantic scurrying like he was trying to finish or hide something, before he'd replied that she could come in and help with his socks. It had taken a lot of effort not to gasp at his bedroom. Palatial rooms like that belonged in films, not real life.

'Yeah, but it took a fucking long time.'

'I could help you.'

'A guy needs some privacy,' he muttered. 'And some bloody dignity.'

'Well, don't worry. I've shifted OAPs with less mobility than you.'

'I bet they weighed a lot less though.'

All the weight on his body was pure muscle. She pulled his wheelchair over and placed it next to the table. 'We can do this. First, you need to swivel around in the same way you got on. Gently does it.'

He pushed himself until he was across the table. Swallowing a breath, Carys placed her palms on his hips and guided him, again trying to desensitise herself from anything other than the mundane action, but it was impossible. Nerve ends sprang to life inside her at the thought of pulling his hips close to hers. *Fuck's sake.* This had to stop.

'Hold there a second and I'll get your trousers.'

'Jesus Christ,' he muttered. 'This is horrific.'

'Don't be silly. It's not like you're on TV or anything, and it's not your fault.'

She bent down and wrestled the sweats onto his ankles, keeping her eyes low and focusing nowhere above his knee even though she wanted to. Her hands trembled as she pulled the waistband up his legs and around his waist. He bit his lip and stared away.

'Now, gently back and into the chair.' She blinked at him and he grimaced. 'I'll, um…' She placed her arm around his broad back, now warm to the touch.

He groaned again as he eased himself into the chair.

'Here's your shirt.' With a gentle tug, she pulled it over his injured shoulder first. He manoeuvred his good arm into place. With a deep breath, she went to fasten the buttons. He grabbed her hand. Their eyes met.

'I can do that myself.'

She blinked and he let her go. 'Great.' Pushing him down the corridor, she ignored the swooping sensation that had started in her stomach when their gazes locked. A tremor of something had passed between them, something that shouldn't be there, something forbidden, but enticing. If she was going to stay here, she needed to stopper these feelings straight away, but how?

Chapter Six

Troy

Troy's pencil scribbled across the page, doodles emerging like sprouting plants. It was manic, messy and unplanned, like the chaos that had landed in his life. He slapped the pencil down and shoved the pad into the drawer. No one got to see this stuff. Without Pippa sharing the room, he could hide it in plain sight. Carys didn't come in here except to make his bed and help him with socks. If he could just reach his damn foot himself, he wouldn't need her in here, period.

He wheeled himself to the window. A gang of paps still crowded around the gates. *Seedy gits.* Was that what was keeping away his teammates? Why had no one visited? Were they all too busy with training and their perfectly uninjured lives?

A knock. Troy clenched his jaw. Now for it. He wheeled himself away from the window. 'Come in.'

Carys's smiling face beamed around. 'Are you ready?'

'As I'll ever be,' he muttered. She picked up his socks and knelt in front of him. He closed his eyes and turned away. This kind of thing got him going in all the wrong places. It was his leg he wanted to rouse into action, nothing else. Why couldn't the agency have found someone less hot? Someone who looked no more appealing than a warthog when they knelt in front of him?

Not a fit chick he could imagine doing all sorts from this position. She could relieve all the tension in his body very quickly. *In my leg. In my fucking leg. That's why she's here.* He ran his hand down his face and groaned.

'Is everything ok?' she said.

'What? Oh… Yes, just, sore, you know?'

'Do you want to bring the massage forward? We could do it before breakfast… I mean, do the massage.'

'I know what you mean.'

She ran her teeth along her lower lip and hovered, rubbing her fingertips together. 'So, do you want to go down now?'

He cleared his throat and covered his mouth with the back of his hand.

'I mean downstairs.'

'Yeah. I know.'

She wheeled him into the hall, stopping at the top of the stairs where she'd already propped his crutches on the railing. Troy manoeuvred himself up, holding the banister. This was the worst part of the day. Getting down these stairs was damn near impossible and every time it was accompanied by visions of himself tumbling to the bottom. Carys walked in front and to the side, her hands out like he was a toddler about to topple. Talk about humiliating.

'Have any of the guys left messages?' he said.

'I don't think so,' said Carys. 'I'll check when we get down.'

'What's got into them? I thought they'd all be round the door to see me.'

'Maybe it's awkward for them.'

'How?'

'They probably don't know what to say. It's like when someone dies and you have to talk to their relatives. Maybe they're nervous. Give them time.'

Troy let out a low growl. 'I've got too much of that.' A hammering on the front door almost sent him careering down. 'What the hell?'

'Shall I answer it?' said Carys.

'Get me down first. No one can get to that door without me opening the gates.'

She frowned and helped him down the last few steps. 'Maybe it's one of your friends. Don't they know the code to get in?'

'No. No one knows it.' Well, Pippa did. But she wouldn't have told anyone, would she? 'See who it is,' he said. 'But keep the chain on. Don't let anyone in.'

Carys crossed the hallway and opened the door into the entrance porch. Troy followed, hobbling as fast as he could, his crutches echoing as they beat on the wood floor. The front door clicked open.

'Hey there. Are you Troy Copeland's nurse?' said a man's voice.

Seriously? Troy made it to the porch.

'Who are you?' said Carys. 'You're not supposed to be in here.'

'Are you living with Troy?'

'Get the fuck off my property,' said Troy. 'I don't know who you are or what you're doing here but go to hell.'

'Can you tell me about your leg?' the man pressed.

'Are you deaf?' said Carys, and Troy drew back. Her face was red and her eyes flashed. 'He said get off his property. You better leave now or I'll make you.' The elfin beauty who looked like a feather could knock her over had been replaced by a possessed pixie ready to bite his arm off. The man was just visible through the crack in the door, an irritating smirk on his face. Troy was well-trained to stay cool around the paps but right now, he'd like to smack the guy's smug face with the end of his crutch.

'I'll have the police on you,' said Troy. Carys looked like she might actually try and physically remove the man, giving the paps exactly the kind of meat they were after. 'Shut the door.'

Carys slammed it in the man's face, then turned to face Troy, leaning on the glass panel. 'Do you think he'll leave? Should we actually call the police?'

'Yup,' said Troy. 'And Chris. I want extra security. That twat must've climbed the fence.'

'Let me see.' Carys made her way to the front window and peered out. 'I hope he gets one of those spikes stuck where it hurts,' she muttered.

'You've got a mean streak,' said Troy, peeking out behind her. She whipped around and their faces came close. Her lips were a hair's breadth from his and taunted him with their delicate pink form. Kissing them was the only thing that would content him, but, Jesus, did he have to keep that idea under wraps. Like on the massage table. Keeping his cool while her hands were all over him required all his mastery. The iceman melted under her warm palms. Screw it, he didn't just melt, he combusted.

Pulling back, he turned away and cleared his throat. 'Get me some breakfast, will you? Then call the police. I'll phone Chris.'

'Er, right, ok.'

She bustled away and Troy leaned on the windowsill, pulling in some very slow and deep breaths. This was only the beginning. She'd been here all of three days and he was already imagining her in his bed. And since when had girls like her attracted him? He'd always gone for glitz and obvious beauty, women like Pippa who sparkled when they entered a room.

Carys was… normal. But there was something about her. *It's just the fact that she gets to touch me.* That was all. He fixed his crutches and started towards the kitchen. It wasn't all though. He wouldn't feel like this if the club physio was massaging the life out of him; that guy had the subtlety of a buffalo next to Carys and the woman they'd had before that wasn't much better. No, this was personal. Something about Carys drew him like a magnet and set him on edge, and he needed to make it stop. She was here to do a job. His brain presented him with an image of exactly what he wanted that to look like and Troy balled his fists. *For Christ's sake, not that kind of job.* His mind was on a one-way street and having her here for six months was going to be torture.

Chapter Seven

Carys

A harsh clanging sound from Troy's bedroom made Carys stop dead midway through scrolling Google images – anything was a diversion from seeing yet more pictures of Troy with his glamorous ex. Carys had seen enough tanned legs, high heels and platinum hair to get exactly what type of woman Troy liked. But that sound chilled her blood. She listened for swearing or other sounds of life. Nothing. She'd been here a week and only been in Troy's room briefly to put on his socks. Everything else, he insisted on doing himself, though it took him forever. A moment like this was what she dreaded. Had he fallen?

'Troy?' She knocked on his door. Still nothing. She barged in and scanned around. The bed was unmade and a cloud of steam billowed out from the open door to the en-suite. Shit. What if he'd slipped in the shower and knocked himself out... or worse? Hastening across the room, she swung around the doorway and came face to face with him, buck naked in his chair, towelling his hair.

'What the fuck are you doing in here?' he snapped, throwing the towel into his lap.

'Nothing, sorry. I heard a crash.'

'That bloody shower seat thing fell over when I got out.'

'Are you ok?'

'Well, you can see for yourself, can't you? Do I look dead?'

She sucked in her lip. What now? Leave him? She should before he blew a fuse and sacked her, but for his own sake, she had to give him a piece of her mind. 'It's really dangerous, you being in the shower on your own like that.'

'So what do you suggest? You want to come in here and wash me?'

Carys swallowed. 'Maybe you should leave your bedroom door open and let me know when you're in there.'

'Sounds like one step down from voyeurism.'

Carys folded her arms. 'I'm suggesting it for your safety, not my own entertainment. I've washed lots of people. Seen one, seen them all, you're no different.' The big fat lie rolled off her tongue. The idea of smoothing shower gel all over him set a fire burning inside her, but he was a grouchy bastard. Hot one minute, cold the next. She didn't need someone like that in her life. He gaped, open mouthed like she'd slapped his face. Clearly, he didn't like anyone insulting his temple of a body.

'If you fall in there and I don't know, how am I supposed to help you? I'd probably get sued.'

He clutched the towel in his lap, his knuckles turning white.

'I'm not sure this job is for me.' How could she go on like this? Calvert Care might not take her back if she quit, but she hadn't done anything wrong so surely she'd get work elsewhere? 'Maybe you should check with the agency and see if someone more suitable has turned up.' She stalked off, crossing his room and slamming the door behind her. The silence in the hall was absolute and throbbed in her ears worse than the crazy noises back her dad's. Her room was neat and tidy. She only had a backpack with her clothes and her tablet, it wouldn't take long to pack. Maybe this was rash, but she couldn't bear the idea of something happening on her watch because Troy was too stubborn to let her do her job. Opening the wardrobe, she pulled out the two dresses she'd hung up.

A knock. 'Carys. Are you in there?'

'Yes,' she said, running her hands under her eyes. Had she been crying? She barely noticed. She didn't want to leave. Not because of the job but because she wanted him to get better and she wanted to be part of that.

'Can I come in?'

'Sure.' She closed the cupboard door. Troy wheeled himself in, still topless, the towel covering his bottom half. His chest was sculpted like the statue of David, perfectly shaped, ripped and incredible. A tremor rippled through her.

'Listen, I'm sorry, ok.'

'Ok. But I can't stay here.'

'Please,' he said, a look of desperation flashing in his eyes. 'I can't be alone. I'll leave the door open like you said.' He rubbed his hand down his face. 'It's Frustrating, you know. You're...'

'I'm what? I'm here to do all these things. If I don't, I feel like I'm neglecting you.'

'I've always been independent. I hate not being able to do easy shit like taking a shower. It's pathetic. And having someone wash me. It's just' – he made tiger claws in the air and growled – 'infuriating.'

'I get that,' Carys said, sitting on the chaise beside where he'd stopped the chair. 'But if I'm going to be here, you have to compromise. Leaving the door open isn't that bad. I promise I won't come in unless you call me or I hear you fall, but at least there's no chance of something happening and me not even knowing you're in there. If something did happen and I had to go for help, the first people I'd run into are the paps. They'd be all over everything. I'd get pulled up for negligence and it would be around the world in seconds.'

'Yeah, yeah, I know. You're right. Ok. Fine.' He sighed and rested his head on his hand. 'Everything's such a mess. I hate this. I hate it.'

Carys leaned forward and put her hand on his thick bicep. His skin burned her cold fingertips with its shower-warm feel and Troy flinched. She pulled away. 'I know that. And it's going to take time.'

'It's not just this. It's everything. I've got no club, no girlfriend… I'm totally screwed.'

'You need a break. Try and forget about all that. Take a time out. Let yourself heal without the stress.'

He dropped his hand and looked at her, his eyes travelling down her face, then her neck, her chest, then back until she felt as naked as him. He stretched out his hand and took hers. 'Thank you,' he said, giving her a gentle squeeze.

'For what?'

'Not leaving. I need you.'

Warmth pooled in her chest like melted chocolate. Did he mean that? He needed her… Obviously in a professional capacity but the sensation was hard to shake. 'It's ok.' She rubbed her thumb over the soft spot on his hand, then let go. This could get a bit too comfortable.

'My parents live in Spain. Maybe I should go stay with them for a few months, that would be a break.'

'Sounds good.' But that would mean a whole new dynamic. Coming to terms with living with Troy was tricky enough. What would his family be like? 'Will they want to look after you?'

'No,' he said, as though it was blatantly obvious. 'You'd have to come with me. My parents aren't exactly the caring type, more the tough love kind. But they have a great house and it's a bungalow, so no stairs, no paps, lots of sunshine and hours to relax.'

'Sounds amazing. Except...' She hesitated. It sounded stupid saying this to an international football player.

'What?'

'I've never been abroad.'

'Really?'

'Yup.'

He sighed and rolled his hand through his hair. 'Come to think of it, they probably won't want me there.'

'Why not?'

'They enjoy the high life. I'd cramp their style,' he said with a bravado that didn't meet his eyes.

'Why don't you look for somewhere closer to home then?'

'You mean the Scottish riviera? Four seasons in one day and all that?'

'That kind of thing.' She pushed her hands under her thighs and pinned them there. The temptation to reach out and touch him was so strong. 'Even that sounds exotic to someone who's only been on holiday twice, once to Largs and the other to Dunoon. It's hardly much to sing about.'

He burst out laughing. It transformed the scowling face, making him instantly softer and more approachable. 'Are you serious?'

'Yes, so you shouldn't laugh. You might hurt my delicate feelings.'

'I'm sorry. Jeez, I want to go travelling now to get you an education.'

She glanced at the door. *I'm not sure I want an education from him... not that kind anyway.* She'd take an anatomy class though.

'Listen, here's an idea. Take this as an apology.' He hung his head in mock mortification and peered at her with begging eyes. 'Why don't you choose somewhere? Not too far but relaxing. Somewhere I can rest up. Anywhere you like, I'll go along with it. Find a place I can stay for three months, preferably without stairs, or with a lift. A rental house would be best, something not too small. I'll get dressed, then call Chris and tell him.'

'Just like that?'

'Why not?' With jerky movements, he wheeled himself back towards the door.

'Won't it affect your recovery if you can't get to the physio appointments?'

'Not if you keep doing a good job.' He held her gaze. 'And you are doing a good job. I'm sorry I snapped. I just feel raw. Going away is a good idea. I need space. I hate those bloody paps pissing around watching my every move. If I take myself off the shelf for a few months, I can heal away from the pressure.' He glanced up. 'This is your hippy mumbo jumbo rubbing off on me.'

She grinned and got to her feet.

'I'll go square it with Chris,' he said. 'And you go stick a pin in the map.'

Carys took a few deep breaths and sucked her lip. She could do this. The fine line between not fussing over Troy and doing her job had widened slightly. And the door that led to everything forbidden still sat ajar. Sometimes the way he looked at her... She shivered. No, she'd imagined it. This was just a job and she'd seen the kind of women he liked. She'd never fit the bill.

Now where to choose? The pressure to pick somewhere good weighed on her as she opened Google maps. Where to start? She knew nothing about anywhere. Her mind fell back to her childhood again – Joanne and her chats about the island she'd grown up on. Carys dragged the map across and looked at them. Not Lewis, Harris, Skye... Nope. Mull. Yes. That was it. She googled it to look at some photos.

It was like nothing she'd ever seen before, not for real. Beaches with white sands and turquoise seas filled the screen. Troy would like this, wouldn't he? The idea of somewhere this remote struck a romantic chord deep within her. This was a place to heal bodies, minds, hearts and souls.

Chapter Eight

Troy

'Did I spy a Nerf gun in the games room?' Carys marched through the living room.

'Yeah, there's a few,' said Troy. 'Why?' Too late. She darted out of the lounge like a whirlwind.

'She's interesting,' said his former teammate Isaac Hobson, leaning back with a cocked eyebrow. Finally, someone had graced him with a visit. Isaac was probably the most laid-back guy on the team and Troy appreciated him showing up.

'She's good at her job,' said Troy, wincing as he cricked his neck, trying to see what Carys was doing.

'She looks like she's on work experience.'

Troy gave a noncommittal nod. He and Isaac sat not looking at each other and Troy flexed his hand on the sofa arm. What the hell were they supposed to talk about?

'What's that noise?' said Isaac.

'Dunno.'

From outside came the dull whine of a motor. Troy frowned through the glass doors but before he spotted anything, the door behind burst open and Carys stormed in, fully armed with the Nerf Rival Phantom Corps Hades and an expression of deep intent.

'Er… What are you doing?' Troy asked.

She marched to the patio door and pushed it open. 'Taking care of business.'

'What?' Troy furrowed his brow as she trotted outside and took aim at something overhead.

Isaac gaped at her. The motorised sound increased and Troy spied a drone whizzing about above the garden, then swooping low as it got closer to the house.

'Do those paps ever stop?' he muttered.

'Is she deranged?' said Isaac.

'Na,' said Troy. The sooner he got away, the better. He was sick of his private life being on display. The perfectly presented private life he'd had with Pippa had been ok, but this injury-induced shitstorm was not for public viewing.

Carys took a potshot and a bright orange bullet narrowly missed the target. 'Bugger,' she muttered.

Troy ran his hand down his face. 'She's something else.' Should he cry with despair or laugh himself silly? People in his life weren't normally this crazy. Would Pippa ever have behaved like that? No bloody way.

'Fucking crackers,' said Isaac. 'She any good with the massages?'

'Meaning what?'

'Nothing. Just wondering if she's doing the job, see'n you're not using the physio rooms.'

'Yeah, she does the job.'

'Does she, aye?'

'Fuck off,' said Troy.

'Ha. I'm pulling your leg, mate.' Isaac got to his feet. When matches and practice weren't on the cards for discussion, there wasn't much else to chat about. 'You could try dating that Lithuanian model who was around for a bit. Can't remember her name, can't pronounce it either. She's a hottie.'

'Yeah. I'll give that a miss until I'm in better shape. You going?'

'I better. Got training in a bit.'

Lucky sod. Troy's stomach churned. 'I'll buzz you out.' He pulled himself to his feet and hobbled after Isaac, hating how upright his teammate looked. He even seemed taller and he definitely wasn't. This sucked.

Troy watched him drive through the crowd of paps. His chest lightened now it was just him and Carys again. The guys were good craic in the locker room but having Isaac here had been… Awkward and strained, almost like Isaac had been sent to pry. There was no chance of Troy putting on a show of how well he was recovering – he could still barely walk for more than five minutes.

He returned slowly to the living room. Carys was still taking potshots at the drone.

'Do you seriously think that's going to work?' he called.

'Have you got a better idea?' She fired again.

His phone buzzed across the glass coffee table as it vibrated and chimed. He grabbed it.

'Hello, Troy,' said Chris. 'How's it going?'

Troy waited for the pleasantries to pass, still watching Carys.

'Do you get what I'm saying?' said Chris.

'What? Eh, sure,' muttered Troy, though he hadn't heard a word. Chris's voice was more monotonous than the drone. 'Ooh,' he said as Carys narrowly missed a direct hit.

'Pardon?' said Chris.

'Nothing.'

'Troy. The season is almost upon us.'

Didn't he know it? It loomed on the horizon like a storm cloud about to burst. It would be the first time in twelve years he wouldn't be part of it.

'The way I see it,' said Chris, 'if you want to take time away from the game to recover, that's your prerogative. You're not tied into the contract. The club has let you go but without it, you're putting yourself in limbo.'

'I'm in limbo anyway,' said Troy. 'I can't get a straight answer from anyone. No one knows how long these injuries will take to heal. I'm not going back to the club while Daryl is about.'

'I'll do what I can but your transfer options aren't great with this injury.'

'Yes, I know, but what exactly is great right now?'

Carys punched the air. 'Got one!'

It had made no impact on the drone, but she beamed as she collected her bullets and loaded it again. She made the *ok* sign with her finger and thumb, and Troy grinned.

'Well, Troy, if you're dead set on taking time away, then here's the deal I think will work best. I'll try to negotiate something for you starting mid-season. It might not be ideal and it might be with a lesser club and a lower salary but it'll mean you can come back slowly. That's the most workable option. I could get something for a year or a year and a half to ease you back in.'

'Do it.'

'Ok,' said Chris.

Troy ended the call and dropped the phone back on the table. It was better than nothing. And right now, he needed something, even to bury his head in the sand. The idea of sitting on the bench watching his teammates for six months while he could barely move made him nauseous. He wanted to bounce back, shock them with his level of fitness and show them all over again he was a genius on the pitch. If it ended up being with a lesser club, so what? Maybe he'd lift them to success like they'd never known before.

'Call the police,' he said through the open French doors.
'I have, but this is fun while we wait. Do you want a shot?'

He scowled at his wasted left shoulder, took a deep breath and balanced on the crutch, then took the rifle from Carys in his right hand. Aiming haphazardly with his one-handed grip, he popped a shot.

Carys doubled over laughing as it pinged way off the mark. 'How did you ever score goals with an aim that bad?'

'Ha bloody ha.' He handed back the rifle.

She fluffed up her wispy hair and it drifted back into place like a feather in the wind, then she smiled at him. He looked away.

'Listen, can you get the number of the estate agent who's renting that Mull property? I want to talk to them.'

She gave him half a frown and raised one eyebrow as he hobbled over to get his phone and passed it to her. Yeah, it looked like sheer laziness. He read her mind. *Your injury didn't affect your fingers, did it?* But finding it himself would take ages. This was why women thought him arrogant and lazy. Asking an employee to do this was marginally better than asking a girlfriend.

'There you go.' Carys handed back the phone with a quizzical expression.

'Thanks.' He took it and turned away, shutting down any chance of her asking him anything. 'When I'm done, I'll come through for lunch,' he said, making it blatantly clear she was dismissed. He hit call and after waiting to be put through to the correct agent, they chatted for a few moments. 'And this is all you have for three months? It's smaller than I'd hoped for.' He cringed inside. *Listen to me!* A three-bedroom bungalow with a gorgeous deck and sea view was too small. A family home for most people. Carys had gazed at it with gooey eyes, like she was admiring the cutest puppy in the basket. Troy hadn't lived anywhere that small since he was eighteen. Surely he could do it if he tried?

'It's the only rental property. If you were looking to buy, we have a property that might suit. It's a large house named Taigh Beinne built six years ago with eight bedrooms. It's currently a B&B and the owners are accepting offers for the furniture to remain in situ. It's in walk-in condition.'

Troy furrowed his brow. 'How much are we talking?'

'The current asking price is eight hundred thousand.'

'Is that all?' Troy said. The estate agent coughed and Troy added. 'I mean, that's a good price. Send me the details, please, and pictures.' *Yup, give me pictures, not some long-winded description.*

'I'll email them directly.'

'Thanks.' Troy ended the call. By the time he'd reached the kitchen, the email had arrived. Carys pulled out a chair at the dining table and helped him into it. He didn't bother trying to stop her. Even if he could do it himself, it was quicker with her help and something about the warmth of her touch lifted his heart in a way he wasn't used to. It brought a deep sense of well-being and comfort. When he was face down on the massage table, his brain got a different message, equally pleasant but a lot less appropriate. Very inappropriate. Most days, he couldn't face the world for several minutes after she was done... he definitely couldn't face Carys. She didn't need to see the full effect her massages had on him.

'Did you agree to anything on the cottage?' She returned to the prep area to toss the salad.

'Not yet.' Troy opened the emails more through guesswork and picture clues than anything else. When he opened the PDF with the house details, his jaw dropped. This was the place. One look and he knew it. New houses were his thing and this was pristine and stylish; white fronted, large windows, French doors onto a patio and an upstairs balcony that overlooked a view he could only dream of: miles of ocean. 'Read this.' He held up his phone and passed it to Carys. She took it and skimmed down.

'Wow,' she said. 'Where's this?'

'On Mull. Close to the rental cottage but it's much more me.'

'You seen the price?' She frowned as she scrolled. 'Eight bedrooms, four public rooms, an office, a dining kitchen, a utility area, a landscaped garden plus a vegetable garden and an orchard.' She glanced up. 'It's for sale, not rent. You realise that, yes?'

'I'm not thick, you know,' he mumbled, though he knew he was. But he didn't need her to discover that. 'I could buy it, live in it for a while, then sell it on. Or I keep it and get someone to run it. Like Andy Murray did at Cromlix. I could name it Copeland's Country House.' His mind kicked into gear and for the first time ever he saw the glimmer of a life beyond football, but he let go and the idea slipped away.

'It seems crazy to me. The cottage was a perfect size. That house looks about the same size as this place.'

'It's not that big,' said Troy. 'If I bought it, I could take a room downstairs and set one up as a gym and my massage room.'

Carys laid the bowls on the table and passed him a napkin folded like a swan. 'You could, yes. But isn't it a bit extreme for three months?'

'That's what I'm saying. This could be an investment for the future.' Troy pulled the bowl of salad towards him. 'Where did you get this?' He lifted the swan napkin.

'I folded it,' said Carys.

'Did you? I thought some fancy machine did the job.'

'Nope, I just use my hands.'

He glanced up at her and her cheeks reddened. She could do any job she wanted on him right now 'just using her hands'.

'I mean… I can show you.' She fumbled about for another napkin. 'My mum… ex stepmum showed me when I was little.'

'Hey. It's ok,' said Troy. 'Show me after. Let's eat.'

Still blushing, she took her seat and picked up her fork.

'It's amazing though,' said Troy, turning over the swan in his hand. Small things like this had passed him by. He was up for buying a mansion on an island he'd never been to, but he didn't know how to appreciate simple yet beautiful things, unless you counted his doodles. Pippa had tutted when he'd closed his sketchbooks and hidden them away when she entered. Maybe she'd stolen a look at them when he'd been in hospital, though she probably didn't care. He swallowed, realising his gaze was still on Carys. An urge to go and get his sketchbooks and show her hit him square in the chest. She wouldn't laugh even if she thought his drawings were terrible.

Her eyes were trained a bit too strongly on her food. She was being sensible. She recognised the danger and wanted to keep away. He had to do the same. 'So, what do you think about the house?' He didn't need her to like it, but he wanted her to.

'I can see you love it,' she said.

'Don't you?'

'I'd be happy with a bedsit in Drumchapel.'

He smirked. He'd always been reckless; maybe that was just another word for stupid. It had got him a name on the pitch. He struck daring goals with devastating effects. Maybe this was a shining example of his idiocy, but he couldn't rid himself of the possibility factor. Was it real?

Was there any way of finding out without trying? 'Let's go for it.'

Chris wasn't pleased. 'If I negotiate a contract, you'll have to be available,' he said.

'And I will be,' Troy said. 'Nothing's going to happen between now and Christmas, is it? I can't train. That gives me four months. I can get helicoptered out if I'm needed somewhere fast.'

'Oh, Troy,' said Chris. 'I just hope this works. Can you prove you're doing physio and following your recovery plan?'

'Sure. Carys will sort that. I want to recover more than anyone, but I don't want to do it in the public eye. The paps are still crawling around and I need space.'

'Ok,' Chris muttered. 'I'll see what I can do regarding negotiations.'

If he didn't get back to football, there was no future. His pie in the sky guesthouse idea was something but in reality, he didn't know how to bring it about. If it came to reading contracts, he was up shit creek. That was Chris's job in the soccer world, but not in the real world. He couldn't go into commentary, journalism, public speaking or any of those things because he couldn't read scripts or risk making some ignorant gaffe.

What had been so clear-cut just months ago was now a mess, but it wasn't all bad. When Carys rolled her knuckles across the plains of his back every day and he drifted into a dream state, he couldn't imagine a much more heavenly place to be.

Chapter Nine

Carys

Carys clung to the steering wheel. She was driving a Porsche, an actual bona fide Porsche. Even sitting in one didn't marry with her existence. Racing her bike down a hill was the quickest she usually got. Hopefully the bike was ok after being sent on ahead with a removal van full of Troy's 'necessities' the previous week.

'Am I the world's slowest Porsche driver?' She leaned forward; raindrops bounced off the road and she squinted at the tail lights of the car in front.

Troy laughed. 'Yeah, but I don't mind. Going fast in this weather is suicide and I've had enough near misses this year already.'

'Oh god, don't remind me.' She'd listed driving as a skill on her CV, when really she'd only driven a handful of times since she passed her test three years before. After being in Troy's employ for nearly two months, she'd confessed she wasn't that confident, especially in this rain, on country roads and with only a vague idea where she was going. Even with the satnav displaying the directions, she wasn't convinced they were on the right road.

Troy hadn't seemed too bothered. 'I trust you,' he'd said and her heartbeat had soared. Going off with him like this was easily the wildest thing she'd ever done. Part of her wanted to imagine they were friends, maybe more, going on a mad adventure, but she had to keep her sensible pants tightly on. This wasn't a lovers' trip to paradise.

'Quite exciting this, isn't it?' said Troy.

'What?' Had he been reading her mind? Sometimes it felt like he knew exactly what she was thinking.

'The weather. I mean it's shit but it adds a bit of adventure to the trip'

'This is not what I'd call an adventure,' said Carys, but butterflies flapped around her tummy. Soon they'd be on Mull – if they weren't washed away or drowned – and they'd have the keys to a phenomenal new house in a new place.

Carys's eyes filled. Unexpected thoughts of Joanne flooded back, how she'd promised to take Carys herself. Memories of her hugs, warm words and funny stories always slapped Carys with powerful emotions but with the added buzz of this trip, it was too much. She dragged her finger under her eye, pushing away a tear with a sniff.

'Are you ok?' said Troy.

'What? Oh, yes, fine.'

'Listen, you never say much about your circumstances or your family. This is ok, isn't it?'

'What do you mean?'

'Moving to the wilderness with me for three months.'

'That's what you're paying me for,' she said.

'Carys.'

She sensed him cocking his head because her eyes were pinned on the road.

'I think we've reached the stage where you can tell me personal stuff. Come on, spill. Am I dragging you away from your home and your family for six months? Is there someone you're going to miss?'

'No. I don't have a boyfriend or a partner. Nothing like that.'

'What about parents? Friends? Come on.'

What, should she tell him her whole damn sordid story? It never sounded real. People were either horrified or sceptical about whether it was even true.

'Carys?' Troy leaned closer. Super distracting when she needed to focus. If he touched her now, he'd find himself in another crash. 'I get you're doing this for the money but it won't stop you missing people.'

'No, Troy,' she said. 'My friends all have their own lives, they won't even notice I've gone.'

'Come on, I don't believe that. You're probably the go-to mate for most of them. I bet they can't get through a day without you.'

Not even close. She scoffed. She had friends but no one in particular, especially after her ex had posted those photos on Instagram. It was the most humiliating moment of her life. Her cheeks burned at the memory. She'd been young and stupid, but she hadn't realised what she'd done would end up losing her all her friends and there was nothing she could do unless she admitted she'd broken the law. She'd never had that one special friend that people should have. It was the same with everyone in her life, she never trusted them to stick around, so she buddied up with lots of people but didn't really get close to anyone. Sometimes it was easier to be alone.

'What about family?' he said. 'No secret kids?'

'Four half-siblings, but they're not a secret, and none of my own, no. They live with my dad and his wife.'

'What about your mum?'

Carys shrugged. May as well spit it out; they'd got this far. 'I never knew her. She dumped me at the side of a road when I was a baby.'

'No way.' His voice was quick and sharp.

'Yes way.' Just as well CVs didn't require family info on them; she'd never have had a job anywhere. 'It happened over twenty-four years ago. I don't remember it and I'm over it.'

'Jesus fecking Christ.' Troy rubbed his cheeks. 'I can't believe it.'

'Well, do. It's true.'

He put his hand out and grasped hers over the wheel. She held her breath. *Need to concentrate. Eyes on road.* Her breathing was haywire. Troy's hand was so warm. She didn't want him to move and if he did, then please let it caress her, hold her.

'Shit.' She rammed on the brakes and they hurtled forward.

'Ow,' Troy yowled as he fell back.

'Sorry,' she said as they ploughed through a huge flood. 'I didn't see it coming.'

'It's ok.' He rubbed his shoulder. 'I didn't realise you'd had such a tough life.'

'It's not that bad. I've also worked with some great people. People who have nothing but are still optimistic, people who are old and have watched their dreams fade and die but still see something in life worth living. Now, I've lived in a mansion and driven a Porsche.'

Troy let out a laugh. 'Living the dream.'

'I take my kicks where I can.'

'Do you?'

'Well, you know what I mean.' Heat bloomed up her neck. Why did she keep saying this kind of thing to him? Or was it him deliberately misunderstanding everything she said? Maybe she did it all the time and that was why she'd ended up with so many failed relationships. People just didn't get her.

'You're funny,' he said, squinting at a flashing sign ahead. 'What did that say? I didn't see it in time to read it.'

She raised an eyebrow. 'Just a weather warning. Like we need it.'

How often had he shoved documents at her and asked her to read them because he 'couldn't be bothered'? And he shied away from writing anything down. He left voice messages rather than typing and moaned when people sent him long texts.

She'd noticed similar things in some centres she'd worked at. Often the clients were illiterate as they'd missed lots of school for whatever reason, but sometimes it was down to undiagnosed dyslexia. Either scenario could apply to Troy. He might have missed school as a teenager if he was heavily involved in football practice. But she daren't ask him. Confessing to having noticed would go down like a brick. The vibes he sent off were louder than a foghorn: *this topic isn't for discussion.*

Rain smeared the windscreen as Carys steered into the ferry lane. It may be almost September but the weather had decided it should be November.

Troy leaned forward, peering into the gloom. 'I can't see a thing. It's like Jurassic Park.'

'If a T-rex comes crashing towards us, I'm out of here,' said Carys. 'That definitely wasn't in my contract.'

Troy flashed her a smile. His chiselled face so frequently had care lines carved into it, to see him smile was a beautiful and joyful thing. Carys returned it and warmth flowed between them. Now more than ever, she wanted to lean forward and let her lips touch his. An electric current surged through her at the thought and she quickly turned away.

A dark shape loomed in the mist, big enough to be a dinosaur, the hulking steel hull of the ferry boat. A creaking and clanking sound followed and Troy looked askance. 'That's the T-rex breaking free. We're in trouble now.'

'Oh, shut up. It's obviously the ramp going down.'

'Is it? Are you sure? Like one hundred and ten per cent sure?' Troy gaped with fake sincerity.

'Haha, whatever.'

As the car in front pulled off, Carys started the engine and edged forward. Driving into the ship's hull was like being swallowed by a whale. Carys focused ahead, not looking at how close the sea was. Pulling up behind another car, she exhaled in a low whistle.

'How the hell am I going to get out of here and onto the deck? There isn't exactly much room. Can I stay in the car?'

'You're not allowed,' said Carys. 'Come on, we'll manage.'

'And all these people.' Troy grabbed a baseball cap from the dash and pulled it low. 'What if someone sees me and posts it on the internet? I don't want any paps following me. I need a break from that.'

'Let's not worry about that just now.' But she couldn't help glancing around as she squeezed between the cars to get to his door. The Porsche stuck out like a sore thumb among the trucks, Land Rovers, people carriers and motorhomes. What if someone did recognise him? She wouldn't know one footballer from another but obviously some people did. She opened his door and helped him swivel his legs out. After readying his crutches, she took his weight for a few seconds as he positioned them. Slowly they made their way to the staircase, Troy clanking along like Captain Hook.

They waited for a couple of elderly people to get in the lift first. Carys smiled at them while Troy kept his head down, covering his face with the peak of his cap. They emerged to cooking smells and a bustle of people jostling into a restaurant area.

'Is it safe to eat here?' asked Troy. 'Or will it kill my regime?'

'You're allowed some leeway,' said Carys. 'It's not like you're playing a match today.'

'Good, because I need somewhere to sit and soon.'

She led him through the glass doors and they took a small window table for two. Carys passed Troy the menu.

'You tell me what I'm allowed.' Troy shoved it back. Yup, there it was again. She tapped the menu. Should she say something? His eyes bored into her, defiantly waiting for her to read it, almost daring her to ask, like he had a short-shrift answer at the ready.

The crossing took just under an hour, but Carys checked the time incessantly. She wanted to make sure they had plenty of time to get back to the car so Troy wasn't rushed, and his paranoia was rubbing off on her. People seemed to be looking their way more than was normal. It could have been the crutches or the fact he looked like he was trying to hide. If he took off the hat, he might not be so obvious.

When they finally took their seats in the Porsche, alarms rang, warning the hull doors were opening. Carys started the engine and lurched forward.

'Steady.' Troy clung to the seat. 'I don't need an insurance job before I'm even on dry land.'

'That wasn't me,' said Carys. 'It's so stormy.'

The first view of the island was a little village shrouded in mist; signs flapped outside the shops and people huddled under the covered walkway for the ferry, nothing much to shout about. A prickle of panic shot through her. What if the pictures were photoshopped and fake? She'd dragged Troy here and he'd spent eight hundred thousand pounds. Not to mention what he'd paid to have a gym and massage room installed, his luggage and her bike shipped over, and for a local company to clean the house and ensure food was waiting. All for a place he hadn't even viewed. Heat rose in Carys's neck along with a burning sensation in her tummy she was sure had nothing to do with the macaroni cheese on the ferry. What if he hated it?

Carys glanced in her mirror. A black car was behind her. It had been since the boat. There was only a limited number of roads from the ferry port but something about the car gave her the creeps. She pulled in and let it whizz past.

'Why did you do that?' said Troy.

'Just manners,' said Carys. 'He was going faster than me and I'm not sure of the roads.' As they wound along the twisty roads through another little village, the mist lifted, but Carys kept glancing in the mirrors. With social media there was no keeping anything a secret, but she wanted to protect Troy from prying eyes as long as she could. Blue sky poked out and the wind carried off tattered clouds at a pace; hills and forests appeared, green and lush. Waterfalls and streams gashed down the hillsides, wild and free. 'It's so pretty,' said Carys.

She drove over a crest and into a glen where a village clustered around an inlet. A white church with a bizarre tower like a dovecote sat on a hillside. Beyond the village, blue sea rolled in with foamy waves like white horses on top.

'Is the house around here somewhere?' asked Troy. 'I've lost track. There's too much to look at.'

'We turn left at the T-junction and it's a little way out of the village.'

A few miles along the coastal road, they spotted it, high on a hill, shining and proud.

'Wow,' said Troy. 'That's my kind of place, alright.'

Carys didn't dare say or even think it but she wanted it to be her kind of place too. Where else could be more beautiful? Once Troy was settled, she could take a couple of hours here and there and cycle around on her bike, a far cry from the city roads. This was a place to be free. She pulled the car into the driveway but didn't move. Neither did Troy. They just gaped at the house. Carys had never seen the like, except on TV when her dad had been watching *Escape to the Country*. 'Shall we go in?' she said.

'I guess.' Troy unbuckled himself and Carys darted around to help him out. A sea breeze touched her cheeks and she inhaled the instant freshness. As she took Troy's weight to help him out of the car, he kept his arm around her for longer than before. Her heart leapt. This was like being pulled in for a hug. It melted her insides and spread to her extremities.

Before she could pull away, warm lips touched her cheek, softly but firmly. 'Thank you,' he said, his nose still pressed to her face above her ear.

'What for?' she said, hardly able to breathe.

'For being alive and finding your way into my life.'

She shifted so she could see him and flicked him a sceptical look. 'Are you ok?' This had to stay light and airy like she didn't care that her very rich boss had just kissed her. 'Has the sea air got to you?'

'Must have.'

'Let's go inside,' she said. If he was a guy from down the road, she'd do something about the feelings swirling around her chest, but he was an international footballer and nothing could happen, no matter how much her heart tugged at her. As soon as their time was up, he'd cast her off like a worn-out shoe. She wasn't cut out for his lifestyle. But whoa. She was letting her mind run away. There was no question of anything like that happening. That was simply a friendly peck after a long journey, nothing more. *Absolutely not.* She strapped his crutches into place.

'What the hell am I going to do here?' Troy gaped around. 'I've never been anywhere so remote.'

'You'll have to learn to enjoy life's simple pleasures.'

'Such as?'

'Think of all the books you could read.' She set the bait; would he bite?

'Seriously? When do I have time to read books?'

'Now. That's the point.'

'I still have a career to save.'

'You can help heal your body by healing the mind.'

'You hippy,' he said.

Chuckling, she led the way to the door and entered the number into the key safe. Flinging open the doors, she half-expected a clone of Troy's Glasgow mansion but this was softer and more homely. A cream carpet covered the floor rather than polished wood. An oak side table and a tartan chair with a basket of books were beside a glass door leading to a corridor.

'I'd like to explore but it'll be a ground floor only tour for a while. My leg feels ready to give way. Honestly, it's ridiculous and frustrating,' he growled.

'Hey. Don't be hard on yourself. You've sat a long time in the car and we haven't done your physio today, so it's not surprising. Let's just relax. I can do your massage and we can explore later. It's not like we don't have plenty of time. Don't worry about training or anything else right now. You've taken a brave step.' She looked into his grey-blue eyes and they shone bright, glistening a little around the tear ducts. He was beautiful when he was vulnerable like this and she understood why he'd kissed her. He'd lost everything and he was counting on her to help him find it again.

Now was the time to focus on him getting better.

even thing and he was traumatised on her to begin but find it
again.
Now was the time to focus on him getting better

Chapter Ten

Troy

Pain. Unbearable pain. It shot from Troy's shoulder, along his arm, across his back and down his leg.

'Stop, just stop,' he groaned.

'I'm not doing anything.' Carys's face was a picture of virtue. Even her freckles glowed innocently, and she batted her eyelids.

'Laughing hurts,' said Troy. 'Like, seriously hurts.' Everything she did made him laugh, smile or want to kiss her. Sometimes all at once.

'Laughter is the best medicine, don't you know?'

'My bones are wrecked.' He rolled his shoulders and gazed out the glass doors across the new garden. The early September greens and yellows glowed in the dappled sunlight. Never had he been so wholly relaxed in a place. No training, no team meetings, no matches to prepare for. Nothing. Just a beautiful house, a stunning view… and Carys.

She padded to the window. 'How about we go and explore the garden?'

With the first day of warm sunshine in a week, it seemed the ideal opportunity, but the paths were rambling and not wheelchair friendly. Even on the crutches, Troy pictured himself going his length. Carys scanned him over and he shrank back. Why did it feel like she was reading his mind or X-raying him? Or stripping him naked? If she wanted to do that, she could have him. He'd lay himself on a plate for her. But, Christ, what was he thinking? Lines were blurring all over the place; he was paying for her kindness and he had to remember that. He couldn't mistake this for interest on her part. She wasn't a woman in the bar, laughing at his jokes and making eyes at him. How could he know if this was real or simply her doing what was in her contract? Every time they got close, she pulled away.

'I know what you're thinking, Troy,'

Do you?

'But it won't be that bad. You can walk and I'll take the chair, so if you need a rest, you can have one. Come on, you can do this.'

Troy hauled himself to his feet. Carys took his arm and helped him position his crutch. How wonderful would it be to stand on his own, keep her arm linked in his and stroll around the garden? But as soon as he could walk on his own, he'd have no need for her. And what then? Would she fancy the life of a footballer's girlfriend? What about a fling? He groaned. That was too risky. If they did it and everything blew up, he'd be back to square one with no one.

'It's ok,' she said

'What?'

'You can do it.' She smiled at him.

'Oh, yeah.' He hobbled forward, testing his weight. When would he be able to do this on his own? Months? Weeks? Days? No one would ever give him a straight answer.

'I'll get the chair while you get to the door,' she said.

He nudged it open with his good shoulder and made his way down the two steps into the neatly kept part of the garden at the front. This kind of garden was ok, as long as he could pay someone to keep it. The rambling part to the side and the back scared him. Things were always better tamed and controlled.

A clattering behind him announced Carys's arrival and she bumped the wheelchair down the steps.

'Just as well I'm not in that,' he muttered.

'You don't fancy joyriding around the paths? A few wheel spins, skids, that kind of thing.'

'And that's different from normal, how?' He raised his eyebrows, watching the grin spread across Carys's cheeks. That smile could sink him. No woman had ever had this effect on him before. He could keep his cool around the most glamorous models from all around the world but not Carys. Every massage sent him over the edge. Did she know her power? Maybe his brain had been affected in the crash. It had turned him into a sap.

'No prisoners next time,' she said.

He limped forwards, smirking, but Carys tapped his arm. 'This way. We've already looked at these flower beds a hundred times. I want to check out the orchard and the veg garden.'

'Is that what you call that wilderness?'

'Stop being a pretty boy.'

'What? How dare you—'

'Shh. Just imagine…' Carys splayed her fingers like she was opening a curtain on her mind. The pains in Troy's legs, back, shoulder and chest diminished as she beamed. Her pale grey eyes twinkled like stars reflecting in a sea of mischief and intrigue. 'This house could be some kind of health retreat. You know what you were saying about it being a B&B? Well, you could push the health side. You've got the gym and the massage area. You could grow veg and harvest your own fruit. You could have mindfulness classes.'

Troy arched an eyebrow but his grin stayed put. 'Could I?' It sounded gorgeous when she put it like that, but completely unrealistic.

'Well, with people to help you run it,' she went on, her cheeks reddening. 'Think of the potential.'

He scoffed. 'You sound like an estate agent.'

They accessed the orchard through a wrought-iron gate with chicken wire attached to it. An archway of twisted willow with tattered bows and long straggly limbs swayed in the breeze. 'This has seen better days.' Carys stretched, grabbing a trailing branch and winding it back into place. Troy admired her lithe shape as she pushed on tiptoes, trying to replace the branch.

'Here.' Troy limped towards her. Stretching over her with his good arm, he slipped the branch into place. Her eyes ran over him and she slid her fingers around the back of her neck. This was the first time he'd felt his own height next to her. He was standing straight, though not for much longer. An urge to seize her and kiss her burned close to the surface. 'Aaargh,' he growled, dropping into the chair.

Carys licked her lips, still watching him, then looked back at the willow arch. 'I went to a willow weaving class with a youth group once. This needs some love.'

So do I. He rubbed his hand across his face and scrunched his eyes shut. When he opened them again, he hoped the world would be back to normal. He'd be in the tunnel, jogging up and down, eager to get on the pitch. And Carys? She'd be a distant memory – he didn't like that bit.

'What's that?'

Troy's eyes sprang open. Something in Carys's voice sounded panicky. Her pupils were wide as she stared through a gap in the trees.

'What?' he said.

'Nothing.' She turned to him and smiled. 'Just the wind moving the bushes. I thought it was a... a deer.' Her eyes darted back to the spot. 'Oh, look at the apples.'

Green and russet apples groaned on stubby bows. Troy got to his feet and scanned the rows of small trees but couldn't help looking back. Had Carys seen something? And if not a deer, maybe a pap? Surely not out here. 'Quite the Miss Green Fingers, aren't you?' he said, hobbling along the overgrown path.

Carys pouted. 'Actually no. I've never had a garden. I'd love to learn though.' She drifted up to a tree and ran a caressing finger over an apple.

Jesus Christ. He forced himself to look away. That action was way too suggestive. The light wind carried sweet scents and rustled the leaves. Troy breathed deep. Carys stooped and picked some daisies, clutching them in her palm like gems.

'My mum used to take me to the park and we'd make daisy chains. I'm not sure I remember how.' She plonked herself on his wheelchair and started threading the flowers together.

'I thought your mum abandoned you when you were a baby?'

'I meant my stepmum. My dad's ex. They split when I was twelve.'

Troy watched for a moment, waiting for more, but she clammed up, keeping her eyes on the daisies. He swung his focus to the sea.

'If it stays nice, let's go to a beach tomorrow,' he said.

'Um... Ok. I'll find a quiet one.'

'Why?' he asked. 'Are you planning on sunbathing starkers?'

'Definitely not,' she said. 'Though you can if you want.'

'It's in your contract to do anything within reason that I ask. If I'm baring all, then it's perfectly reasonable for you to do the same.'

She smirked at the daisies. 'Too cold, so I'd say it's unreasonable.'

'You've never had an ice-bath. Now that's cold.' His phone vibrated in his back pocket and he fumbled for it. So far reception had been poor and he'd hardly spoken to anyone. He screwed up his face at Shaun Eddery's picture.

'Hi, Troy. How's it going, mate?'

'As well as can be expected. Why?'

'No reason. Just wanted to hear your voice. I miss those dulcet tones bossing us about.'

Troy huffed and shook his head. 'Seriously?'

'Yeah. It's not the same without you. Daryl's a shit captain.'

'He's taken over as captain? How did I miss that?'

'What's happened to you, man? I wondered when you would react. Where you been?'

Troy shrugged as if Shaun was right in front of him. 'I've had more important shit to worry about. So, how'd that come about?'

'Dunno, because we have zero respect for the dick after what he did to you.'

'Thanks, mate. I'm glad I got out. I couldn't have stomached watching his smug mug gloating over me.'

'It's worse than that. He sits in the car with Pippa before he comes in for practice. He's all over her. I'm surprised you haven't seen the pics. The paps are having a field day. It's plastered over social media.'

'I haven't looked.' He didn't want to go down that rabbit hole. It would boil his blood.

'So, are you making good progress?' asked Shaun. 'Isaac said you were looking a bit down when he saw you.'

'Well, it's hardly a picnic in the park. This is the longest I've been on my feet since June.' What did the idiots think he was doing? They really had no idea how bad these injuries were. Or they were in a position to sweep it under the carpet.

Carys placed a crown of daisies on her head and fluttered her lashes. Give her a set of wings and she'd be a flower fairy. She jumped up and pushed the chair in Troy's direction. He accepted the seat as she all but rammed it into his backside. 'That's better,' he muttered as his limbs relaxed.

'What is?' said Shaun.

'I sat down.'

'Aw man, it sounds awful. Has Chris found anywhere for you yet?'

'He's still negotiating. He's good at what he does, so I'm leaving it to him to work his magic.' The pangs of worry surged like a great wave again. Chris could negotiate the best deal in the world but that didn't mean Troy would be fit enough to play. He may never be fit enough again. Why was he sitting here in an orchard while his nurse made daisy chains? Getting fit should be top priority.

But as soon as Shaun was off the phone and Carys started chatting again, the niggling urge flickered and died. Recovery happened in different ways and this was part of it. Wasn't it? Or was Carys on her airy-fairy planet, leading him into all sorts of crazy plans that weren't helping with anything?

*

The following day, Carys drove them south towards a beach she'd read about.

'It's called Uisken Bay and it's far enough off the main road to be away from the tourists, but it has a car park nearby and it isn't a long walk, so the guidebook says,' Carys informed him on the way.

Sunshine streamed in the window. Troy lounged back and watched the scenery.

'It hopefully won't be too busy,' said Carys, checking her mirror. 'Hang on.' She indicated and pulled over.

'What?'

'Just letting someone pass. I'm not keen on these single-track roads. I'd rather have the cars in front than behind.'

A black car whizzed by.

'This road only goes to the beach,' said Carys. 'So they must be going there too.'

'Hmm.' Troy flexed his fingers and his toes. Maybe it was his imagination but he felt more supple than before. 'I see some houses, maybe they live there. Let's hope. I'm not going starkers but I still don't want anyone to see me.'

'I've packed extra shorts, so you can go for a dip. The seawater will do you good.'

'And how am I getting the shorts on? If you think I'm getting changed on the beach, then forget it. It takes me about two hours to get dressed.'

'Well, I could help you.'

'No.' That would be too torturous for words. 'I'd feel like Prince bloody Charles or something.'

'Oh, get over yourself,' said Carys, but her cheeks glowed red.

He folded his arms and stared out the window. This wasn't about her seeing him starkers. He would have been the same with anyone. It was bad enough for her to help him with clothes after the massage. Dressing was too personal, too intimate. And she had power over his body. He couldn't control himself when she touched him. She made him smile, she lifted his moods and she was there, present, when he needed someone. Was it simply a side effect of proximity? Being close to her every day was bound to have an impact. He narrowed his eyes and gave himself an internal nod. *Yup, that's my story and I'm sticking to it.*

By the time they reached the beach, the sun had gathered heat and it felt almost tropical. 'So, we arrived in August and it was chucking it down like the middle of winter. Now it's September and it's like midsummer,' he muttered.

'That good old Scottish weather again,' said Carys.

Two other cars were parked in the small uneven parking area, including the black one that had passed them, but whoever they belonged to must have walked elsewhere as the beach was empty. Troy scanned around. A few houses overlooked the bay, a bit too close for comfort. Even out here, someone might recognise him. He hobbled across the stony surface as Carys grabbed some bags from the boot.

The second he stepped onto the beach, the sand yielded under his feet. 'Ok. Call me Prince Charles, but will you take off my shoes and socks?'

Carys gave him a coy smile as she knelt in the sand in front of him and unlaced his shoes. His jaw set and he fixed his stare on a house on the hill behind the beach. His insides clenched and his groin twitched. What must this look like? He wanted to thread his fingers into her hair and draw her close. *Fuck's sake.* He almost growled aloud. *Keep a lid on it.* He met beautiful women all the time. A perk of the job. But natural women, kind women, caring women, they were harder to come by. The WAGs and prospective WAGs could be those things once you'd waded past the superficial. Not with Carys. She was just as she was. Artless. And now she was kneeling in the sand in front of him. Could she please hurry up?

As she wrestled with his right shoe, he placed his weight on his left crutch and his shoulder and chest smarted. With great effort, he straightened his left foot and spread the load onto it. Carys pulled off the shoe, then whipped off the sock.

'Ok, foot down,' she said. He eased it into the soft sand, enjoying the relief of pressure from his bad leg but savouring more the tingling warmth of the golden grains as they engulfed him to the ankle. Carys removed his other shoe and sock, then peered up. *Don't look at me like that.* 'Do you want your trousers rolled up, Your Highness?'

He scowled heavenward, partly resigned to her teasing and partly to stop his eyes lingering on her chest. The breeze had stopped and the air was suddenly intense. 'Yeah, thanks, wench.'

She smirked and very deliberately pushed up her cleavage with her wrists. Then, with a wink, she started rolling up his trouser legs. Even in his most unattractive sweats – the only trousers he could get on – there was something seductive in the way her fingertips twisted and lodged them above his knee. Forcing his gaze away wasn't an option any more. As she finished the second leg, she swung forward as she got to her feet and he almost toppled over as her face came close to his waist. 'Christ, watch what you're doing,' he muttered.

'Sorry. So, are you going in?' The patch of pink on her cheeks betrayed her embarrassment.

'Maybe.' He scanned around again. Crickets or something were clicking in the grass but no one was in sight.

'What is it?' asked Carys with a frown.

'I dunno. Do you think people in the houses are watching? They might take pictures and sell them to the paps?'

'No one will recognise you from that distance.' She kicked off her white pumps, but her eyes wandered over the grassy bank in front of the houses. 'Come on.' She led the way to the sea. Her pale blue dress fluttered as she walked. She cast off her thin white cardigan and set it on the sand beside her shoes.

Troy's eyes grew busy following each dainty move she made with that pixie body. Not watching where he was going, he stumbled on a dune. Shit, the wheelchair was in the car. Pushing it on the sand wouldn't work, but he was bloody stranded and helpless. What if he got stuck here and had to crawl back? Heat burned his neck and branded his face with humiliation. 'Argghh!' he growled. Seething bile formed in his stomach.

Carys glanced back and frowned. 'What's wrong?'

Troy's jaw set and his facial muscles spasmed. This wasn't him. Who was he now but a pathetic invalid? He was perving on a girl who probably thought him a loser.

'Troy?' Carys gave him a quizzical look as she strolled back. 'It's ok,' she murmured, placing her hand under his good elbow. 'If you don't want to go in, I'm not going to force you. Like I could. You're too strong and too stubborn.'

He couldn't speak but he shook his head. This wasn't something she could make light of.

'Do you need the chair?'

'No.'

From the corner of his eye, he caught her frown. 'What then?'

'I don't want the chair, I don't want these fucking crutches, I don't want a nurse, I want to be able to walk and run, do my training, live my goddamn life, not be a twisted cripple.' He squeezed his eyes shut.

'Of course you don't want any of these things.' The pressure on his elbow intensified and she held him firm. 'I can't change what's happened and neither can you. And I know it sounds meh if I say look on the bright side, but really, Troy, looking for positives is the best way. You will get better.'

'Will I? Do you know that?'

'Yes, I do. I can't promise you'll ever be exactly as you were before, but you're already better than you were. You've walked this far without a rest. You did the same yesterday. So, cut yourself some slack. You're used to a fast-paced lifestyle and working with a team. It's hard to think about yourself without feeling like you're letting the side down. But you're not. You need this time, so take it. Enjoy it. This is a tiny moment in your life. Let it be what it is.'

Her eyes were wide and pleading. How did someone so young have such wisdom? Everything she said resonated and while he couldn't completely shake the anger at being thrown into this mess in the first place, he accepted her words and let her lead him forward. 'You should get a job working for a football club. If you can talk me off a ledge, you can work magic.'

She patted his arm. 'No, Troy. I don't fancy that at all. I'd hate to be in the public eye with every move being watched and people printing lies about me every few days. Something like that happened to me once and it was awful. How you can do it day in, day out baffles me. I don't know how you stand it.'

'Learned to live with it, I guess.'

'Let's channel some positive energy.' She stroked her wispy hair behind her ear and tossed back her head. Her exposed neck begged to be kissed.

'Carys. Can I...' *Kiss you? Please.* He swallowed and leaned closer. 'Can we...' *Be together as more than injured dude and nurse?* Cool waves rolled gently over his toes and ankles. He inhaled the clear air. 'I... Nothing.'

Her dress flared gently in the sea breeze. The delicacy of the movement struck him deep. 'What is it?'

'Really, it's nothing.' How could he say everything he wanted to when she'd just dismissed a life in the public eye? That was the only life he knew.

Chapter Eleven

Carys

Carys slung a mesh bag over her shoulder. The little orchard might never yield a crop for anything more than one apple and berry smoothie or a granola crumble, but it was enough. She smiled at her pickings. At the rear orchard fence, tangled bramble bushes pushed their way over, adding their wild fruits to the cultivated ones. Carys took out a Tupperware box and plucked the ripe berries. Purple stains covered her fingertips as she loaded the container.

The simple joy of knowing these fruits were grown here was special. She was so used to grabbing things from convenience stores in the city and not checking where they came from that this was a novelty. She threw back her head. This was a kind of place she'd never even dreamt of before. Everything was natural and free. But Troy was her priority. Maybe once her time was done with him, she could consider a lifestyle change, but now she took a few moments to breathe. She didn't want to think about a life without Troy.

On the path between the orchard and the house, newly fallen brown and yellow leaves dotted the gravel. Somehow in the city, these signs were easy to miss or dismiss in the fast-paced hubbub of life. Now they were all around. Proper autumn trees in vibrant colours, greenery on the hills turning brown and a sense of change sweeping in on

Margaret Amatt

the rushing clouds. A few miles along the main road, Carys had spotted a box with eggs for sale at the end of a farm track. For the first time in weeks, she took her bike out. As she freewheeled around the corner, she spotted a black car parked in a passing place.

She jumped off the bike and slung it on the ground beside the egg box. Was she being super-paranoid in thinking that was the same car she'd seen on the beach road a few days before? Must be a coincidence and even if it was the same car, this was an island, there weren't that many people. All the same, it made her feel edgy. She collected a box of eggs and left some money in the tin. Once they were strapped on the bike, she pedalled back, though it was much tougher as most of it was uphill.

Troy roared with laughter as she opened the front door, sweating and out of puff. He wasn't anywhere in sight, but she assumed he was in the living room talking to one of his friends or teammates. She pulled off her helmet and nipped into the kitchen with her eggs and the pickings from earlier. She'd accumulated enough material to start a healthy eating menu with something different for every day of the week, almost the month. Her mind whizzed over possibilities. Maybe if Troy turned this house into a B&B after he left, he would let her stay and work in it. Troy had one goal – to heal and get back to football but Carys's future was up in the air.

Some papers lay on the dining table and Carys squinted at them. They were covered in doodles, elaborate lines twisted together to form very stylised pictures, similar to adult colouring books. Had Troy done them?

The clunk of his crutches in the hall made her look up. She abandoned the drawings and started washing the berries. A tremor fizzed through her as he approached. Take away the employer, take away the football superstar, and what was left was a man Carys liked just as a man. When the pretence and barriers fell away, Troy was a fun guy, sometimes as explosive as his reputation but also gentle and warm. She felt a kindred spirit in him, someone who had lots of friends but no one close. But he was so out of her world.

'Hey.' He limped in. 'Check this out.' He briefly lifted one crutch and held it out, then gingerly took a couple of steps before grabbing the table for support.

'Very good,' said Carys. 'But be careful not to aggravate it.'

'Spoilsport.' His gaze landed on the drawings and he shuffled around, folded them up and shoved them in his pocket.

'They're good,' said Carys. 'Did you do them?'

'What? Oh, yeah. I was just messing about. Where were you? You were ages.' He pushed with his crutches, manoeuvring himself onto a barstool across the kitchen island from her. His expression said the subject of the drawings was closed.

'I picked all this in the orchard and got some eggs from the farm down the road. I'm noting some ideas of what we could do with it.' Her tablet sat open. Every day her book grew. She'd reached the stage of believing one day she might get it published, though after googling the process, she'd laid off; it made her head spin. 'Maybe something in the vegetable beds is usable but I'm not sure what's in there. I'm not very knowledgeable about plants.'

'More than I am,' said Troy. 'If it's green, it's a plant. That's all I know.'

Carys cocked her head. 'I'm sure you could learn. I'd like to but I'm not sure how. I need to get an identification app.'

Troy pulled a bewildered face.

99

'Who were you phoning?' It wasn't her business but it didn't feel wrong to ask.

'No one,' he said.

'Sorry, I thought I heard you laughing.'

'I was watching TV. I never watch anything normally. There's some funny shit on. I was too young for *Friends* the first time around but it's seriously funny.'

'Yeah, it is.'

'We should binge-watch them one day. I've never had a TV binge day.'

His look of boyish excitement made her grin. Most guys she knew spent every non-workday on a TV binge. 'I'll schedule it into your recovery plan. Tell you what, why don't you do it this Saturday? There's an Autumn Produce Market in Tobermory. I'd like to nip along and see if there's any local produce I could use in the menus. It's not really your thing, so you could TV binge without me.'

Troy folded his arms. 'Why wouldn't it be my thing?' he asked in a mock put-out voice.

'There'll be lots of people, potentially fans ready to pounce on you.' She glanced up from washing the apples to spy his reaction.

'Yeah, ok. Does that mean you want to skip out on the binge-watching?'

'After living with my dad, I'd be happy never to watch TV again, ever.'

Troy chuckled and Carys smiled. When he was chilled and relaxed, his eyes glittered with mischief and colour returned to his cheeks. So much life was in him, but as soon as they did anything geared to his recovery, the grim expression reappeared, presumably the steely determination that had got him so far in his career.

*

Even set up for his binge date, Troy didn't quite manage to pull off the look. He was missing the potbelly, the bleary morning after face and the grungy clothes. Still, he seemed as happy as a pig in muck, or a child who'd been granted a sick day when they were actually fine and just wanted chill-time. Carys had her coat and bag on. Kiss him goodbye? She shouldn't – of course, she bloody shouldn't – but it felt odd leaving him on his own after so many weeks together. She'd barely been apart from him. All their shopping had been delivered or she'd grabbed stuff on the way back from their trips to the beach or the woods. Troy would stay in the car, head down and hat pulled low. The ride to the farm gate was as far as she'd been without him.

Remembering he didn't like fussing, Carys didn't ask if he'd be ok. 'Call me if there's any problem. It's only half an hour away,' she said.

'I'll be fine.' He pointed the remote control at the giant screen, smirking.

Sitting behind the Porsche wheel without Troy at her side was odd. And she had his credit card – his housekeeping one anyway. He was generous with his budget. She shuffled in the seat and chewed her lip. This was like robbery or at least fraud. Since when did Carys McTeague have the right to drive a car like this or have unlimited funds?

Since now, apparently. She pressed the start button and whizzed down the short driveway. It wasn't a long way to the town but the roads were twisty and hilly.

A steep road curled into the main street of Tobermory. Carys glanced in her rear-view mirror and frowned. The black car again. 'I should've checked the numberplate,' she muttered, turning into the car park at the bottom of the hill. The car didn't follow but carried on along the main street of the harbour town, famous for its brightly painted multicoloured houses. They beamed in the low autumn sunshine, forming a curved backdrop to the street as Carys got out, still looking for the black car. *Just a coincidence.* There were loads of black cars about.

She took out a bundle of shopping bags and made her way to the promenade. To her right, the sea lapped at a large marina full of boats and yachts. The street ended with a slipway and a small ferry terminal.

Halfway along the road, a pier jutted out at a curious four-sided clock tower with a pointy roof. All the clock faces were at different times. Carys laughed to herself. Such was the pace of life here. There was no set time. Everything happened when it was ready. On the pier and across the road close to the town hall were long tables with canopies and gazebos. A banner strung from the town hall proclaimed: Autumn Produce Market.

Carys strolled along the pier first, her eyes popping at the huge barrels and boxes of fish. Where to start? After browsing every stall but buying nothing, she crossed the road to the next row. People bustled along, crowding around and chattering. A dark green gazebo was first and inside was a small table with neatly packaged boxes of vegetables and a pile of colourful books with a child's drawing on the front.

'Would you like to buy our school recipe book?' asked a girl as Carys was reading the stall's name; it belonged to a local primary school.

'Could I look at it first?'

'Yes.' The girl lifted a book and handed it to her. 'All the money we get will go to our school for new playground equipment. The books are five pounds and you can also buy a box of vegetables from our school garden.' The girl took a huge breath and pulled a half-smile.

Carys grinned back. The girl was too cute with her sale's pitch and no way would Troy grudge a few pounds from his budget to help a local school. 'Ok, yes,' said Carys.

The girl clapped and almost did a little dance as she skipped behind the table.

'Do you take cards?'

'I think so, but I have to get my teacher to do it. She's there, I'll get her.'

Carys watched as the girl passed a couple of people, swishing her long ponytail. She approached a woman with a brownish bob, streaked with some greys, talking to a man. The girl waited silently, tapping her foot and keeping her eyes fixed on the woman.

'I need the money for the stall,' the man said to the teacher. He was tall, dark-haired and good-looking but had a shrewd expression.

'Sorry, Calum,' she said. 'You need to invoice the headteacher.'

'I already did.' He thrust his hands into his blazer pockets. 'She really should have paid beforehand.'

'I know that, but I'm just here to look after the stall. She's the one to sort the money out with.'

The man sighed. 'Honestly, this is the reason I hate getting roped into jobs like this. It's more trouble than it's worth.'

'You have a reputation when it comes to debt collecting,' said the teacher. 'They probably thought you were the best man for the job.'

'Yeah. Great.' His eyes moved away from the teacher. 'I think that lass is waiting to talk to you.'

The teacher spun around. 'Is everything all right, Catelyn?'

'A lady wants to pay with a card.'

'Oh, of course.' The teacher hurried over. 'Hello. Sorry to keep you waiting. We have a card machine we borrowed but it's not very quick I'm afraid.'

'I'm not in a rush,' said Carys.

The teacher booted up the machine and held it, waiting. 'Are you on holiday this weekend?'

'I'm working here for the next few months, but I'm off today.' She glanced sideways. A man was peering over the vegetable table with his back to her, though she felt sure he was listening. Was it the same man who'd been asking about money?

'Lovely,' said the teacher. 'In a hotel?'

'No. I'm a carer. I'm working with someone who's here to recover from an accident.' Her eyes were still on the man's back. He turned slightly and she realised it was someone different but she thought she'd seen him before.

'Oh, that sounds stressful.'

'Some days are better than others,' said Carys. The man had gone. She refocused on the teacher. 'The house has a great garden and I'm trying to learn how to grow things. It's keeping me busy.'

'Mrs Hansen showed us how to grow all this,' said the little girl.

The teacher smiled. 'I love gardening and growing things. I've taken that passion into school with me.'

'I went to school in inner city Glasgow and growing cress on a paper towel was the only thing we ever did.'

The teacher grinned as she handed the card machine to Carys. 'We're so lucky here to have the countryside at our disposal, but an island can be a harsh climate for growing things. We're blessed with the gulf stream, which means it's rare to get very low temperatures or snow for a prolonged period. But there's a lot of wind and that can cause damage to plants.'

'Yes, I've noticed interesting weather since we arrived. So, what kind of things could I plant that wouldn't blow over?'

'You've missed the best time for planting unfortunately. Will you still be here in the spring?'

Carys sucked on her lip and shook her head. 'We're here until January. If the recovery goes well.'

'Hmm.' The teacher rubbed her chin. 'There are a few things you could grow. Could you pop back and we could chat about it later? It's just there's a queue forming.'

'Oh, oops,' said Carys, blinking around. 'Sorry.'

'Not at all, I'm happy to help, but these kids are great salespeople. How about I give you my number, drop me a message with any questions? I live on the island, so I'll always be about.'

She took a slip of paper out of a box at the gazebo edge and scribbled a phone number and the name *Fenella Hansen*.

'My name's Carys, in case you wonder who the mad person sending you messages is.'

Fenella smiled. 'I look forward to the questions, Carys,' she said.

Carys left the gazebo with her book and a box of veg. Her mind harked back to the man. Was he someone she'd met before or was her mind playing tricks on her? *I'm getting as paranoid as Troy.* It was hard enough getting him to relax. She didn't want to jeopardise it for something that was likely nothing. She made her way along the other stalls, purchasing some gorgeous bread loaves and deciding not to mention anything to Troy about the man and the car.

When she had Troy in tow, she only had the briefest chance to investigate as she ran errands but today, she was free. Past the end of the market stalls, she spied a striking window display in a shop named The Island Florist. Red, gold and orange blooms, mingled with pumpkins and gourds of all shapes and sizes, were decked around a wheelbarrow, wellies and garden tools.

She could get a nice bouquet for the window in the hallway. An earthy aroma struck her as she entered the shop and she heard people chatting at the till as she browsed the central displays. Something about the voice made her glance up. Her eyes homed in on the woman behind the counter. A smiling face she hadn't seen for years was ringing up someone's purchase. A face that stirred every emotion in her. That face had smiled at her while its owner hugged her and told her stories, had commiserated with her when things had gone wrong at school, and had vanished from her life without a trace. Mum... Joanne.

Carys blinked, woke from her trance and found herself stomping out of the shop, across the road and towards the car. A numb cold spread from her chest outwards. *She* was here. After leaving Lee she'd come home. *So much for wanting to come back for me!*

Carys started the engine and drove towards the house, a storm of emotions swirling around her head. Witnessing Joanne happy and content was like having a cold knife run through her. Subconsciously, she'd wished Joanne was a sad, lonely woman, filled with deep regret and sorrow at what she'd done, not someone casually going about daily life.

TV sounds and Troy's laughter greeted her as she came in and unloaded the shopping. She leaned on the worktop and breathed deeply.

'It is you, good, just checking in case you were a mad intruder.'

Carys jumped. Troy stood at the door. She hadn't heard his crutches. Quickly, she swept a finger under her eye. Why was she crying? How long had she been crying?

'Hey? What's wrong?' Troy frowned, hovering in the doorway.

'Nothing. Just the fish oil.'

'That's not true. Tell me.' Troy hobbled forward and leaned on the island. 'Is it because you're stuck here with me? Do you want to go home?'

Carys shook her head. 'It's nothing like that.' Should she tell him? It sounded so petty compared to his problems.

'What then? Have you spent all my money at the candyfloss stall?'

Carys managed a little smile. 'No.' She rubbed her face. 'It's nothing, really. Me being silly, that's all.'

Troy made his way slowly around the kitchen island. Carys's heartbeat raced. What was he doing? He approached with a furrowed brow. Propping one crutch on the island, he placed his arm around her shoulder. 'Whatever it is, you can tell me.'

Carys didn't reply. She closed her eyes, inhaling his cool citrus aroma. She leaned on him, letting the gentle circling motion of his fingertips on her shoulder lull her, but she couldn't fully relax. He was still her boss first and foremost, however much she'd love to crumple in his arms.

'When you're ready,' Troy said. 'It doesn't have to be today, or tomorrow, or even next week. But you and me are stuck here together. We're all we have right now. And you've done everything to help me, the least I can do is listen.' Troy leaned over and placed a kiss on her forehead.

'Thank you,' Carys whispered, barely resisting the urge to cave and melt into him. 'But really, I'm fine.'

Chapter Twelve

Troy

'Oh my god. No.' Carys clutched her face, staring at her tablet. 'No, no, no. Not again.'

'What is it?'

'Read this.' She shoved her tablet at him and hid her face.

Troy stared at the screen. As always, the words and letters jumbled about. Red banner at the top. A headline. Was it a news article? Carys slammed her hands on the table and ground her teeth. Maybe given a very long time, he could work it out, but with her staring, he couldn't.

'I don't know,' he said. The heat in the back of his neck burned like a rash.

'Don't know what?'

'What you want me to do with it.'

'Read it.'

He swallowed and scrolled down, looking for pictures. 'Holy shit. Is that us?'

'Yes.'

'Oh, fuck no.' Photos of them on the beach from a few days ago punctuated the article. They weren't the greatest quality and had obviously been taken from some way back but people would know it was him. Several of the pictures looked extremely suggestive with Carys on her knees in front of him and the two of them staring at each other by the water's edge.

'A friend, or so-called, sent me that, asking if it was me,' said Carys. 'They've plastered it all over Instagram. Oh, god, this is all my fault.'

'How do you work that out?'

'I kept seeing a car, then there was this man the other day. I didn't tell you. I didn't want to bother you over nothing. Ugh.' She threw her face into her hands. 'I thought I'd seen him before. I think it was that pap who broke into your drive in Glasgow. He must have followed us here.'

Troy grimaced at the tablet. 'That doesn't make it your fault. It's part of my life unfortunately.'

'But it's not mine, Troy. And you see what the article is suggesting?'

He gave a non-committal shrug.

'That I'm a slut who's lured you away from football. That's what everyone will think.'

'I'm sure they won't, not people who really know you. But these fucking paps are doing my dinger in.'

'What if someone from the agency reads it? I'll lose my job. Or what if my dad sees it? And now everyone will know where you are. I don't want my name out there and everyone thinking I'm... Well, that we're...'

'Together. No. You don't want that, do you?'

'Well, do you? Isn't it bad for your career?'

'Depends. I dunno. I'll see what Chris says.' He rapped his finger on the table. 'So does it actually say your name?'

'No, but everyone will have seen it now. Jaylee posted it on Instagram, saying she was sure it was me. And, Jesus, Troy, it looks like I'm... You know.'

'Yeah. I know what it looks like, but you weren't, were you? If your agency people say anything, I'll set them straight.'

She covered her face. 'This is horrible. It's like my worst nightmare coming true – again.'

'Look, let's not panic. I'll call Chris and see if there's anything he can do. What else does it say about us?'

Carys let her hands fall and frowned slightly. 'Didn't you read it?'

Troy internally recoiled and cinched his shoulders; the left one hurt like a bitch.

'Can you not read?'

'What do you mean?' he snapped.

'Nothing. I just wondered if you were dyslexic or something. Sometimes… I don't know.' She bit into her lip. Perhaps the ferocity of his stare had taken her aback.

Troy clenched his fists. 'Fine, ok, you're right. I can't. That's the kind of fuckwit you've been assigned to.' He hauled himself to his feet. 'Not only do I come with bloody paps chasing me around but I can't even read the shit they churn out about me. Maybe it's just as well.' He threw out his hands and pulled a face to shrug it off, like he did when he lost matches. This was the same. A small loss today and he'd be back fighting tomorrow. 'I'm going to call Chris. He might have news about a contract too.'

'Troy, please. Wait a bit. Not being able to read doesn't make you a fuckwit. Your choice in TV does, but that's different.' She gave him a weak smile.

He tilted his head and cast her a look. Was that her pathetic attempt to lighten his mood? 'No? Well, that's what my teachers said. My family thinks so. I play football because I can't do anything else.'

'And look how successful you are. They can read but they aren't half as successful as you, are they? You've used the skills you have and made the most of them.'

'Yeah, but I still need to read. What if that article said something damning about me? It's clearly upset you.'

'Because I'm not used to it. I had a bad experience in the past and I lost a lot of friends.'

'Did you?' Troy sighed and ran his hands through his hair. 'Tell me.'

'It's humiliating.'

'Yeah. I know how that feels, after Pippa.'

Carys sighed. 'I was only twenty-one. I had this boyfriend who really wanted to date Lissy, a friend of mine. I obviously didn't realise that or I wouldn't have gone out with him. Lissy was dating this other guy called Jack. Jack and my ex were friends but they also constantly pulled pranks on each other and all that crap.'

'They sound like my teammates.'

'Yup. One day my ex said he had to go around to Jack's for something. I went with him, only Jack wasn't in. I climbed in the window and opened the door from the inside.'

'You broke into the house?'

Carys nodded, her cheeks reddening. 'I thought we were going to get whatever it was my ex wanted, but once we were in there...' She covered her face. 'This is so embarrassing. He persuaded me to... do it with him in Jack's bedroom.'

'What? As in shag him?'

'Yes.' Carys looked away, her lips drawn in.

'Whoa.' Troy let out a low whistle. The thought of her doing that with someone who sounded like a dickhead made him want to hunt the guy down and smack his thoughtless mug.

'He said it would be funny. It was really stupid but then he started being ridiculous and taking photos on his phone. I told him to delete them. I thought he was going to send them to Jack like he'd somehow got one over on him. But it was worse. He got into Jack's Instagram account and posted photos of me in Jack's room… wearing… well, not much, and acting like Jack had sent them himself. He tagged me in it, saying this was his new girl and he couldn't wait for us to go public. Then he put, "sorry, Lissy, we're done".'

'Jesus Christ. Didn't Jack take them down?'

'He did, but it was too late. All my friends saw them. Lissy dumped him and didn't believe he hadn't put them up. They all believed it. They dropped me and Jack. Jack didn't know who'd put up the photos and I didn't dare say anything because my ex said if I told anyone he'd report me for breaking in.'

Troy cocked his head. 'Aw, Carys. That's horrible.'

'They all think I'm a slapper.' Her face fell and she looked like she might cry. 'And now this.'

'Hey. You're nothing like.' He stretched out and took both her hands 'People like that just aren't—'

'Worth it. I know.'

'They're really not. I'll do everything I can to make sure everyone knows those photos are twisted and not what they seem. I'll get Chris to make a statement right now.'

She looked into his eyes and smiled, then slipped her hands out of his. 'Thanks.' She cast around like she really wanted to talk about something else. 'Why don't you practise reading? I'm happy to help you. We could do that as well as the physio. You know, brain exercise.'

Troy rubbed his temple. 'Sounds terrifying.'

'Like running laps around a football pitch probably terrifies your family and all your ex-teachers… and me.'

'Maybe. But it's pointless.'

'You can't know that unless you try. I met a kind lady at the Autumn Market. She's a teacher and I've been messaging her about the garden. I bet she could help.'

'I don't need everyone knowing about me,' he barked.

'I'm talking about one person, Troy. And she doesn't strike me as a football fan. I won't say who you are. I'll just ask if she has any ideas.'

Troy's ears were ringing. 'You know I'm thirty, right? I'm too old.'

'You only think thirty sounds old because you think in football terms. I've worked with ninety-year-olds who don't think they're old.'

She had a point. In football terms, he was close to the end. But she might have thrown him a lifeline. If he could read, doors would open. Post-football doors. What kind of effort would it involve though? 'Will I need to see this woman?'

'Would it be bad if you did? She could give you some private tutoring and help me with the garden.'

Carys's expression said she would ask whether he liked it or not. She had her mission face on – better than the one she had after seeing the article. If she planned on employing someone as a tutor, she'd have to make sure she signed confidentiality agreements. Troy couldn't risk his secret getting out to the masses, especially with a pesky pap lurking on the island. What would the fans think if they knew their hero was learning to read with a primary school teacher? If they thought he was having sexy times on a beach with a beautiful woman, so be it. That didn't bother him half as much, though, for Carys's sake, he'd get Chris on the case.

He was no stranger to working hard but the thought of reading lessons paralysed his brain. He watched Carys call the woman while he called Chris. Chris had no power to stop the paps posting that kind of thing unless it was libellous or life endangering but he was prepared to put out a statement about what actually happened on the beach.

Carys ended her call shortly after him and bounced her fists together. 'Excellent. She's coming over at the weekend to check out the garden and she'll do a quick reading assessment with you.'

'A what? Are you insane?' She had his interests at heart but what misery was she signing him up for? She swooped into the seat next to him and rested her palm on his good thigh. He almost leapt off the chair, though his muscle-protecting reflex kicked in just in time to stop him from doing himself further damage. He could barely control himself at the best of times. Now, here she was, holding his leg, smiling at him, all twinkly eyes, freckles, and glossy strawberry blonde hair. This kind of behaviour was leading his mind through all sorts of forbidden doors.

'Fenella is a lovely lady,' she said. 'She's like someone's mum, in fact, she is someone's mum; she told me she has grown-up sons. She'll be kind and won't pressure you at all. She just wants to see what level you're at, then she'll suggest some books and ideas.'

'For fuck's sake,' Troy muttered. 'Like I'm six years old? She's going to patronise me?'

'It won't be like that. Stop fretting.'

'Right. Like you're going to stop fretting about that article?'

'I'll try if you do.'

He shook his head. 'Honestly, I think you're a wicked fairy. You can make me do anything.'

Right now, he fancied his chances of beating Real Madrid at home with two men on the bench more than letting this woman hear him read.

The weekend swung around as fast as if the Real Madrid game was actually on. If his leg was in better shape, Troy would have paced, but attempting it with his crutches made him dizzy and sore.

'Did you tell her who I was?' he said.

'No,' said Carys. 'I told her your name was Troy and you would prefer if she didn't speak to anyone about why she was here.'

'Prefer? I insist. She needs to sign something.'

'Fine. I'll get her to sign something but that makes it more obvious you're famous. I can bet she won't know who you are.'

The doorbell rang before he could protest. It was too late now and he couldn't have Chris write up a contract. Carys and her crackpot ideas would be the end of him. Their voices rang from the hall and Carys popped her head around.

'Will this do?' She held up a piece of paper covered in handwriting.

'You know I can't bloody read it,' he muttered.

'It says, *I, Fenella Hansen, solemnly swear not to mention anything to anybody about what I'm doing at this house other than helping Carys with the garden.*'

Troy rolled his eyes. 'I guess it'll have to, though it's hardly official.'

A woman appeared behind Carys. She was middle-aged with neatly cut hair and a kind smile.

Maybe she only looked like a teacher because he already knew she was, but Troy was convinced he'd still have known had he seen her cold. The sight put the fear of death into him.

'You must be Troy,' she said. 'I'm Fenella, nice to meet you.' She walked forward and shook his hand.

'Hi,' he said.

'I completely understand you don't want me gossiping about what I'm doing here. And, I assure you, I won't say a word. I've taught a lot of children over the years and have three of my own, though they're all grown now, so I know how important it is not to tittle-tattle. I'll treat whatever I do with you as I would a pupil in my class. Which means I won't talk about it with anyone.'

'Except me,' said Carys, 'because I'll be working with him.'

'We'll count you as a member of staff,' said Fenella.

Troy held his breath, feeling like some kind of protégé or science experiment. Where to look? Teachers made him want to either hide or play up, but he had to ditch those thoughts if he wanted to do this. *Dammit, I can do it.* 'Right.'

'Shall we start now?' asked Fenella. 'Or do you want me to do the garden first?'

'Let's get it over with,' muttered Troy.

'Not a great attitude,' said Carys with a stern look.

'Sorry.' Troy rubbed his forehead. Having a teacher in the house put his hackles up. They always hated him and thought him an idiot. Now he was a thirty-year-old getting remedial work.

'It's quite all right,' said Fenella. 'None of this can be easy. It's a brave step even admitting to it. Getting help when you need it isn't bad, but it's probably intimidating, embarrassing and maybe even a bit scary.'

'Very,' said Troy.

'Well, I've brought some books and some flashcards. Ignore the subject matter; these are books for children but only to gauge whereabouts you are. Once we know, you'll be able to order reading packs geared more for adults, so you won't have to resort to reading about what Biff and Chip are getting up to this week.'

Troy smirked. 'I remember them.'

116

'Me too,' said Carys.

'Yes, they've been around a long time.'

Troy sat at the breakfast bar and Fenella pulled up beside him and took out a manila folder.

'Should I go?' said Carys. 'You might not want me listening.'

Troy glanced at her and drew his eyebrows together. 'No, stay. I need you here.' And he wanted her. Truthfully, he wanted her beside him all the time. She was his human crutch and when she was pulled away his whole world collapsed. 'You need to see this too, so you can help with my lessons.'

'Ok.' She bounced onto a seat opposite and sat like the class swot, ready for her daily instructions.

Fenella opened her folder and laid a card on the table. 'So, can you read that?'

His forehead tensed. 'Cat.'

'Good,' said Fenella. 'What about this?' She placed another card.

'Go... no... er...' Troy swallowed. 'Gone?'

'Yes. So, did you see that as *go*, first?'

He nodded.

'Ok, this one?'

Troy stared at each letter, pulling them together carefully. 'House.'

After several more minutes working through the cards, Fenella pulled out a book. How idiotic did he look, sounding his way slowly through a book that was probably designed for five-year-olds? He glanced at Carys and she sent him a smile of encouragement. The impact hit him deep; her approval was everything. He had to do this. For himself and his future. And for Carys too. Already he saw the pride in her eyes. She may never see him holding a trophy but he could damn well do this for her.

Could and would. Anything to see that smile.

Chapter Thirteen

Carys

Carys lifted a card off the table and knocked Troy on the head with it. 'These cards are for kids; as if the word bitch would be on it.'

'Ok, birch.' He rubbed his head. 'And ow.'

'Typical footballer,' Carys muttered.

'What?'

'Making a meal out of the tiniest bump. Like that card would actually have hurt you.'

He plucked at the cuff of his hoody. 'Don't know what you mean.'

'Bunch of babies, that's what footballers are.'

'Hey, I'm not milking this nearly enough then.' He clutched his face like he was suffering a crippling migraine and groaned.

'Oh, stop it. Now, try this one.'

She wasn't an expert but, among his nonsense, Troy seemed to be making progress. She was happy for any excuse to work with him. It lessened the pain of knowing those hideous pictures were out in the world. All the evil memories had come back. She never wanted to go through that again. She'd never felt so helpless and dirty when her ex had betrayed her. She'd acted like a criminal and the photos were the kind everyone dreaded. The photos of her and Troy weren't quite so explicit but who knew how many millions of people had seen them? Knowing Troy was on her side made all the difference. There was something safe about him. Even with all the uncertainty about the future and the knowledge that paps would always want a piece of him, she trusted him. It was a strange feeling.

When they were done, she cleared up the cards. 'Fenella told me about an estate not far from here,' she said. 'It has a walled garden and they're selling produce to local people.'

Troy chuckled.

'What are you laughing at?'

'I've never known anyone to get so excited about vegetables. It's like some kind of fetish with you.'

'No. I just like the idea of no air miles.' She shoved the cards into the box, feeling the heat in her cheeks. Maybe she sounded like an idiot.

'You're such a hippy.'

'No…' she protested but Troy was beaming from ear to ear.

'I don't mind. I like it. But you're going pumpkin shopping on your own.'

She bit her lip. 'But what about… Well, if the paps are about?'

'And what? They get a photo of you handling the aubergines?'

'Troy, be serious.' She glared at him. How could he make light of this after what she'd told him and with his paranoia at being recognised?

'Won't it be worse if I'm there and they try to get a photo of us both fondling the peaches?'

'Right, stop that.'

He dropped his head on the table and laughed. 'Sorry.'

'I just don't want to leave you on your own.'

'I'm not a baby.' He looked up and met her eyes. 'Though I don't really want you to leave me on my own either.'

A butterfly storm burst in her chest as he smiled. If she could stop the world and hold onto this second, things couldn't get much better. The look he was giving her sent her spinning into another dimension. Somewhere they were allowed to be together; where Troy wasn't her employer and she was someone who wanted the lifestyle of a world-class footballer's partner, and didn't care if her photo was plastered over the internet in the most unflattering and compromising positions.

After lunch, they headed for the room on the ground floor that was kitted out for Troy's massage. Carys watched as he limped towards the door. His back looked straighter and he was walking easier. A double-edged sword dangled above her – on the one side, the hope Troy was on the mend, on the other, the knowledge their parting would swiftly follow.

Troy propped himself on one crutch and wrestled off his t-shirt. Carys wrung her fingers to stop herself from rushing to help him, not because he didn't like her fussing but because she wanted to do it for her own pleasure. She'd never tire of looking at those abs. A few seconds more and she'd have that body at her mercy. As he wrestled with his trousers, Carys blinked and seized a bottle of massage oil from the shelf. Whatever she did, she had to keep her eyes away. Once he was lying down, she could kid herself he was just another client. *Yeah right.* Had that tactic ever worked before?

She turned as he was wriggling into place. Nope, this was no ordinary man. He was Troy Copeland, football legend with a godlike body, and he was laid on a plate just for her. If she chose to enjoy this as much as she could, was it so bad? Was it wrong to enjoy her work? She smoothed the oil over her palms, rubbing them together before placing them on Troy's shoulders. His soft groan and accompanying exhale brought a smile to her lips. He was enjoying this as much as her. Words weren't necessary. She kneaded his taut muscles, gently working on his wounded shoulder, then moving to his spine. It hadn't suffered in the accident like the rest of him but Carys knew the importance of keeping it strong and straight, especially when he was heavily favouring one leg.

Each stroke affirmed the deep sense of awe she had for this body. If only he could reciprocate. She'd love to take her turn on the table, rest on her back, let him slowly undress her, place kisses down her neck, touch her and lay his body over hers. 'Mmm.' She let out a whimper, her hand stilled on his shoulder.

Troy groaned. 'Oh god.'

'Are you… ok?' She swallowed and tried to breathe normally.

'Fine,' he mumbled. 'Leave me here for a bit.'

'Don't you want me to do the front… Your shoulder?'

'No… It's fine.'

'Ok.' She put on the relaxing music and glanced back at him. His back rose and fell deeply. She bit back the desire to bend over and kiss his cheek, just above the spot where a little stubble had grown. Would he object? Like a statue, she stood, hovering, considering.

'Relax,' she whispered as close to his ear as she dared, giving his shoulders one last squeeze. He moaned again and didn't open his eyes.

She quietly closed the door on her way out.

It was almost an hour before he emerged. He'd showered and was in fresh clothes.

'You didn't tell me you were in the shower,' she said. 'Lucky I heard it running.'

'I forgot.'

'Hmm.' She peered at him. 'Are you ok?'

'Fine.' He adjusted the slightly open neckline of his shirt. His eyes didn't quite meet hers. 'So, are you going to the walled garden place?'

Carys checked the time. 'Yes. Are you sure you don't want to come?'

'I'm good.'

She still felt bad leaving him on his own, so she decided to be quick. According to Fenella, it wasn't far from the house, on an estate called Ardnish, but like everywhere on the island, it took longer to drive than usual with all the twisty roads.

Her thoughts whirred over Troy and how she could stop herself ravishing him. She wanted him so badly now, her body ached with it. She passed through two large stone gateposts and stopped. Where now? Tracks led off the main path in both directions.

Then she spotted a small sign poking out the ground with Walled Garden written in fancy lettering. She spun the Porsche around the corner and slowly edged along the bumpy track. Another track forked off to the right, leading to a small stone cottage close to the edge of a cliff. Outside, two vehicles were parked and some people were chatting. Carys stopped the Porsche and got out. She wanted to check she was in the right place and not riding roughshod over someone's land.

A young woman wearing a bright yellow coat and spotty wellies waved to the group, then headed towards Carys.

'Hi,' said Carys.

The woman smiled broadly with her red lips. 'Can I help you?'

'I heard I could get some local produce at the walled garden, but I don't know where it is?'

'Oh, no problem. I can sort that for you.'

'Are you Georgia?' Carys asked. Georgia Rose was the name Fenella had given her. 'The owner?'

The woman grinned and let out a half-laugh. 'I am Georgia, but it's my fiancé who owns the estate. I can help you with stuff from the walled garden.'

'Great.'

'Are you Carys?'

She nodded. 'How do you know that?' Her cheeks burned. Maybe she'd seen the article. If anyone here saw it and learned her name, they'd put two and two together. What would they make of it? Those photos looked like she was kneeling in front of Troy, gazing into his eyes like she was about to pull down his fly. In one of them she was pushing up her breasts from when she'd been pretending to be a bawdy serving wench. Altogether they looked like something completely different from what had actually happened. Whatever she felt about Troy, she'd never compromise him in public... or herself.

'I had a message from Fenella saying you might come round.'

'Oh, good.'

'Nice car.' Georgia examined the Porsche.

'It isn't mine,' said Carys. 'It belongs to my employer.'

'Who's your employer?' Georgia asked.

'I'm not allowed to say,' said Carys. This was getting worse.

'Really?' Georgia's eyes widened and she opened her mouth.

'Yeah. I'm his carer. He's recovering from a car crash.'

'Oh, gosh,' said Georgia. 'That sounds awful.'

'He's doing well,' said Carys.

'That's good.'

The path fell before them, winding gently to a more cultivated area and Carys glimpsed the garden's outer wall. A pretty cottage built in the same stone formed the near corner and beside it was an arched gateway. A breeze picked up from the sea, ruffling Carys's hair and she zipped her puffa jacket to her chin.

'At the moment, there's too much produce for the estate,' said Georgia. 'But not enough to go commercial. That's why we're keeping it as word of mouth until we expand. We supply a couple of local hotels but mostly ad hoc.' Georgia pushed open the gate and Carys strolled inside.

Parts of the wall had collapsed and broken equipment was piled in various spots but other than that, it was like a sweet shop and she was the kid with the pocket money. She wandered towards a raised bed where leafy greens and purple plants sprouted. Behind it were tall, winding bean plants, and a few paces forward, a low bed full of squashes with a tumbling mass of trailing vines.

'This is amazing,' said Carys. 'I'd like to grow things but it would be on a much smaller scale.'

'Where are you based?' asked Georgia.

'I can't really say that either,' said Carys. Was this overkill? She should go back to Troy. She missed him. Nothing felt right without him.

'Of course,' said Georgia. 'Sorry.'

'But it's a house I think would be great as a health resort or a retreat. I'd like to be self-sufficient, but I have to convince my employer.' Every time Carys said that phrase, an odd twinge assailed her. Troy wasn't like an employer anymore, he was so much more.

'We could help you out with supplies,' said Georgia. 'If your stocks run low or you need extra.' She pushed open the door to another building built into the wall at a lower section. Inside was a cold, stone-floored room. A wooden table on one side was laden with freshly cut produce. On the other side was a small disused hearth. 'You can choose anything you like from here.'

Carys wanted to spend time browsing but she needed to get back to Troy. Georgia chatted about people on the island who could help Carys and helped her put the produce in a crate. 'And there's Joanne,' said Georgia.

'Who?' Now she had Carys's full attention.

'She's the owner of The Island Florist in Tobermory, she'll know where to buy plants, though probably more decorative than edible.'

'Is she nice?'

If Georgia thought it was a weird question, she made no outward sign of it. 'Yes, really nice. Very approachable, she'd definitely help. She has a lovely family too.'

'Kids?'

'A son. I think he's about eight.'

So she had her own family now after all the miscarriages. No wonder, she hadn't tried to come back. She'd made a new life.

'Go see her, even to look around the shop. It's gorgeous.'

'I, er… Ok.'

'Honestly, she won't mind helping. She's lovely. I never see her without a smile.'

Just as Carys remembered her. What pain had she been hiding back then? And what now? The idea of running a health retreat with Troy was little more than a fool's hope. He wouldn't really do that. No way would he give up his career for this. Carys wasn't sure she dared ask him if he'd keep it and let her run it. Knowing Joanne was on the island put a different spin on things. Did she want to live so close to someone she'd once called mum? Someone who'd kissed her goodbye and promised to come back for her soon, then never shown face again.

Chapter Fourteen

Troy

'Aaargh!' Troy yelled. His leg buckled under him and he lunged for the side unit in the hallway. With scrabbling fingertips, he gripped it, steadying himself. Where was Carys? After she'd buggered off to the walled garden the previous week, he hadn't seen her half as much. Had she forgotten he was paying her to look after him? All she talked about was kooky ideas for this place when her real concern should be him. *Where the hell is she?* Either his fingertips or his leg was about to give way and he'd be left writhing on the carpet.

'Troy?' Carys rubbed her hands down the side of her jeans, hastening out of the kitchen. 'Are you ok?'

'Do I look ok?'

'Not really. What are you doing?' She hurried over, pushing herself under his arm, taking his weight and placing her arm firmly around his waist.

He ground his teeth. 'I was trying to walk. That's what I'm here to do.' Her proximity was arousing the nerve endings inside him as she always did but adrenaline was clouding his brain. He didn't want to feel anything, he couldn't afford to. 'Maybe you've forgotten.'

'Of course I haven't.' Her lips fell and she looked like he'd stabbed her. 'You don't like me fussing over you, so

I've been giving you space. But I'm sorry if I've neglected my duties.'

That word stung more than anything. Suddenly he was a duty. After they'd been getting on so well. Far too well. Their daily massages were like some kind of foreplay where he was strapped to a bed forbidden to move. He could hardly bear the torture of not being allowed to touch her in return. Now, he was back to being the paid employer. Maybe that was exactly how it should be.

He steadied his ragged breathing.

She guided him slowly towards the bottom step where he'd propped his crutches and didn't glance at him as she retrieved them and helped him strap them onto his arms.

'So, what would you like to do now?' She blinked a few times before making eye contact.

He bit the inside of his lip and squinted away. 'Ok, don't be like that.'

'Like what?'

'Like that. You haven't neglected your duties. I…' He threw back his head. 'Ugh. It's so frustrating. I need to get this leg working and nothing is happening.'

'It is, just not fast enough for your liking.'

'Yeah.' She was right but it didn't help. He took a step forward, clinging to the crutches and winced. 'I've made it worse. It feels sorer than it did.'

'You've maybe strained it. We should go to the hospital.'

'Are you serious?'

'Yes.'

'You're not being over the top because of what I said?'

'No, I mean it. That leg is one of your most precious assets. Let's get it checked just in case.'

'Well, you better call Chris and have him arrange a helicopter.'

Carys's eyes roamed up his leg, lingering on his upper thigh. 'That's you being over the top. Let's trust the local hospital.'

Troy clenched his fists around the crutches. The appeal of not leaving the island won the battle in his brain but the idea of all the nosey people who might be hanging around a waiting room made his skin crawl.

Back in the passenger seat, he pulled his baseball cap low as Carys drove the Porsche across the island to the hospital. What kind of place would it be?

When they pulled up outside a modern building with a landscaped car park, Troy breathed a sigh of relief. Carys got out of the driving seat and dashed to open his door so quickly she must have put jetpacks on her trainers.

'I can manage,' he muttered.

'I should help,' she said. 'It's my job.'

'Ok, that's going to wear thin.'

She gave a half-shrug. 'That's why you pay me, and I don't want to lose my job.' She'd turned her blade and forced it in a little deeper. Nothing she'd said was a lie, but it hurt and it was his own fault. Why had he allowed her to get close? Everything had shifted in their dynamic after a few silly words and Troy wasn't sure he could get back what they'd had… or if it was wise to try.

Carys stalked ahead and opened the door, holding it as he limped in. He stopped and looked at her. For a few highly charged seconds, they stared. The urge to seize her and kiss her was only tempered by the fact he'd literally fall flat on his face if he did.

She blinked first, approached the reception desk and chatted to the attendant before she directed Troy to a seat. He manoeuvred himself into position and put his legs out in front. The left one was bound with the grey and black strapping he wore over his sweats. He pulled his cap low and kept his head down. 'Did you tell the woman who I was?' he muttered.

'Yes,' said Carys. 'I had to. But they're all signed up to confidentiality here. So even if she recognises you, she isn't allowed to say anything. I thought this all went with who you are. That's what you told me. Why are you still so bothered?'

'I dunno. I don't care if it's on the internet.'

'Is it that different?'

He shrugged. *Ouch*. He had to stop doing that. Maybe because he'd never been able to read the articles, they'd never bothered him. Real people, on the other hand, could and would judge. In the club, they were all in the same boat, teammates and sometimes pals, but in the world outside everything was different. He wasn't sure he knew how to speak to ordinary people any more. Everyone he mixed with was from the football world.

Peering out from under the peak of his cap, he realised they were the only people there. Carys got up from the seat and strolled to the other side of the waiting room. She riffled through the magazines, then browsed the posters on the noticeboard.

'Here's something for you,' she said.

Troy squinted towards her. 'What does it say?'

'Community Christmas party. Sounds right up your street, think of all the new friends you could make.'

'Shut up. That's not funny.'

'Troy Copeland.' A woman with long dark hair pulled into a ponytail put her head around the door and Troy hauled himself to his feet.

'Do you want me to come too?' Carys asked.

'Yes,' said Troy. They followed the woman along a short corridor into a neatly laid out consultation room. Troy took a seat and stretched his strapped leg out in front.

'I'm Dee and I'm the duty nurse,' said the woman. 'If you can tell me what the problem is, I'll assess you and see how best we can help you today.'

'My leg,' said Troy. 'I've got a compound fracture in my femur and this morning… Well, I tried to walk without my crutches and I stumbled. I need to know it's not broken again.'

'Does it feel worse than it did?'

'Yes, a bit.'

'Ok. So, if we can get you on the table. I'll do a quick exam.'

'Don't I need an x-ray?'

'You might do, but we'll try this first.'

With some shuffling about, Troy got himself onto the bed. The nurse helped. Troy glowered and gritted his teeth as Carys smirked at her phone. Who was she in touch with? He lay back and closed his eyes. Curse his possessive mind. She had a right to be in touch with people aside from him, but a tremor of jealousy shook him.

Dee prised off the strapping and took off Troy's trousers. Even that didn't get Carys's attention. Was he that dull? Had she seen it so often before he was nothing? Maybe he should cough but Dee took hold of his thigh. She didn't have Carys's magic touch; in fact, this was verging on brutal. Dee's thumb dug into his skin.

'So, your leg feels fine,' she said. 'There's some colouration but it's more likely to be the remainder of the initial bruising.'

'Yeah,' said Troy.

'As your leg heals, the muscles and the tendons will tighten. So, if you've fallen awkwardly, the chances are you've pulled something. If you'd broken it again, you'd be in a lot more pain.'

'So, I don't need an X-ray?'

'I can set one up if you're desperate but I don't think it's necessary. I can also arrange for a doctor to see you if you'd like a second opinion.'

'I'm sure it'll be fine,' said Carys. 'We just wanted to check.'

Troy pulled himself into a sitting position. 'But when will I be able to walk on it again? It's not getting better.'

He caught Carys's eye. Her brows raised and almost met in the middle. What was she looking at him like that for?

'I don't know the exact details of this break,' said Dee. 'But every fracture is different and the healing process can take time.'

'This has been since June,' said Troy. 'We're in November now.'

'And what did your consultant say?'

Troy let out a sigh. 'He told me to keep up the physio. But he didn't give me a very detailed time frame.'

'Troy.' Carys placed her arm on his wrist. 'You're a lot more mobile than you were. It's hard for you to see that, but really, it is getting better.'

'Too slow,' muttered Troy.

'If it was a bad break,' said Dee, 'it will take a long time.'

'It broke in two places,' said Carys. 'And some of it shattered.'

Dee pulled a pout and gave a knowing nod. 'That can't mend overnight. Your muscle tone felt good and there's no swelling or new bruising. Once everything's knitted together again, you'll be able to put weight on it. But until then, don't put undue stress on it. And keep up the physio. Where are you getting that?'

'I do it,' said Carys.

'I can recommend professionals on the island if it feels too much for you.'

'I'm trained to do it,' said Carys.

'Oh, that was lucky.' Dee moved around the bed to help Troy with his trousers. 'If you're going to break a bone, it helps to have a physiotherapist for a girlfriend.'

Troy glanced at Carys and smirked.

'I'm not his girlfriend,' said Carys.

'Oh.' Dee looked up. 'My apologies, I just assumed.'

'I'm his carer,' said Carys. Troy rolled his eyes.

'Perfect,' said Dee. 'So you're in good hands. Don't hesitate to come back if there are further problems though. Or make an appointment at the surgery. There's a quick form to fill out if you're visitors but that's all.'

The familiar cold sweat spread across Troy's forehead. A form? He breathed, remembering he had Carys to help.

Dee strapped him up, ratcheting the Velcro fastenings like she wanted to stop the blood flow. The second he was out of the room, he stopped in the corridor and loosened the top one.

'Are you ok?' said Carys.

'That nurse was a bit rough. Can you loosen the lower one? Any tighter and my leg will fall off.'

Carys bent down and adjusted them. Troy inhaled sharply at her touch, passing it off as a wince. She was getting to him as much as ever. Did she have any idea of the emotions and desires she stirred in him?

'Thanks, girlfriend.' He kept his tone jolly; he had to, otherwise he would do something crazy like kiss those pink lips or bury his face in that soft hair. If she wrapped her arms around him, he would melt and she could soothe away the aches of his body.

'Don't even go there,' said Carys.

'You don't fancy the life of a WAG then?'

'Definitely not. I can't imagine anything worse.'

And there it was. A direct hit to his heart and all his secret wishes. A half-smile played on her lips but he knew she wasn't joking. She was homegrown with her fruit trees and vegetable beds. He wouldn't change her, but it meant he couldn't have her either.

He put his hand on her arm and she moved to steady him but he gripped her firmly. 'I'm sorry, Carys. I shouldn't have said anything earlier. You do a great a job and you've become a good friend too. And I'm really glad.'

'About what?'

'That you're you.' He looked her up and down. 'And you're amazing, just the way you are.'

He limped to the car and got in, pulling his cap low over his face.

Chapter Fifteen

Carys

The lithe contours of Troy's foot were impressive even through the soft rib of his sock. How many goals had this foot been responsible for? Now it was in Carys's hands again. Troy perched on the opposite end of the bench in the custom-installed gym, his right foot firmly on the floor, his left leg stretched along the bench. Carys gently pushed his toes, straightening them.

The bruising on his leg had almost gone, as the nurse had observed. But a long scar ran down his thigh, protruding from beneath his gym shorts to his knee. Soft, pale hairs covered his leg. Carys ran her palms up his shin, pressuring his pallid skin until a gentle colour returned to it. She reached his kneecap, then stopped.

How could she kid herself this was just another massage? After his parting shot at the hospital the day before, she wasn't sure what to say to him. He'd barely spoken two words since, unless they were strictly professional. Every second in his presence got harder and harder. The idea of sliding her hands up his thigh from this position sent her heart rate skyrocketing. She swallowed and placed her palms on either side of the scarred thigh. Pressing with her thumbs, she began working on it, unable to meet his eyes.

He leaned back onto his hands, arched his neck and let out a groan. It didn't help. Carys's pulse pounded in her ears. That noise had to be because she was relieving the pain or making it worse. Just that. Anything – but not that he was enjoying this. He couldn't. He mustn't. It would be unprofessional for him to get that kind of pleasure from this. Her thumbs trembled as she moved closer to the hem of his shorts.

'Ok, stop,' said Troy.

Carys lifted her hands and held them in front of her like she'd been arrested. 'What's wrong?'

'That's... Not helping. Let's do the next exercise. I don't like that.' His voice was breathy and he didn't look at her. He didn't like it? Or maybe he liked it a bit too much?

'Ok.' Carys sat back. 'Keep your leg stretched out and push your foot into my palm.'

Troy grunted as he pushed forward. His face crinkled around his grey-blue eyes with the effort. Was it the strain of pushing? He still didn't meet her eyes.

'Now gently pull your heel along the bench. Bend your knee. Pull it as far as you can.'

Taking a deep inhale, Troy bent his knee and slowly his heel moved. With a low growl and another determined breath, he moved it further. 'That's really good,' said Carys. Finally, their gazes connected and he gave her a grim smile. His chest heaved as he held his leg in place.

'Can I put it down yet?'

'Try and hold it a few seconds more' She shuffled along the bench and placed her palms on his thigh again. He flinched and let out a growl, like she was about to torture him. 'Relax,' she said. 'Just relax.' She pressed her thumbs into the tense musculature at the back of his thighs.

'Are you kidding?' he muttered. 'I seriously can't.'

'Easy does it,' she said, helping him lower his leg. 'How does that feel?'

'Dunno.' He rubbed his forehead and puffed slowly, like he'd overdone some strenuous exercise.

'That was a good workout.' Carys got to her feet and retrieved his crutches.

'You think?'

'Considering the circumstances, yes.'

'We barely scratched the surface.' He rubbed his hands along the length of his thigh, applying a lot more pressure than he'd allowed her to. Something told her the workout he was imagining wasn't one she was contracted to do. She repressed a tremor, blocking out the visions of those hands working on her rather than his own thigh.

'Maybe we should get a Christmas tree,' she said.

'Ok, that's random.'

Yes, it was, but the need to change the subject had driven her to the first thing that popped into her head. 'It's November, Christmas isn't that far off.'

'Fine, Christmas it is,' said Troy. 'Get a tree if you want. And while we're on this random subject, what do you want to do for Christmas? Do you want time off?'

'Um.' Carys fiddled with a crutch as she passed it to him. She should have thought this through. Her dad might like her home but Kat wouldn't exactly welcome her back into the fold at a time when money was tight – no matter how much she offered to pay. 'I should stay with you,' she said. 'It's my job and I don't mind.'

'What if I go to Spain to see my parents?'

'Then won't you need me to help you on the plane?'

'I guess.' He pulled himself to his feet and looked taller and more upright than usual. 'But if you want to go home to your family, I won't stop you.'

'Thanks. I'll let you know.' But the idea of staying here and cosying up in front of the fire with Troy for a quiet Christmas together was more appealing than anything else.

'Who were you messaging when I was getting examined yesterday?' His voice sounded casual but Carys had a feeling he'd been burning to ask her for the last twenty-four hours and had only just mustered the nerve. Was he jealous?

'Georgia Rose.'

'Who?'

'The woman I met at the walled garden. She's really nice. I might go to that community party with her and meet some more people. It's time I made some new friends.'

'Seriously?'

'I mean, only if you don't mind.'

'What happened to not wanting to leave me in case the paps break in and get photos of me starkers?'

'If it's a problem, I'll stay here.'

His good shoulder flinched and he pulled a *why should I care* face. 'Go if you want. You're allowed nights off.'

'You know what would be even better?' said Carys.

'What?'

'If you came too.'

'No way.'

'Why not?'

'Why do you think? All the superficial attention. Or it might be full of Rangers fans. I can't risk it.'

'I don't get it. It's nowhere near as many people who will have read stuff about you on the internet.'

'Yeah, but I don't have to talk to them.'

'Suit yourself, but everyone I've met here has been really friendly and it wouldn't do any harm for us to go somewhere different.'

'They won't be my kind of people.'

'If you hide away like a hermit all the time, no one's going to be your kind of person.'

Troy rolled his eyes and grunted like a wounded bear.

Over the next couple of weeks, the strengthening exercises on his thigh worked wonders. Each day, it was less of a struggle for him to move. But the tension building in Carys's chest was at fever point. Manipulating an athletic body was all she was doing, but the feel of his velvet skin stretched over his muscular legs tickled her senses a little too much. The signals her brain received mingled with the desire to follow the path further up his thigh and around his tight bum. Then she'd straddle him and he'd kiss her and… No! She had to stop. Just stop.

When she wasn't thinking about jumping him, her mind dwelt instead on the party. For the most part, she was looking forward to it, but what about Joanne? Would she be there? How would it be if they met? Every level of awkward could arise and Carys swallowed back a cold, sick feeling. Was it too late to say no? She'd almost welcome Troy forbidding her to go.

'What's up?' he asked.

Carys blinked. How long had she been massaging Troy's toes and gazing at his shin?

They were back on the bench, ready for his workout.

'Nothing.'

Troy cocked his head and raised an eyebrow, totally unconvinced. 'I know you well enough now to know that's not true. You seem distant. Tell me what's going on. Is it those pictures? Are people still bothering you about them?'

She gave a brief headshake and placed her palms on his calf, ready to work on it. No one had mentioned the photos for a while… not to her face anyway.

'Stop,' he said. 'I don't want you to do anything until you tell me what's going on. This has been a few days now.

You're not yourself. Is it me? Have I done something wrong? I know I said some stuff… I didn't mean to offend you.'

'It's not you,' she lied.

Part of it was. She couldn't forget the words he'd said. She'd dreamt of boyfriends saying things like that to her but hadn't expected it from Troy. What to make of it? There was the possibility he said it to get her back on side again after he'd been so grouchy but she couldn't be sure. He thought she was amazing. In what way? Was it flirting? It was too big to think about. Her mind kept harping back to Joanne. The lingering niggle that had gnawed away at her for the last twelve years. Now it might all come to a head. She let her hand fall and her shoulders slumped.

'If I tell you…'

'Tell me, Carys. Whatever it is.'

'Well, remember I once told you I had a stepmum.'

'Yeah.' His brow furrowed. 'She split with your dad years ago.'

'Twelve years ago. She was my mum in every way, she just didn't give birth to me. She and my dad sometimes argued, I know they did, and my dad is a really lazy man. But… One day she walked out. No explanation, nothing. Dad said she was bitter because she couldn't have her own kids.'

'I'm so sorry,' he said.

'When we were together, she talked about the place she grew up. It was here. Mull. That's why I wanted to come here. Curiosity.' She raised her eyes to his.

'Jesus Christ.' Troy pinched the bridge of his nose.

'I'm sorry. I didn't know where else to choose.'

'I don't mind. Is this what's been upsetting you? Would you rather be somewhere else?'

'She's here.'

'What? Have you seen her?'

'The day I went to the market, I caught a glimpse of her in the florist.'

Troy gritted his teeth and partly using his hands to support his leg, he hoisted it off the bench. 'Did she see you?'

'No.'

'So, what now?' He pushed himself along, so he was next to her.

'What do you mean?'

'What do you want to do next? Do you want to see her?'

'That's just it. I don't know. I've committed to going to this party. What if I see her there and it all goes horribly wrong?'

Troy put his arm around her shoulder and the deep pressure of his hold brought a wave of tears. 'It's ok. Jesus, Carys, you've had a shitty life. I don't know how you keep that pecker up all the time.'

'There's no point in moping, is there?'

'Isn't there? You're talking to the king of moping, remember?' Troy squeezed her and she smiled, allowing herself to rest her forehead on him. Ah, that smell. The refreshing and tangy scent of his branded deodorant working with his freshly laundered t-shirt and the proximity of his skin set her nerve ends alight. This was a place she could find solace and never want to leave.

'You're such a good person,' said Troy. His soft words skimmed her ear and Carys wanted to plant a kiss on that lightly stubbled cheek. She could even brave the consequences of where it might lead because she needed it. 'You always put others first. Do this for you. Who cares if she's there or not? She's the one who's got to answer for her actions, not you.'

Carys nodded and he pulled her closer. The sadness was still there but the comfort of Troy's embrace was overwhelming. She glanced up at him, taking in the kaleidoscopic depth of his eyes, his perfectly straight nose, his chiselled cheekbones, and finally his lips. Who moved first wasn't clear, but Carys felt his lips touch hers at the same moment she went for his. Hot blood rushed through her and she closed her eyes, savouring every second. It was soft and tender but scorching too. He slid his fingers into her hair and tugged her closer, deepening the contact with her mouth.

'Jesus,' he muttered, pulling back to breathe.

Carys edged out of his grip. 'I'm sorry, Troy. I got carried away... I was upset and...'

'It's cool. All cool.' He held up his hand and rolled his shoulders. 'When you're ready, we'll do it.'

'Do what?' Heat flamed in her cheeks. What did he mean? He wanted to take her to bed or have her right here? She wanted him too but could they do that? Wouldn't she be in big shit? She could lose her job. Lose everything. Was it worth it?

'We'll go to the party. What did you think I meant?'

'Oh... Nothing.' She'd almost put her foot right in it. 'But what? You'll come with me?'

'Yes, Carys.'

'You'll actually come to the party?'

He brushed his fingertips up her arm and pulled her close again. His lips touched her forehead so softly it was more of a graze than a kiss but it set off another chain reaction. A shiver of pleasure coursed through her. 'Yes,' he murmured. His warm breath tickled her skin. 'For you, I'll come to the party.'

Chapter Sixteen

Troy

Brightly coloured Christmas lights twinkled from the tiny tree in the corner of Troy's bedroom. He didn't normally bother with it. Did anyone put trees in their bedrooms? Carys apparently, and she thought he should have one too.

Troy liked wearing a kilt for special occasions, but with the leg brace, it wasn't practical. A suit wasn't much better. Black jeans and an ultra-white shirt were the best bet, though he still looked ridiculous with the girdle and what resembled Velcro suspenders all down his leg.

With one crutch propping him up, he adjusted his cufflinks and rotated to examine his figure. He wasn't as trim as he used to be. No one else would notice but the toning brought about from daily training was a lot less perfect. Once he could walk again, it wasn't just the leg he needed to get into shape.

His mind leapt back to this time last year when Pippa had ordered a massive tree for the Glasgow mansion and bedecked the house in several tons of glitter. Music had pounded from the entertainment area in the basement and cars had pulled up, bringing his teammates and other friends. Paps crawled the streets, their cameras flashing like beacons, trying to get the juiciest shots of the exclusive guests. What a contrast to the utter quiet surrounding this house.

Troy let out a sigh. All that was part and parcel of his lifestyle. It made enjoying this seem even more important because, pleasant as it was, it couldn't last once he was back on the pitch.

He hobbled out of his ground-floor room and frowned. Not wanting to risk a stumble on the night of the party, he didn't try, but he felt like he could walk. His leg was stronger. Still, best not to test the theory. Carys wouldn't appreciate a hospital run tonight.

His eyes flicked to the top of the stairs and an adrenaline rush hit him like a bus, but he held his ground. Carys drifted down in a plain black dress that skimmed her dainty figure and brushed the top of her knees. Silver pumps were her concession to comfort and were so her.

Since their kiss in the gym, they'd tiptoed around the subject like it was a sleeping tiger, just waiting for the right moment to wake up and tear them to shreds. There was so much of Carys waiting to be unlocked but jumping over the carer–client hurdle was a tough ask. She looked gorgeous, more stunning than any of the models he'd dated or seen his mates date. Heat burned in his veins as he watched her. More than ever, he longed to toss away his crutches and take her in his arms. He'd never been much of a dancer but he imagined taking her hand and waltzing her around the hall.

He swallowed as she approached, wearing the dress he'd insisted she bought. Carys, in her usual way, would have been quite happy with a top from three years ago, but he was determined. She deserved the world and a new dress was the least he could get her. 'You look… beautiful,' he said. Her cheeks bloomed their customary pink and she gnawed on her lower lip.

'Don't embarrass me,' she said. 'I feel weird enough in this as it is.'

'Honestly. You look great.'

'Am I WAG-like enough for you to be seen out with me?'

He flipped her a wry smile. 'More than. I don't mind what you wear. I wanted you to have that for yourself, not for my benefit.' He took her in again. How perfectly the dress fitted her, the neckline low enough to be tantalising without being tacky. 'But I'm not complaining.'

'Me neither.' She skimmed him up and down and it was his turn to feel the heat. Why? People did that to him all the time. He was used to having his body on display. Being objectified was part of his life but this was more. Carys was like a lithe panther sizing up a potential mate. Was he good enough? He wasn't the king of the jungle anymore. He was broken and wounded. She could do better. Six months ago, he'd have taken on anyone but now what was he?

'I'm going to try just one crutch tonight,' he said.

'Are you sure?'

'I feel much stronger.' Maybe it was his ego talking.

'Let's go then.' She linked her arm through his and led him to the door. This was an everyday move. She'd take his weight, lead him, support him, but tonight it felt like more. She was his girl, on his arm.

Carys drove across the island in pitch black. For the first time, Troy appreciated how far away from everything they were.

'This really is an extreme getaway. I don't think I've ever been anywhere so dark.' He peered out at the thousands of stars dotting the sky above. 'It's incredible.'

'Isn't it?' said Carys. 'Imagine if you did have Taigh Beinne as a health resort. There's enough space in front of the orchard to build a couple of cabins. You could have them like saunas or with hot tubs. It would be awesome, sitting out there with a view of the sea in summer and the stars in winter.'

Even in the dark, her face lit up as she chatted about her favourite baby. For a moment, football was a memory and Troy was fully present in her dreams. They ran a retreat, they welcomed guests and wowed them with healthy food grown on site and training programs developed personally by him. He could meet people without having to hide. His name attracted them in the first place, but when they met him, they'd discover he was just a guy who enjoyed simple pleasures – nothing fancy.

'It sounds perfect,' he murmured.

It took them over half an hour to reach the Glen Lodge Hotel where the party was being held. As they headed down the driveway, a two-storey building came into view, lit by external lamps and lights at the windows, a warm and welcoming sight.

Troy blinked in surprise. He'd expected a rundown community centre but this country chic hotel was much better. The nerves wouldn't dissipate completely but he was momentarily relieved.

'Are you sure about this?' said Carys.

'Yup.' He unclicked his belt and opened the door. He'd perfected the art of getting out of the car.

Climbing the stone steps to the front door presented more of a challenge.

'There's a ramp,' said Carys.

'I can do it.' One foot in front of the other. The leg was getting stronger. It had to be getting stronger. Chris had given him an ultimatum on three contracts and he needed to choose one and sign before the end of January.

Carys took his free hand as they reached the top. Her fingers were cold – her grip a little too firm. He applied pressure, letting her know he was there if she needed him.

An older woman with short white hair greeted them at the reception desk and directed them through a set of swinging double doors. Together they entered a large room with a highly polished dance floor in the middle. Around the side, tables were laid and several people were already seated.

Carys drifted to an empty table and pulled out a chair.

'I should be doing that for you,' he mumbled.

'Don't be ridiculous.'

Instinct nudged Troy to put his head down and not make eye contact with anyone, but manners told him not to. Carys had barely hung her wrap across the back of her chair when a young woman came over and tapped her shoulder.

'Oh, hi, Georgia,' Carys said.

'You made it.' Georgia beamed and embraced Carys like an old friend. 'And you're not alone.'

Troy smiled at the woman, who was obviously trying hard not to look at his leg.

'This is…' Carys hesitated. 'My employer.'

Troy burst out laughing, tempering it straight away by shoving his hand to his mouth. 'Sorry. Carys is the ultimate professional. My name's Troy.'

'Hi,' said the woman. 'I'm Georgia.'

Troy leaned over to shake her hand. 'Sorry, I would get up.'

'I can see you're somewhat incapacitated,' said Georgia. 'I take it you won't be dancing.'

'I doubt it.'

'Well, I can send some people to whiz you off your feet,' she said to Carys, 'so don't worry. Archie, my fiancé, is an amazing dancer. Sorry, Troy, you'll just have to watch.'

'Probably best if Fred Astaire is in the mix.'

'Oh, gosh, yes,' said Carys. 'Don't send anyone who's a good dancer my way. I'm terrible. Zimmer-Zumba is my standard.'

Georgia laughed. 'What is that?'

'I used to teach the residents Zumba when I worked in a care home.'

If ninety-year-olds on Zimmer frames could dance with Carys, then Troy Copeland bloody well could. Even in front of all these people or if paps were lining the walls, he would try. He had to.

Carys waved to Georgia as she headed away. Troy watched her approach a group close to the bar. A tall man with dark auburn hair slipped his arm around her shoulder. 'Is that Fred Astaire?' said Troy.

'I guess,' said Carys.

'He looks well suave,' said Troy.

'So do you.' Carys smirked.

'I'm anything but,' said Troy. 'I've made money but my family are from Paisley. We lived on a housing estate when I was a boy and it definitely wasn't posh.'

'You still look suave.' She eyed him over.

'Are you taking the piss?'

She shook her head. 'I think you know I'm not.' She held his gaze, her teeth grazing her lower lip before she looked away.

Might she come with him? He knew the answer too well. She didn't want a life in the public eye and if he forced that on her, she wouldn't be the same person.

More people came in and the swing doors barely shut before they were pushed open again. Some couples, some older people, some groups, a few with children. A man, a woman and a boy about ten years old were next. Carys clenched the table edge until her fingertips blanched. The woman at the door was laughing as the man helped her adjust the wrap on her shoulder. She beamed about, pointing out someone to the boy, then scanning around as if checking for her friends. Her eyes brushed over Carys and stopped. She blinked and frowned, then turned her back to them.

Carys revolved slowly to face Troy, her skin very pale; only her freckles and a pink tinge on her cheeks gave her any colour. 'That's her.' Her voice was soft. 'She saw me, then she looked away. We should go. I can't stand it.'

Troy peered over Carys's shoulder. 'Sit tight, she's coming over.'

Chapter Seventeen

Carys

Carys didn't dare to move or breathe, her gaze fixed on Troy. She was counting on him now to let her know what was happening.

'Excuse me.' A woman's voice spoke and Carys's insides froze; her blood had ceased pumping and the world stopped spinning. Troy stretched out and took her hand. The warmth barely penetrated.

'Hi,' he said.

'Hi,' said the woman's voice. 'Carys?'

Slowly, very slowly, like she was melting one frozen nanosecond at a time, Carys turned. The face was the same, narrow with almost almond eyes and sharply angled eyebrows. A few more creases lined her smiling lips and her dark curly hair had lost a little of its shine but the vibrancy twinkling from her grey irises was alight and more alive than ever.

'Hi,' said Carys, though her voice seemed to come from far away, through the music and chat.

Joanne raised her shapely eyebrows. 'You don't remember me, do you?'

'Of course I do.' Like she'd ever forget her mum? She turned away quickly, wiping back tears as they flowed freely. Troy's grip intensified. She'd forgotten about it but realised it was the only thing anchoring her to reality.

'Why are you here? I never thought I'd see you again.'
Carys couldn't look at her.

'She's here with me,' said Troy. 'I'm not sure this is a good place to talk.'

'I guess not,' said Joanne. 'But… No, you're probably right.'

Carys glanced up. 'Wait. One thing…' Her eyes swam as she looked at Joanne. The woman who'd been her mum for ten years. The only mum she'd ever known.

'Anything,' said Joanne. Her eyelashes sparkled and she pinched her lips together.

'Why didn't you come back?'

Joanne cocked her head, pressing her fingers to her mouth. 'I tried. Didn't you know?'

Carys shook her head. 'Dad said you were bitter, but I don't get why you didn't call.'

Joanne ran her hand down her face. 'I'm truly sorry.' She took a deep breath. 'Can I sit?'

'Yeah,' said Troy.

Joanne pulled out a chair next to Carys. Carys stared into the face she hadn't seen for so many years.

'I tried to come back for you but Lee didn't want me to have any contact with you. He was angry with me. This might be tough to hear but he was sleeping with Kat before we split up. She was already pregnant when she moved in. I was in hospital after a miscarriage when it started. It was awful. You were my daughter in everything except genetics. I brought you up, but Lee was having none of it. He falsely accused me of all sorts, then had a restraining order taken out. I wasn't allowed to see you.'

'Oh god.' Carys covered her face. 'I knew things were bad with the two of you. I heard the fights, but I didn't think he'd go that far. How could he?' Why had he thought it was ok to separate a twelve-year-old from the only mum she'd ever known?

'Lee was a tough guy to live with.'

'Yeah, I know.'

'But for all his faults, he always loved you. He was so protective of you. I was too scared to cross him. I tried all the official routes to get access to you but I had no rights. I wasn't your biological mother. When he married Kat, things got worse. Everyone I went to thought I was some crazy woman trying to abduct a child and Lee played on that. No one would listen. In the end, I moved back here to be with my family. I couldn't take any more.'

'Didn't you want to get in touch now she's older?' asked Troy.

'I did. I saw you on Facebook but I didn't dare press friend or message. I knew Lee would have poisoned your mind against me. And... Well, I can see that's what's happened. It's still my word against his and my story always sounds like a lie.'

Tears flooded down Carys's face.

'Hey,' said Troy. 'Maybe we should stop this.'

'Ok,' said Joanne. 'But I want you to know that not a day's gone by when I haven't regretted walking out on you.' Her voice faltered and tears clouded her eyes.

Carys knew the helplessness only too well. She'd felt the same when her ex had lied about her and no one believed her. Despite everything her dad had told her, she knew Joanne was telling the truth. It made sense. Joanne's love had been so real. Nothing could have kept her away... nothing except Lee and the law.

Joanne scraped back her chair and got up. Carys wiped her eyes and got to her feet too. 'Please, please don't go. Not again... Please, Mum.'

'Oh, Carys.' Joanne turned back. 'I never wanted to.'

They looked at each other, then Joanne opened her arms and Carys fell into her embrace. Carys forgot where she was. The music and chat seemed a vague backdrop. She was back with her mum… 'I missed you.'

Joanne held her tight. 'Oh gosh, me too. I'm so glad you're here. Of all the places. What brought you here?'

'I remembered your stories. I always wanted to visit. I never thought I'd actually see you.'

'Is everything ok?' a man's voice spoke.

'Fine.' Joanne rubbed her tears from her eyes but kept Carys in her arms. 'This is Carys.'

'Carys?' said the man. 'The Carys? Your… daughter.'

Joanne glanced at her. 'Yes.'

'Wow, that's a bit of a shock,' said the man.

'Hey. Would you all like to sit down?' said Troy.

Carys blinked and her focus fell back to the table. Troy wasn't smiling but his face was more passive than angry. Was he being sarky? No way would he want strangers to sit with him. His horror of the general public shimmied to the forefront of her mind. This would be his worst nightmare. But all she wanted to do was cling to her mum and never let her go again.

'Troy… Are you sure?' Carys gaped at him.

'Absolutely,' said Troy, his smile turning warm and genuine.

Joanne beamed at him. 'Are you two…?'

'No,' said Carys, quickly. 'He's my boss. I'm his carer.'

Troy half-rolled his eyes, then patted his strapped leg.

'Oh, I see,' said Joanne. 'This is my husband, Ewan, and my son, Rowan.'

Ewan embraced Carys like a long-lost friend. 'It's a delight to meet you in person.' Carys was drowned by his hug but not in a bad way. It was the kind of hug she imagined people getting from cheerful uncles, not something she had any experience of. Her only uncle was constantly in and out of prison and not someone she ever wanted to hug.

'Thanks,' said Carys. 'And hi, Rowan.'

'Hi,' said the boy, but his eyes fell on Troy. 'Oh my god,' he said.

'My gosh,' Joanne corrected, ruffling his hair. 'And don't stare.'

'But that's Troy Copeland, Mum.'

'Who? Sorry,' Joanne said to Troy. But Ewan was gaping too, evidently putting pieces together in his mind.

'Yes,' said Troy, raising his hand as if owning up to a misdeed. 'That's me. I'm Troy Copeland. Nice to meet you.' He pushed out his hand to shake Rowan's first and the boy gaped.

'Should I know who you are?' said Joanne.

'Probably not,' said Troy.

'He's the Celtic frontman, or he was,' said Ewan, shaking his hand. 'How's the leg? And why are you on Mull?'

'Long story,' said Troy. 'Sit down and we can chat.'

Carys frowned. He really meant it?

Ewan took the seat next to Troy, and Rowan, using his dad as a safety barrier, continued to goggle at Troy, then he whispered loud enough for everyone to hear, 'My friend told me he saw him in a Porsche in Tobermory. I thought he was fibbing.'

'Shh.' Joanne batted him as she sat next to Carys.

'I did read a rumour you were here,' said Ewan. 'A gossipy sort of thing.'

Carys ground her teeth. He'd seen that? What would he think of her? Had Joanne seen it too? Maybe her card was marked before they'd even had a chance to talk properly.

'Well, it got that bit right,' said Troy. 'I'm here, but the rest of it was the usual rubbish the paps make up.'

Joanne beckoned Carys closer.

'I honestly can't apologise enough,' she said.

'Don't,' said Carys. 'You couldn't have stayed with my dad. I know what he's like.'

'I should have done. For your sake.'

Carys blinked through her misty gaze, looking at Joanne, trying to erase the years of sadness and fathom new possibilities.

Joanne took Carys's free hand. 'Is it too late?'

'For what?'

'To try again. I'd have you back in a second.'

'But you have your own family now,' she said.

'There's always room for more happiness, Carys. And I feel like we've been given a second chance.'

'Yes. I'd like that.'

Joanne leaned in and hugged her. Together they cried in each other's arms, forgetful again that the party was happening around them, that others were talking at their table and that years had gone by since they last did this.

'I don't remember the last time I was this emotional. And in public too,' said Carys. If the paps were here now, they could take all the pictures they wanted. This didn't feel like something she was going to regret.

'Big deals like this don't happen every day.'

'Thankfully,' said Carys, smiling. Joanne broke into a grin and they continued to take each other in for a few moments.

Ewan's booming laugh made Carys bump back to the table. She glanced back at Troy, a knot of tension forming in her stomach again. *Oh god.* She'd thrust him into the very situation he'd been trying to avoid. He was surrounded by groupies. Other people had come over to talk to him and were hanging around, some putting themselves forward, others hanging back. Troy didn't seem bothered. Was he just hiding it really well? He was grinning and laughing. When Carys tuned in, it didn't even sound like they were talking about football.

'Yeah, that was my sister, not me.'

Carys blinked in surprise. He hadn't even spoken to her much about his family and here he was telling perfect strangers about them.

'She used to want to be a pro,' he said.

'Troy…' Carys frowned at him. 'That doesn't sound…' She motioned her head towards Rowan '…suitable.'

He stared for a moment, then realisation dawned on him. 'My sister wanted to be a professional golfer,' he said. 'That's what I meant. These folks were asking.'

'I thought I read somewhere he first wanted to be a golfer,' a man said. 'I was offering him a game when he's better.'

'Oh, right,' said Carys.

Rowan wrinkled his nose like they were all mad.

'Ewan seems nice,' Carys whispered as the guys fell back into chat.

'He's so great.'

'I'm glad,' said Carys. 'After my dad, you deserve the best.'

Joanne took her hand and squeezed it. 'So, how did you get in with a famous footballer?'

'It's just a job,' said Carys, her chest compressing. *Yes, just work.* 'My contract's only until January. He's hoping to be well on track to recovery by then.'

The lights dimmed and music struck up. Gradually the crowd around Troy waned and Rowan ran off. Carys spotted him with two other boys, hiding behind a table and pointing at Troy. After a few dances, Ewan took Joanne to the floor and Carys watched with a smile.

'Are you ok?' said Troy, leaning over.

'I think so. It's all a bit overwhelming. Are you?'

Troy smirked. 'Actually, yeah. These folks are full of good craic'

'Seriously? I thought you were joking when you said they could sit here. Are you mad with me?'

'No, not at all. It's cool.' He leaned forward, his grey-blue irises twinkling with the reflected lights. 'Seriously. I swear. It's like you said, I'll never find my kind of people if I hide myself away.'

'You actually listen to what I say?'

'Every word.'

Carys fiddled with her sparkly nails. This was the first time she'd dressed up in ages. She didn't come close to a footballer's glamorous girlfriend but just sitting with Troy filled her with a new sense of self and for a moment she dropped the *I'm his carer* persona and enjoyed sharing a table with him. He was talented, smart, fun and determined. Throw away the fame and he was her perfect man. She'd love to be seen with him… When it was appropriate. She just didn't want the whole world seeing them whenever they fancied.

'Shall we dance?' said Troy.

'You and me?'

'That's why I'm asking.'

'Even though you're…'

'What? Your boss? Crippled? Too suave for you?'

Carys smiled. 'All of the above.'

Grabbing his crutch, Troy pulled himself to his feet. 'Let me show you what I can do when the motivation's there.' He put out his hand and she took it, rising to her feet and feeling like a real-life Cinderella.

He took three deliberate breaths, then rested his crutch on the table.

'What are you doing?' said Carys.

'We're doing this without props,' he said.

She took his arm, but she was barely supporting him. Still breathing hard, he made it to the dance floor edge. 'Nothing too acrobatic,' he said. Carys spun to face him and wrapped one arm around his back. He placed his left palm on her waist, then linked his right fingers with hers. 'At least if I fall, you'll catch me.'

'You won't fall,' said Carys. She closed her eyes and rested on his gorgeous, firm chest as they gently swayed on the spot. He breathed a little more heavily as the dance went on, but he kept going. Carys's soul flooded with contentment. First Joanne, now Troy. A perfect moment in time. It couldn't get much better. The music softened towards its finale. Troy shifted his hands, slipping both of them behind her and encasing her in his strong grip, then dipped down and placed a kiss on her forehead. Her heart rate picked up. That moment she'd thought couldn't get any better just did.

'You deserve to be happy,' said Troy, his breath whispering over the spot he'd kissed.

'What do you mean?' said Carys, desperation flooding the words.

Troy put his fingers to his lips. 'Just that. Right now, I need to sit. Like seriously need to.'

Carys extricated herself from his grip and fetched his crutch. He hobbled back to the chair. Joanne and Ewan were sitting already.

'I hope you won't think me rude,' said Troy. 'But I need to get home. This has been quite an outing for me and I feel wasted. Who'd have thought it after one dance.'

'Not at all,' said Ewan. 'You take care of the leg, mate. And I look forward to finding out where you're signing for next.'

'But we'll see you again,' said Carys, her eyes darting to Joanne. 'Won't we?'

'Of course.' Joanne pressed Carys's hand in hers. 'I'm not going anywhere this time. You have my number and you know where I am.' She got to her feet and pulled Carys into a hug. It was such a warm motherly hug Carys didn't want it to end. Twelve years of missing her mum poured into it. Joanne rubbed her back. 'Come and see me any time. I'm so looking forward to it.'

Carys smiled at her, sure her face must look totally tripped out and goofy. But she suddenly had an overpowering sense that everything would be ok. The sense only a mum could give. How she'd missed it. 'I'll call soon,' said Carys.

'Excellent.' Joanne kissed her cheek. 'It's hard letting you go again.'

'But we won't be far apart this time.' Carys leaned in and hugged her again before leaving with Troy. She kept her arm in his, helping him to the car. His walking had slowed and it took some time getting down the steps and across the darkened carpark. Somewhere behind, the sea lapped on an invisible shore.

'I hope you don't mind leaving,' said Troy. 'But I overdid it with the dancing.'

'It's fine,' said Carys, her mind wheeling over the night's events. Her mum was back in her life. The possibilities were endless and exciting.

As she drove towards the house, Troy massaged his thigh. 'Was I stupid to dance without my crutch?'

'Maybe a bit.'

'It wasn't technically even dancing,' he said. 'I barely moved.'

'But you were supporting your own weight and that's pretty good.' The pang of conflict struck again, as it always did whenever Carys thought about what would happen once Troy was fully fit, but now it didn't feel so terrifying – not now she had Joanne again. And she wanted to make sure she did. She was determined to make lots of calls and not let the connection fall away. It was too important.

The steep driveway to the house was pitch black. Carys steered the Porsche slowly up. The automatic light flicked on and she helped Troy out. He stumbled slightly and she caught him, taking his weight.

'I owe you so much,' he said.

'What's brought this on?' said Carys.

'Seeing you so happy. You've given me a slice of that too. I'll miss you when we're done here.'

'Don't, Troy. I can't think about that right now.'

'Yeah, I guess. I shouldn't spoil your evening with my troubles.'

'They're not just your troubles,' said Carys. 'Do you think I won't feel it too?'

'I didn't mean that, I know you will.'

The automatic light flipped off as they stood still, leaving only the stars above shining and everything else in utter darkness.

'If you think I won't miss you too,' said Carys, 'then you've got something wrong somewhere. Of course I will.'

She would have said more but Troy's weight was pressing on her, his face was close, though she could barely make it out, and all she wanted to do was touch those lips with her own. Pushing onto tiptoe, she found exactly the spot she wanted, and he was ready, like he'd been leaning in to do the same. Their mouths met and Carys kissed him, ignoring the fact he was her employer and a famous footballer. Now he was just a man she desperately wanted to kiss. And if he'd kissed hundreds of other women with more finesse or better technique than her, she didn't care. This was her moment.

Troy's crutch clattered to the ground and he slipped both his hands around Carys's waist, pulling her closer, running them up and down the sides of her body. His tongue flicked against her teeth and she moaned, matching his need. He edged closer and the Porsche's chilled metal pressed against her back. He pulled her top lip between his, kissing it, then her bottom lip, until she was giddy and barely able to breathe. But she was terrified to stop. When she did, that would be it. They would sweep this moment under the carpet like they'd done before and go back to the way they'd been. It was the only way. Wasn't it?

Fearing she might pass out, Carys pulled back and filled her lungs with cold air. She couldn't collapse. Troy wasn't in a fit state to help her and one of them had to keep their head.

'You deserve to be happy,' Troy whispered.

'So you said.'

'I mean it. And I'll help you any way I can.' Troy's cold fingertip touched her cheek. 'If it means letting you stay on here, then that's cool with me.'

'But what about you?'

'Let's not worry about that.' He stroked her cheek and she melted some more. 'I enjoyed the kiss,' he said. 'But I'm stuck.'

'How do you mean?'

'My crutch is on the ground.'

'Oh.' She swallowed. 'Lean on the car and I'll get it.' She fumbled for it and placed it under his arm. The security light flicked back on again and seeing Troy's face crushed some of her courage. 'I enjoyed it too,' she said. 'But we shouldn't really… I mean—'

'Yeah. I know.' Troy gave a half-shrug as he hobbled towards the door. 'But I'm not sorry.'

Carys locked the car and followed him towards the front door. With a trembling finger, she touched her lips. Some women would fight with handbags at dawn to have kissed Troy Copeland like that but they didn't know the real Troy. Carys would take a kiss from him again in a second if she believed they had any kind of future, but how could they?

Their worlds were at opposite ends of a spectrum. With each step Troy took he got closer to returning to his world and Carys got further away.

Chapter Eighteen

Troy

Troy sucked the end of his pen and stared at the blank white space. He didn't remember ever being in this position before. What did people write in Christmas cards? He'd gone straight from his parents writing them to his agent's assistant doing it on his behalf. Now, he not only had to do it himself but he needed to get the wording right.

Carys was special and he was drawn to her more than anyone he'd ever been involved with. He'd done as she wanted after the party and left the kiss at the car. But he'd have kissed her again and again. He'd have taken her to bed and made love to her every night, even if his leg had fallen off. But she didn't want to get involved with someone like him.

'How can I persuade her?' he muttered. If she came with him, he wouldn't force her to go to matches or functions if she didn't want to. Would that work for her? He needed to ask her but that was going to be difficult. He was no stranger to asking women out but he'd always known they'd say yes. Carys could easily say no, in fact, she would say no. She'd already told him. This was hopeless. His pen started moving around the card, doodling until a picture appeared, all lines and swirls, building to make a Christmas scene in his own style. Words didn't flow, but drawings did. Carys wouldn't laugh. She'd spotted his doodles before and said they were good. Even if they were amateurish, she'd appreciate the thought.

He wasn't sure what he was doing for Christmas and it was getting close. Carys seemed to be waiting for him to make a decision before she made one for herself. He'd had offers from his parents, his uncle and several friends but none of them appealed as much as staying here with Carys. She could whip up a healthy Christmas lunch – or ditch it and they could stuff their faces on the traditional for a day like everyone else.

She strolled into the kitchen and Troy lifted a book and slipped the card under it. 'Hey,' he said.

'How are you getting on with that?'

'Not bad,' said Troy, patting the book. 'We should send Mrs Hansen something for Christmas. She's kind to have done all this for me.'

'Yeah, that's a nice idea. I'll sort it.' She sat opposite him. 'Troy, I need to ask you something.'

'Fire away.'

'You know you said I could go home for Christmas?'

'Yes.' His stomach slumped. He had said that, but he didn't want her to go anywhere. He wanted her with him. Always.

'Would it be ok, if you're going somewhere for a few days, for me to stay on the island and spend Christmas with my mum?'

Troy nodded and opened his mouth, not sure what to say to get the right feelings across. Of course, he didn't grudge her spending Christmas with the mum she thought she'd lost. And he liked Joanne, Ewan and Rowan. They were good people. 'Yeah, sure. I, er… think I'll go to my sister's house.'

'Great. There's so much we have to catch up on but at the same time it's like we've never been apart.'

'It's so great.' He could see how much it meant to her.

'But that means we have to figure out how to get you to your sister's.'

Troy flipped a little smile. 'Yeah. Don't you worry about that. Chris can arrange something.'

'Are you sure?'

'Definitely. You make your plans and enjoy yourself.'

Her watery smile pierced straight through him and slammed into his lower gut.

She got to her feet and bustled off to prepare dinner, and he slipped out a scrap piece of paper. He needed to practise before he wrote the real thing. *Dear Carys. You have changed my life. I can never say how much. Thank you for being you. Love from Troy.*

Did that say enough? Could he ever find words to speak for his heart? The pencil moved across the paper, finishing the doodles and making an intricate frame. Creating something for Carys was important.

Later he wrapped a little gift box, stuck the card to it and left it by the Christmas tree. Now to convince her to go to Joanne's early on Christmas Eve, so he could pretend Chris was sending the helicopter. He wasn't really going anywhere. She'd never know, but he couldn't face it.

*

On Christmas Eve, Carys packed her overnight bag ready for the short trip to Joanne's house in Tobermory. 'It's hardly worth staying,' she said. 'I could drive there in the morning.'

'This is more fun,' said Troy. 'She probably wants to tuck you up and sprinkle magic dust in your eyes. And when you wake up, there'll be a stocking filled with presents.'

'Maybe. Or maybe I just want to have a drink tonight and not have to drive back.'

'Exactly that.' Troy edged towards her slowly without using his crutch. He swung his arm around her. 'Take care and merry Christmas.'

She patted his back, tilting her chin and studying him. 'When are you leaving?'

'Soon,' said Troy. The urge to kiss her lips burned deep. 'Chris will message.'

'I hope it goes ok.'

'It will. See you on Boxing Day.'

'Bye, Troy, and merry Christmas.' She pushed onto tiptoes and kissed him on the cheek. He closed his eyes, savouring the warmth, but he didn't respond. How could he? There was so much he wanted to pour into a kiss but this wasn't the time. There may never be a time.

Holding onto the doorframe, Troy watched her drive away in his Porsche, his stomach slumping to his feet. Perhaps she expected the helicopter to fly over at any second. His parents thought he was spending Christmas with friends. His friends thought he was visiting his uncle in London and Chris thought he and Carys were having a quiet Christmas together. No one knew the truth. What would his fans make of Troy Copeland spending Christmas alone?

Carys, the queen of meal prep, had enough food in the freezer to last several months, so that wouldn't be an issue. But as she disappeared along the road and out of sight, a raft of loneliness struck him in the gut. It was only two days, and he didn't have a particular love of Christmas one way or another, but without Carys he was empty. He hobbled into the living room, where the tree winked at him. Underneath, he saw his little gift and card for Carys. He'd forgotten to give it to her.

'Fuck.' He slumped onto the sofa, wanting to cry. Was that pathetic? It would be more sensible to use the time to call around and send messages. First, his parents. After enquiring about his leg, they told him about their Christmas plans. Had it been that long since they last talked? They hadn't seen fit to call and ask him… and neither had he until now. He sighed as he ended the call. They were enjoying life without kids. He and his sister had always felt like a burden. His parents encouraged his football because long training sessions kept him out of their way and meant they didn't have to entertain an energetic and troublesome child. Now they were free and couldn't make it any more obvious how thrilled they were.

He tried his sister next but the phone rang off, so he left her a voice message wishing her a merry Christmas and asking what she had planned this year. Why hadn't he thought to invite her here, especially when he'd spent the last week pretending he was going to Glasgow to spend Christmas with her? She wouldn't have come. She'd be living the party life with her friends.

With the calls and messages out of the way, Troy lounged back and placed his arm along the sofa. He'd have to bite the bullet and put on a Christmas movie. What else was there to do than mope? Shuffling along, he grabbed the remote control and aimed it at the TV.

Something clicked. *What was that?* Burglars? Paps? 'Jesus Christ,' he muttered, lunging for his crutch as footsteps clacked across the hall. His own real-life *Home Alone*. Could he get to his feet quietly? He wasn't exactly prepped for a fight. As he staggered up, the door swung open.

'Carys.'

'Holy crap, Troy.' Carys jumped and her hand leapt to her chest. 'What are you doing here?'

'Eh, same question.'

'I forgot my Christmas present,' said Carys. 'I spotted it under the tree last night and I wanted to open it on Christmas Day.' She smiled and her eyes were wide and innocent, her cheeks pink from the cold air outside and her wispy hair tucked under a bobble hat. 'Has the helicopter not arrived yet?'

Troy rubbed his hand across his face and slumped back down. 'No.'

'Why? What happened? Has there been a mix-up?'

He shook his head. 'I'm not going. I'm staying here.'

Carys pulled off her gloves. 'But why?'

'I was never going. I wanted you to go and enjoy yourself. I still do. I'm fine here.'

'No way, Troy.' She sat beside him and rested her palm on his knee. 'I can't leave you here on your own at Christmas.'

He put his hand on hers and held it. 'It's cool. You have a family to go to.'

'Come with me,' she said. 'They won't mind. They like you.'

'No, this is your thing. I don't want to intrude.'

'You won't be intruding. Let's forget I work for you. Come as my friend. Please.' Her pale grey eyes pleaded with him. He couldn't deny her anything when she looked at him like that.

'Ok. But call Joanne and check it's cool.'

She affectionately squeezed his knee and got to her feet to call. Troy leaned back and sighed as Carys explained the situation. Faintly, he heard Joanne's chirpy voice agreeing to everything.

'I better pack some clothes,' he said.

'No, it's better than that,' said Carys.

'How do you mean?'

'They don't have room at their house for anyone else so they're packing everything in the car and coming here.'

'What?'

'Yup. Mum's scraping Rowan off the ceiling. Santa's just come early.'

'What do you mean?'

'He's getting to spend Christmas with his favourite footballer in a mansion.' Carys looked at him as though it was obvious.

'Isn't it a lot of work? I feel like I've caused a whole lot more trouble.'

'Don't sweat it, Troy. They're thrilled. I'm going to drive back and help them. They have some secret presents to stash away.' She winked. 'Where better to hide them than in his idol's Porsche?'

Troy's quiet Christmas was about to be knocked out of the park into a whirlwind of insanity.

By the time Carys returned with the three guests, Troy had worked himself into a state. This wasn't simply three near-strangers in his house for Christmas. One of them was Carys's mum. And even though Carys had told him Joanne was only forty-five – just fifteen years older than him – it felt like he was about to spend Christmas with the in-laws and his every move would be under scrutiny – a different kind of scrutiny than he was used to.

With a tremendous effort, he got to his feet and made his way to the entrance hall.

'Hello.' Ewan clapped him on the arm. 'You've made our lad's Christmas. And mine.'

'Mine too,' said Joanne. She stepped forward and hugged Troy. 'The oven's on the blink and I was panicking about ruining the turkey.'

'And now you've got Carys to cook it,' said Troy, flipping a wink at Carys.

170

'I'll settle for a working oven, but Carys is probably better at cooking than me.'

'She's a whizz in the kitchen, all right,' said Troy. 'Would you like a tour?' he asked, focusing on Rowan. 'I could show you the gym.'

'Can I?' Rowan's eyes almost burst from their sockets.

Imagining the house through the eyes of an excited nine-year-old gave Troy the boost he needed. He shrugged off the worry and embraced the craziness. As evening drew in, Carys, Joanne and Ewan started prepping a buffet and Troy sat with Rowan discussing every goal he'd scored in great detail. Before the feast was laid out, they changed into Christmas pyjamas.

'You'll have to wear whatever you normally wear,' said Carys, catching his arm before he headed for his downstairs room.

'Oh yeah?' He raised his eyebrow. 'How do you know I don't sleep naked?'

'Really, Troy.' Her cheeks glowed pink.

He winked. 'Do you seriously want me to appear in my birthday suit?'

Carys scanned him up and down and her lips curled. 'I wouldn't object, but I'm not sure it's appropriate for the others.'

'Maybe not. But how about later I put on a bow tie and give you an early Christmas present?'

Leaning in closer, Carys whispered, 'Have you been drinking? Are you propositioning me?'

Troy made a face. 'I might have had a whisky or two, and as for the other bit… What's better than a Christmas prepositional thing?'

'Oh, get lost and go put on your jammies.'

Troy smirked and hobbled towards his bedroom, sniggering. He did sleep naked! Boxers and a t-shirt were the best he could do. He looked like he was back in his kit, only now he had a scarred leg. Back on the pitch, that would be a souvenir of his triumph.

When he got to the living room, everyone else was huddled on one sofa. Ewan at the end with daddy elf pyjamas, Rowan next in his elf junior pyjamas, Joanne beside him in her mummy elf pyjamas, then Carys. Her red striped shorts barely covered anything and the tiny t-shirt with a glittery pug in a Santa hat stretched a little too perfectly over her beautifully formed chest. Troy's fingertips flexed. How much would he like to run them over the contours of her body? She patted the free part of the cushion beside her.

'Cosy in,' she said.

Troy squeezed in beside her, his thigh butting up against hers. She smiled. Joanne leaned forward and pulled out fleecy blankets from a bag. 'Fill up your plates,' she said, 'then we'll snuggle up and get the film on.'

With his plate balanced on the sofa arm, Troy helped Carys pull a blanket over the two of them. Now he wished the others would disappear. If they were alone like this, all his Christmas wishes would come true.

He hadn't watched *Home Alone* since he was little but found himself laughing out loud at all of it. Maybe it was the fun of seeing it through Rowan's eyes. Whatever it was, he forgot the world outside. When Carys's head touched his shoulder, he didn't wince despite it being his injured one. He leaned over so his temple rested on her hair. Under the blanket, he found her thigh and slid his palm over it. She inhaled sharply, holding her head stiff against the sofa back. He carried on across her lap until he found her hand. He took it, laced his fingers through hers, and held it firmly. *Merry Christmas to me.*

Chapter Nineteen

Carys

Rowan's excitement at spotting piles of presents magically appearing under Troy's Christmas tree was a film-worthy moment. Joanne and Ewan smiled, passing proud glances at each other as Rowan rampaged through the presents, throwing paper everywhere.

Carys's fingertips trembled as she peeled back the shiny wrapping on the little gift from Troy. His eyes bored through her.

The carpet was soft under her legs. She glimpsed the edge of a shiny dark purple box that reflected the Christmas tree lights, and the swooping butterflies in her tummy intensified. Something told her a lot of thought had gone into this gift. How should she react? Was anyone else looking? A quick scan told her the others were engrossed in their own gifts. Carys hadn't been given anything special since she was little, her dad's only child. He made a big show of spending too much and buying her everything from flashing trainers to bikes with streamers on the handlebars, realistic prams and hundreds of dolls. After Joanne left and the other children arrived, Carys got 'too big' for presents. She was lucky if he slipped a tenner into an envelope for her. The last few years, she'd worked Christmas Day, taking the shift no one else wanted, dressing up as an elf and having fun with children in care homes or old people in their nursing homes. Sharing their happiness had brought her joy too.

But now she was faced with something new. Falling asleep on Troy's shoulder during the film the night before had provided magical vibes; opening his card to find a beautiful hand-drawn picture and handwritten message had left her tingling all over. She'd spotted his drawings – doodles, as he called them – before, but he'd always hidden them away. He couldn't do that anymore. They were amazing. Perhaps she could find an outlet for them. Maybe a local gallery would display them. It could be a New Year mission. But this wasn't the time. This was the time for more magic, heart-stopping magic. She dug deep and pulled out the box. Her entire hand was shaking now. Prising the box open, she blinked at a glint of silver. Slowly, she raised a delicate chain from the box. Sparkling from the centre was a tiny, jewelled star cut in a whimsical, hypnotic shape. The chain was like fluid in her fingertips. Carys hardly owned any jewellery, except a few bangles from Primark and earrings from Claire's Accessories, but this necklace sang money. Too much money.

Folded in the box was a slip of paper featuring another of his doodles, making a Christmassy border around the words:

You shine like a star, your light is so bright it spills onto everyone else, filling their hearts with joy and love.

Merry Christmas, Carys

Love, Troy

She raised her fingers to her lips as she read the words. He'd written them himself. She lifted her eyes to him. He glanced back from his place on the sofa, rubbing his knuckle with his fingertips, his eyebrows drawn up uncertainly.

Getting to her feet, Carys parked herself beside him and threw her arms around him. 'This is so beautiful,' she said.

'I mean it,' he said.

'I know.' She gazed at it. 'But it must have cost a fortune.'

'Who cares,' said Troy. 'You're worth every penny. Here.' He took it from her, slid his hands behind her and brushed her fine hair off her neck. 'Turn around and I'll put it on you.'

She did, gasping as the cool pendant dropped on her throat. Troy's fingers grazed her skin as he fastened the clasp, leaving a trail of goosebumps. Carys touched the star and spun back to face him.

'Suits you,' he said.

Carys smiled, unable to drag her eyes from him. 'I didn't really get you much, just the baking.'

'Which I'm sure is delicious.'

'Because you pretty much have everything.'

'Yeah.' He let out a short laugh. 'Everything money can buy.' With a brief check that the others were still busy with Rowan's unwrapping, he leaned in and placed a quick kiss on her cheek. Carys's hand leapt to the necklace again; she didn't think she'd ever stop touching it.

'Has Santa been good to you then?' Troy asked Rowan, blinking his gaze away from Carys.

'Yeah,' he shouted from amidst a pile of paper.

Joanne withdrew to the sofa beside them. 'It doesn't matter what he gets, the excitement of being in your house over Christmas will be enough. I can't thank you enough.'

'Not a problem,' said Troy. 'Carys is like family now. And you're part of hers, so we'll go with that.'

Joanne smiled, her eyes darting to Carys's neck. 'Oh, that's beautiful,' she said.

'Troy gave it to me.' Carys fingered it.

'So lovely,' said Joanne. 'It was fate that brought you together and then back to me.'

'But we're not together,' said Carys. They weren't. And she couldn't kid herself. It wasn't going to happen and every happy thing that did would be offset by the tragedy of Troy leaving. She had to protect her heart. If Troy wanted a place in her soul, he had it, but he wasn't sticking around. She'd be abandoned like the last sprout at the dinner table.

'I know,' said Joanne, laying her hand on Carys's arm. 'But you know what I mean.'

Christmas Day passed in the blink of an eye. The fun didn't stop. Ewan filled every quiet moment with a hilarious story.

'Like the time when my mate and I were hiding from a wifey we didn't want to talk to and we snuck into the back of a van to hide. Then it drove off.' He doubled up laughing.

Joanne gave Carys a half-exasperated grin while Troy and Rowan chuckled. If it wasn't Ewan making them laugh, it was Troy giving them inside gossip from the football scene and Joanne's endless supply of insane games.

Charades had them all in stitches and when they played Name That Tune, Carys curled up crying at Troy's attempt at 'Grease Lightning'.

Everyone lent a hand with lunch and Troy insisted on his own special way of cooking sprouts.

'You might even convince Rowan to eat them,' said Joanne.

'Why do we put ourselves through sprout torture every year?' said Ewan.

'I quite like them,' said Carys.

'That's because you're the vegetable queen.' Troy picked some sprouts off the stalk. He was standing unaided, almost upright, so much taller and stronger.

'Those are fresh from the walled garden,' Carys informed him. 'So they should be pretty tasty.'

Behind, Rowan sat at the table surrounded by his new presents. Troy pointed at one of his books. 'That looks good.'

'*The Twits*,' said Rowan. 'Mum's going to help me read it.'

'Cool,' said Troy. 'I've heard of that, but I haven't read it. Who wrote it?'

'Roald Dahl,' said Ewan.

'Ah yes. I'm not a great reader,' said Troy, plucking more sprouts from the stalk. He glanced at Carys and she smiled. This was new. Since when did he discuss his reading and writing issues?

'Neither is Rowan,' said Joanne under her breath. 'He's dyslexic and we're trying to get him to enjoy books. Some of his friends are reading the Roald Dahl books on their own and he's not even close. But I don't want him to be afraid of reading.'

'I know how he feels,' said Troy.

Joanne looked up.

'I'm the same. It's only since I met Carys I've admitted how big a problem it's been all my life. I'm probably at the same level as Rowan.'

'Really?' said Ewan. 'I didn't know that.'

'No one does,' said Troy.

'Can I tell Rowan?' Joanne asked, loading the sprouts into the pan.

'Yeah. Why not? I guess I shouldn't be ashamed of it. It's just hard to change my mindset. I've always panicked people will think I'm thick.'

'Now they'll know you're brave,' said Carys. 'Facing your demons head on.'

Troy's smile sent her heart racing again.

After lunch, Carys lolled back in her seat. She'd eaten more in one meal than she had in the rest of the month. Piles of dirty dishes lay on the table. She could leave them until the morning but she would regret it. Standing was an effort but she did it, lifting a pile of plates and staggering to the kitchen. The others followed and everyone chipped in loading the dishwasher.

'That's great you're helping Troy with the dyslexia,' said Joanne. 'Rowan's teacher is very good and I'm trying to raise awareness.'

'It's important.' Carys yawned and stretched; wine always made her sleepy. 'It's so common. I've seen it so often in children's homes.'

'Exactly. Do you think Troy would help with an awareness campaign? It would give us so much more clout with a name like his behind us.'

'He might,' said Carys. 'He's just coming to terms with it himself, but he's involved with other charities, so there'd be no harm in asking.'

'There's a meeting in April. I wonder if he'd be up for saying a few words.'

'I can ask him,' said Carys. But by the time she'd got to the living room, the wine had filtered into every pore and she was so tired could barely remember her own name, let alone what she was meant to be asking Troy.

*

Troy's strength was increasing daily. In between Christmas and New Year, Carys drove him around the island and they found beautiful spots for chilly walks. She didn't bring the wheelchair anymore, and more and more

Troy would pass her the crutch and have a go hobbling on his own.

'You're doing so well,' Carys said, her eyes brimming with proud tears while her heart wept. Soon he'd be strong enough to run, then run and kick, then play football matches again. Their time would be up.

'It feels so much better,' he said, rolling his shoulders and standing tall. 'But I don't want to jinx it or overdo it, so you better give me the crutch back.'

Come Hogmanay, they travelled to Tobermory to watch the midnight fireworks from Joanne's house up on the hill. Everyone in the street had gathered along the low wall that bordered one side of the lane. Below it was another row of houses. The slope was so steep, they were above the roofs from this position and looked out over the darkened marina, lit only by a few twinkling streetlamps.

As Joanne chatted to Rowan, Carys took Troy by the arm and tugged him away.

'What is it?' he asked.

'I forgot. Mum asked me on Christmas Day if I'd ask you to help with her dyslexia campaign.'

'Oh, right.' He rubbed his chin. 'I guess. What does it involve?'

'Nothing much, just lending your name to it and maybe saying a few words to inspire the kids.'

'Yeah, I guess I could do that.'

Carys smiled. Somehow that gave her a little lifeline; a way to keep Troy even after he was back playing football.

Across the still bay, the sound of bagpipes floated on the light breeze. Down on the promenade was a procession they couldn't see from their lofty position. They listened until the music stopped, watching the miniscule figures wind their way towards the clock tower. Carys checked the time. Almost midnight. After a beat, more noise from below carried their way, a countdown. The people lining the street joined in.

'…Eight, seven, six, five, four, three, two, one!'

A colossal blast heralded the first firework, and the new year arrived with a bang. The sky was lit with bright colours bursting above the marina and reflecting in the inky black sea.

'Isn't it traditional to kiss someone at New Year?' whispered Troy, leaning in so only Carys heard.

'I wouldn't know,' said Carys, but her blood was racing. 'Normally I'm working and none of the people I work with are usually kissing material.'

'Not even this time?' Troy side-eyed her and smirked.

'Maybe this time I could make an exception.'

He dipped in and claimed her lips, slow and deep. Carys closed her eyes, letting her senses focus on the taste of his mouth. It didn't last nearly long enough. Carys straightened herself out, aware of the eyes of many people, ostensibly watching the fireworks but actually roaming her way.

After trying so hard to keep the lid on that little can of worms, she'd blasted it off again in a few seconds. *Great work, Carys. Great work.*

Chapter Twenty

Troy

Troy placed the weight on the floor and leaned forward on the bench, panting. His shoulder had almost been forgotten because his leg was always the priority, but with his recovery going so well, he wanted to test himself. Before the injuries, he could have lifted much heavier weights but it was a start. Throughout January, he pushed himself to do more.

Carys watched, biting into her lip and frowning. 'That's enough, Troy. You're pushing it as it is. If you do too much too soon, you'll risk damaging it again.

'Ok. I'll stop there.' But it felt good. Damn good. Every day, his strength was returning. Carys might be right not to push it, but it was like a caged animal was waking inside him, ready to burst out, and he couldn't keep it locked away any longer.

The adrenaline pushed him to greater things with his reading too. After his chat with Rowan, he'd started trying to read *The Twits*. Exercising his brain helped release some pent-up energy.

'This is actually a good story,' he said, propping it on the table as he ate his lunch. Carys was always on hand to help decode the tricky bits but the challenge of doing it himself kept him going.

'I need to nip to the florist and see Mum,' Carys said, stacking some dishes and putting them in the cupboard. 'She's using some plants from here for foliage in her bouquets. Do you want to come with me?'

'Yeah. Ok.' He closed the book and stretched. A few twinges rattled his bones but they were barely noticeable. Everything was finally getting back to normal.

Troy left his crutch in the car and walked the short distance from the car park along the promenade to the florist. He didn't bother with his baseball cap. Since the Christmas party, people on the island knew a famous footballer was living among them but no one really bothered him. Occasionally a young person would point and stare but he could deal with it.

His phone bleeped and he checked it. Shaun Eddery flashed on the screen. Troy smirked. He'd read the name without thinking. He pushed play on the voice note and held the phone to his ear.

'Have you seen Insta today, mate?' said Shaun's voice. 'Someone's posted a picture of you snogging a girl and it's all linked up to that one where the girl gave you a BJ on a beach. Daryl's fucking milking it. He thinks you've lost the plot. Don't read his comments or you'll want to kill him. He says he knew you were finished even before the accident and you're just using this as an excuse. Git. I hate the bastard. And Pippa's on there too. She agrees and says you were always hiding behind your bravado and she's pleased you've faced up and left the game before you embarrassed yourself.'

Troy lowered the phone and glared at it.

'Everything ok?' asked Carys, pushing open the florist door.

He should reply but the words were jammed by rage. Sometimes Shaun didn't know when to shut up, but Daryl.

He thinks I'm finished? He'd thought that before the accident. And Pippa? What did she mean embarrass himself? That was it. The red rag was flapping in front of him and he was ready to charge it down. If he worked a miracle and persuaded Carys to go back with him, she'd walk straight into the middle of this shitstorm. Her worst nightmare.

The shop smelled earthy and fresh, too calm and pleasant for how Troy felt. Winter bouquets in cool colours lined the work surface, dwarfing Joanne as she peered out from behind them. Carys placed the basket of greenery on the long wooden table next to a pile of ribbon and a pair of long-bladed scissors, her eyes still roaming over Troy, her expression slightly puzzled.

'Oh, these look great,' said Joanne. 'Exactly what I need.' She reached out and hugged Carys. 'And how are you, Troy? You're walking so well.'

'Yeah, thanks. I feel so much stronger.' His reply was instinctive but his gaze roamed to his phone and he opened Instagram. It took ages to load and his focus shifted back to Joanne.

'Oh, that's good to hear.' She lifted the basket of greenery and carefully placed the sprigs and twigs onto sheets of paper. Taking the scissors, she snipped a stem and placed it beside another, her head wavering from side to side as she admired the effect. 'And, before I forget,' she glanced at Troy, 'I have the information about the dyslexia conference. The organisers were over the moon when they heard you would speak. I've given them your details; I hope that was ok. They'll contact you directly and agree on the formalities with you. Hopefully it'll fit your schedule because you might be back playing by then.'

Joanne kept on talking as she searched for something behind the counter. Troy's fists balled. He'd found the picture. It was a grainy black-and-white shot of him with Carys at New Year. *Fuck*. And wait… He hadn't agreed to speak at a conference – had he? He'd said he would say a few motivational words to the kids, maybe go to a local primary school and chat to a few children. He couldn't speak at a conference. Press conferences about football were bad enough. People joked about him being a man of few words. The films were cringey: him sitting back with his cap pulled low, giving monosyllabic answers, dreading to say too much in case he used a wrong word and let his illiterate brain get the better of him.

Daryl's comments swam beneath the pictures. He barely made sense of them but he got the gist. Joanne handed him a letter. His stress levels were so high, the words jumped around. How did they expect him to talk to a hoard of scholars about his troubles? Taking a deep breath, he concentrated. Slowly, the words came together. 'It's in Glasgow?' He passed the letter to Carys.

'On the twenty-fourth of April,' said Carys. 'At the SECC.'

At the Scottish Exhibition and Conference Centre? One of the biggest venues in the country? Everyone would want to hear Troy Copeland talk about his failings. No way could he let that go public. Not after Daryl's words. No, no, no. Daryl would have a field day, so would Pippa and all the other doubters. Troy imagined their smug laughter as they branded him for the thicko he was. She'd congratulated him for not embarrassing himself, but he already had. He'd been so thick he hadn't even noticed his fiancée sneaking around with his teammate or heard what they were saying behind his back. *They thought I was finished? I'll show them. I'll show those bastards.*

'Right,' said Troy. 'I'll let you know.' He staggered backwards out of the shop, not waiting for Carys. He couldn't walk quickly enough to put any distance between them, but the amazing feeling of being able to conquer the world was back. Talking to hundreds of people about dyslexia was a sure-fire way to make a fool of himself but getting back to the pitch wasn't. They wouldn't know what hit them when he got back.

'Troy,' Carys called, catching up with him. 'Are you ok?'

He didn't answer but carried on towards the car. She put her hand on his arm.

'Ow,' he said and, like the footballer he was, rubbed it like she'd yanked it from the socket rather than gently touched it. He desisted at the expression on her face. 'I can't do that conference thing.' His eyes wandered over the marina behind. He couldn't meet Carys's gaze.

'Ok. I'm sure Mum won't mind. But what's changed your mind?'

'Nothing. It just doesn't fit with me and what I'm doing.' He scratched his hand through his hair. It was getting long on top and could do with a good trim. 'I didn't realise that's what it was and I'm not ok with speaking to that many people. And you know what, it's not important. This is what's important.' He slapped his thigh, sending a tremor of pain down it. 'I need to talk to Chris. I've had long enough to decide which contract I'm going with. The deadline is coming up. I need to sign it today.'

'Today?' said Carys. 'What's got into you?'

He stopped. 'Do you want to read what they're all saying about me? I can't read it, I'm too stressed, but Shaun gave me the gist.' The words came out louder than he meant them to, but he'd had enough. 'I'm a footballer. This little holiday has been good. In fact, it's been the best recovery I could have had, but I need to get back now.'

Carys's beautiful lucid eyes shut down. No twinkles or shining light glowed, no tears fell. Nothing gave a clue to how she felt. Maybe she was just accepting. Troy stiffened his jaw and tramped on. This was how it had to be. He was a footballer and he was going back to where he belonged and where he knew what to do. Once he was back on the pitch, it would wipe the smirk off all the critics.

As he got into the car, he pulled out his phone and scrolled for Chris's number. Silently, Carys drove out of the carpark, taking the road towards the place that had been their island home for four months now. He'd healed and learned but that would soon be a tiny memory boat sailing on the ocean of his career. He ignored the pain forming in his chest. Troy Copeland was going back to the pitch and he was going to be one hundred per cent fighting fit and two hundred per cent focused.

Chapter Twenty-One

Carys

Not for the first time in her life, the searing pain of loss ripped through Carys. Troy was still in the house but he was as good as gone. His voice rang through the rooms, laughing and talking too loudly about his new contract. Gone was the man she'd dragged here in September and a brash football icon had stepped into his shoes. The face was the same but very little else. Even with the slight limp, he swaggered. His Roald Dahl book lay abandoned on the table and all he wanted to talk about was his training schedule and his new teammates. The doctor had okayed him to drive and he could razz around in the Porsche again.

In a vain hope he might change his mind about doing the conference, Carys hadn't told her mum he didn't want to do it. But hope faded with every second. Kids with dyslexia were something far removed from his plans. If one day he lent his name to a dyslexia charity, it would be under studio conditions with a perfectly posed photo and a professional article. Nothing from the real man who hid in the shadow of his overconfident football persona.

Taking out her phone, Carys called her mum from the kitchen. Troy's voice was still echoing out of the living room as her call connected.

'Hey,' said Joanne. 'Are you ok?'

'Not really,' said Carys.

Margaret Amatt

'Oh no, what's happened?'

Carys sighed. 'Troy can't do the conference.'

'Oh, well, that's ok. Has he signed with another club?'

'Yes, but I'm not allowed to say where.'

'Oh, Carys. I don't mind where. I just feel sad for you.'

'For me?'

'Well, yes. You'll miss him.'

Carys sucked her lips between her teeth, damming the emotion waiting to spill out. 'Is it that obvious?'

'Yes,' said Joanne.

'Great,' muttered Carys.

'You'll always have a home here if you choose to stay,' said Joanne. 'I know it won't be the same without him.'

'Oh god, don't. I'll start crying. I'd love to stay with you, Mum.' Tears welled in her eyes.

'Oh, Carys. See how things play out with Troy because no matter what happens there, I'll be here for you.'

'Thank you. He already said I could stay on at the house and run it as a health retreat, but I can't. Not on my own. It's too big and he's the one with the money. We need to be able to talk about it and work together.' It was something she'd dreamed for both of them, in her fantasy where Troy wasn't her boss or a famous footballer.

'I understand,' said Joanne. 'And maybe he'd be better selling. Then you can let it go and move on.'

Carys sat at the table and put her head in her hands. 'You're right. I can't stay here.'

'And...' Joanne paused for so long, Carys frowned at the screen. Had she been cut off? 'Is there no chance of you going with him?'

'To do what? He won't need a carer once he's back with a team. They have all the people on site. He'll have physios and trainers. He can even hire a chef.'

188

'I didn't really mean that,' said Joanne. 'I meant as his girlfriend.'

Carys scoffed and ran her fingers through her hair. 'No. I don't fit the high heels or know how to apply the fancy make-up.'

Troy's voice had stopped in the living room and the house was oddly quiet without it. Had he gone outside? Maybe he was doing a video tour of the garden with his new teammates. They were the kind of people he belonged with.

'He's too famous and too important for me. I don't want that life.' She wanted a life with him here but that wasn't going to happen. Not now. 'I can't live like that with no privacy and everyone knowing our business. You see all those horrific things on the internet about me?'

'I can understand you not wanting it,' said Joanne. 'But I felt sure there would be a way. He seems to like you so much.'

A noise in the doorway made Carys glance up. Troy stood, hand at his mouth like he'd cleared his throat. Heat rose in her neck. Had he overheard?

'I have to go,' she said to Joanne. 'Speak later.' She ended the call and held Troy's gaze.

'I'm sorry,' he said.

'About what?'

'You and me.'

Carys busied herself not looking at him. 'Was there ever really a you and me? Other than the work?'

'Yes, Carys, there was.' He glanced at his feet and for a second the vulnerable Troy returned but when he peered up his eyes were steely and determined. 'There still is, or there could be.'

She shook her head. 'Not really.'

'Yes, really. Stop hiding from it… I mean, wouldn't you even consider it?'

'Consider what?' She gulped in too much air. What was he doing? Couldn't he just leave? Didn't he know that was what people always did to her? Why was he dragging it out like this when he knew she couldn't go with him?

'Come with me, please. Even for a little while, no strings, see how it goes.'

'I can't.' She shook her head. 'I… I just can't.'

He ran his fingers through his hair. 'Fine. Chris is sending a helicopter this afternoon. I'm meeting my new teammates. I won't be back until tomorrow. Then we need to discuss what you want to do about this place.'

'Sell it,' she said. 'I don't want it.'

He arched his eyebrow. 'Ok. You don't even want to think about it? I'm perfectly happy for you to run this place as a retreat. I always liked the idea.'

'I've been thinking about it for the last four months, that's why I know what to do. I don't need to think about it… I need to *stop* thinking about it.'

'Ok, fine.' He wavered at the door. 'I'll still pay you to the end of your contract but, just so you know, I'm moving back to Glasgow soon.'

'I know.' She had to hold herself together and be professional. 'When you're away this afternoon, can I use the Porsche?' she asked.

'Sure. Use anything. You know… I… I'll…' He raised a finger in the air. 'Oh never mind.' He turned on his heel and left.

Carys snatched the car keys and scooted out. As she drove, she didn't glance back. Tears obscured her vision. She had to get to her mum. Once she was there, she could pour out her soul but Troy wasn't going to see her. Only a mum would know what to do. Carys finally had one again and she needed her more than ever.

Chapter Twenty-Two

Troy

Waiting for the helicopter, Troy used his new mobility to pace like a caged tiger. He was doing the right thing. Wasn't he? Getting back into football was the number one priority.

He'd overheard Carys's words. She confirmed she didn't want his lifestyle and he came with it, like it or lump it. His chest tightened. He'd asked her to come. He'd really wanted to tell her exactly how he felt but he couldn't spit the words out. They needed to talk properly but his brain was so full of football and his new team that he couldn't see past it. Once this first meeting was out of the way, he could sort things out.

His phone beeped and he glared at it. He couldn't take any more smart remarks from former teammates. The press had got hold of the Instagram pictures and speculation about his retirement was rife, along with the colourful reports on his private life. Daryl's comments made him sick; the prick who'd almost killed him now thought it ok to talk like he'd done Troy a favour getting him out of the game before he faded away.

CHRIS: Technical issues and bad weather forecast. Can't do the flight today. Watch this space for tomorrow.

'Fucking great!' Troy launched the phone across the floor. Now he was stuck here with no Carys, no car, a head bursting with crap and no one to offload it to.

He flung open the door and the misty January air nipped his cheeks as he hobbled down the step towards the orchard. This place was all Carys. A smile broke through his vile mood as he remembered her wheeling him round here in the autumn, spouting her grand plans. For a moment it had seemed real, but it hadn't been. Not really. She deserved someone better. He had all the money in the world, could buy her anything she wanted, but he couldn't provide the life she deserved. Carys was a happy, carefree spirit. Living the life of a footballer's girlfriend would tether her to the daily grind of paparazzi and exposure. Expectations and judgement were an everyday thing and they'd crush her. He had to accept her choice and see that she was right. She'd made the decision and not only should he respect it but he should honour it without bitterness.

Was he doomed only to find love when it was someone he couldn't have? How unfair.

The sound of an engine jolted him and he spied two cars coming up the drive. The Porsche led the way and Joanne's silver car followed. Carys was back. For the second time in less than a month, she'd discover him not on the helicopter he was supposed to be going on – only this time it was genuine.

Hiding in the garden felt like a wise move, but also a coward's move and Troy Copeland wasn't a coward. He approached the house as fast as he could along the wet and slippery path. He had to take care, one misstep here and he could slide and put his recovery back weeks. The door was ajar and he pushed it open. Voices rang from upstairs.

'Carys,' he shouted up the stairs. The voices stopped and Carys appeared, leaning over the banister.

'Troy? Why are you here? Where's the helicopter? Did you make up a story again?' Her brow was creased and Troy couldn't read any amusement in her expression.

'No. Chris messaged. It can't get here today.'

She hopped down the stairs. 'Listen,' she said. 'We both knew this day was coming and it was never going to be easy. Mum's here and we're taking my stuff back to her house. I'm not leaving the island when you go. I'm staying with her.'

Troy nodded and laced his fingers together. 'Right. Well, you belong here. You have your mum now, it's perfect.' His jaw was stiff.

She glanced at her feet. 'Not perfect, but I think I can make it work.'

He placed his hands on her upper arms and took a deep breath. 'Maybe you could come and watch a game sometime, bring Joanne and Rowan and Ewan. I'll take you out after and we'll have a meal somewhere fancy.' *Oh Jesus,* why was he parading his money in her face? This wasn't what he wanted.

'I'd like that,' she said, maintaining eye contact until Troy found breathing difficult. 'We all would.' She stumbled out of his hold. 'Do you need me to stay now the helicopter's been cancelled?'

'Yes, Carys. I want you here all the time. I never want to be without you. But I can't have that. My money doesn't buy that. I'm fit again. I can drive. I don't need a carer. I want you... As my equal, my friend, my—'

'Troy... What...?' Her mouth fell open, her grey eyes boring into his soul, perhaps trying to detect a lie but it was all true. 'I can't come with you, you know I can't.'

'So you said.'

'Like you won't stay here with me,' she said. Her eyes filled with tears.

He stood like a plank, thoughts whirring around his head. Staying here had never been a serious consideration, more an airy-fairy dream, but Carys had a point. Why were his dreams more important than hers? He swallowed, remembering all the negative publicity and doubt that had showered over him in the past few weeks. He had to go back and prove them all wrong. It was his destiny, with or without Carys.

'I'm sorry,' he said. 'But…' He glanced up the stairs, Joanne was still up there, hopefully not listening. He leaned in closer. 'I can't let you go without telling you.'

'Telling me what?' she whispered, her eyes wide, almost fearful.

'That I love you.'

'What?' She stepped back, clutching her face. 'No, Troy. No. That's a stupid thing to say, you can't.'

He blinked and looked away. 'Wow. Ok.' Stupid? Now she thought he was stupid. After all those months helping him get over his difficulties, she decided he was stupid after all. And why? Because he had feelings? Fuck yes. She was so right. He'd been so damn good at bottling up those pesky emotions all his life and that was exactly what he needed to do again.

'I don't mean you're stupid, you know that's not what I meant. But saying that when you're about to leave.'

'Pa,' he said with a shrug. 'Don't bother backpedalling now. You're right. It was a stupid thing to say and I'm stupid for ever thinking it. You get what you need and I'll see you about.'

He turned and stalked into his room, slamming the door behind him.

Chapter Twenty-Three

Carys

If the world was still spinning, Carys couldn't feel it. She couldn't feel anything. Numbness spread through her whole body. Joanne finished loading the boot, then frowned.

'Are you getting in?'

'Yes.' Carys climbed into the passenger seat and slumped against the window. Troy had said the three little words she'd waited all her life to hear. And what had she done? Cast it back in his face. Unforgivable. She deserved the names her ex-friends had thrown at her. She was nothing but a thoughtless bitch. How could she have called him stupid? That wasn't what she'd meant. It was just such an awful time to hear those words. How could she live knowing he felt like that? When she felt the same. The pressure to go with him was too great. That was what she'd thought stupid. The timing. The tension. But she'd scuppered it. No need to wonder what she'd done wrong this time, even she couldn't miss it.

Joanne drove towards Tobermory, casting sidelong looks at Carys. 'What happened with Troy? Is he angry?'

'I don't know. Maybe. Upset, I think.'

'Did he want you to go with him?'

'Yes. Do you think I should? Am I being ridiculous?'

Joanne shook her head. 'I don't know. It's a tough decision. Once he's back playing football, that'll be his life and you'll have to accept it. It's not a lifestyle I'd want but that's not to say it's not for everyone.

Carys's phone vibrated. She fished around for it, frowning when she saw Calvert Care on the screen. The agency?

'Hello?'

'Is that Carys McTeague?' said a woman.

'Yes.'

'Good morning, it's Jenny from Calvert Care.'

'Oh, hi.' She relaxed, remembering Jenny from when she first signed the confidentiality papers.

'Hi.' There was a pause and Carys sucked her lip. What was this all about? Did they have another job for her already? Officially she was still assigned to Troy. 'Unfortunately, Carys, we've been forced to make a difficult decision and we're going to have to release you from Calvert Care.'

'But... Why?'

'Certain news reports and articles have been brought to our attention and we can't endorse that kind of behaviour from any of our employees, so we'll have to let you go.'

'But those articles were fake. They twisted everything. All I was doing was my job.'

'Hmm,' said Jenny. 'I'm sorry but it's too risky. We can provide references based on your previous jobs but that's all.'

'Right.'

'Ok, well, thank you and goodbye.'

Carys laid the phone on her knee and stared at it. Could this get any worse?

'Are you ok?' asked Joanne.

'I've just been sacked. The agency saw those pictures of me with Troy on the beach. Christ.' She slapped her hand on her head. 'I was doing what I was getting paid to do. I was helping him get ready for paddling. Can you believe it? I've been fired because there are photos on the internet of me doing what I was supposed to be doing.'

'Oh, Carys.'

'This is why I can't go with Troy.' She stared out the window. 'I hate it. I can't live with this kind of thing hanging over me day after day.'

The florist shop smelt like heaven and looked like an indoor garden, exactly the kind of thing she would usually love, but nothing felt right. Carys needed to keep busy or she'd go crazy thinking about Troy and beating herself up for things that might have been if she had enough guts to go for them.

Joanne chatted as she opened the back room. Carys followed her in and carried some boxes into the main shop ready to help fix bouquets for the new window display. She knew her mum was doing her best to cheer her but nothing was working.

When her phone rang an hour later, she welcomed an excuse to escape into the cool back room again.

'Hi, Dad.' She was pleasantly surprised. He so rarely phoned.

'You've never been working for that wanker?' Lee shouted down the phone.

'What?' said Carys. 'How do you know?'

'All over the fucking news so it is. My daughter and the Celtic striker. I'll never hear the end of it.'

'I don't get it… Is my name on the news?'

'Obviously. And not just your name. The reporters have had a field day digging up everything about you. All the old court cases for when I had to prove I was your dad to get you out the home. They've made you sound like quite the little sob story with your being dumped at the side of the road.'

'No way.'

'Yes. And they've dug up the dirt on Jimmy, my dick of a brother. Got his story in there too. Painted our family as a bunch of criminals and you as some tragic princess off to find her footballer prince.'

'Oh my god.' Carys covered her face. This was horrific.

'Your photo's all over the place. Filthy what they caught you up to.'

'That isn't what happened. I was... Oh, never mind.' The truth sounded so weak compared to the mighty lies of the media.

'Well, now the eejit's signed for The Saints, that'll bring him down a peg or two. They're the crappiest team in history.'

'Listen, I have to go.' She thrust her phone into her back pocket and traipsed back into the main shop.

'Carys.' Joanne cocked her head and sighed. 'Is everything ok?'

'No.'

'Oh no.' Joanne rushed to her and threw her arms around her, holding her and letting her cry it out.

'I don't know what to do,' said Carys. 'Dad says there's all kinds of stories on the news about me. Things about me and Troy. Stuff about the past... They know I was dumped as a baby. Now, everyone will know. I'm a pathetic bit of baggage that can be chucked away.'

'No, no,' said Joanne, rubbing her back. 'You're not at all. Is that what you think? Your real mum abandoned you because she was a teenager on drugs, she didn't know what to do with you or herself.'

'Do you know her?' Carys pulled back and gaped.

'Not really. I met her once with Lee. That was when she told him she'd lied that she'd miscarried his baby and actually left you at the side of the road. He was furious, you know what he gets like. I thought he was going to kill her.'

'Oh my god.'

'I dragged him away and suggested instead of wasting his anger trying to get revenge on her that we tried to find you.'

'It was your idea?'

Joanne nodded. 'I couldn't stand the idea of a little girl being in care when we were able to look after you. It wasn't easy finding you and it was really lucky you hadn't been adopted. You were in foster care and Lee had to go through paternity tests and we had to prove we were fit people to have you. But we did it and I'd do the same again. The only thing I regret is that I walked away ten years later.'

'I don't blame you for that.' Carys shook her head at her feet. 'I won't lie and say I was ok about it. I wasn't. I was devastated. But I get it. I know my dad, I know what a slob he is. I don't get how you stuck it for so long.'

'I stuck it for you.' Joanne's eyes teared up and Carys nodded. 'And I should have held out longer, but he was sleeping around. When Kat got pregnant, I couldn't stand it. I'd had so many miscarriages and all the while Lee was off with other women. We argued and I said I wanted to take you with me. He went ballistic and that's when it all kicked off.'

'He should never have done that.'

'I wanted us to have you and be a real family but Lee thought I was attacking him by trying to take you. All I wanted was the right to see you – as a real mum would have had. So please, don't think no one wants you or cares. It's not true.'

'You are a real mum. You're my real mum.'

'That means the world to me,' said Joanne, taking her hand. 'You were the best part of my time with Lee. And you found a way back.' She gave her a watery smile. 'But if you want to go after Troy, please do. Life's too short. We've found each other again and we'll not lose touch now. So if you want to chase him, then do it.'

Carys didn't look up.

Years of her life had been filled with the knowledge she'd been dumped by two mothers. It had never gone away or got better. She carried it with her as part of herself and the same would apply to Troy. He would live in her heart forever. It was unbearable that she'd never see him again or, if she did, it wouldn't feel right. The circumstances would make her someone he'd once known, an old acquaintance he was obliged to give free tickets for his matches to or to take out for a meal once in a blue moon. Was that any better than letting him go?

Chapter Twenty-Four

Troy

The house was boxed up, the removal van filled. Chris had arranged everything much quicker than Troy expected. He'd been airlifted to his Glasgow house and travelled with Chris to his new club in Perth for most of the end of January and early February. Now he was back on Mull for the final stage. But the house wasn't on the market. He couldn't bring himself to sell it yet.

After he got the Porsche off the island, he would close this chapter of his life. Almost. He'd turned down Chris's offer to send someone for the car; he needed to be here in person this last time because he needed to see Carys. Somehow the paps had got her name and slapped every story they could find about her all over the internet. 'Fuck's sake.' He slammed his hands into his face. It was all his fault. He'd dragged her down to the place she least wanted to be. He couldn't blame her for not wanting to be in his life, but he had to see her and try and make it right.

So far, he'd managed individual training with the physio and club doctor on hand, but a return to the pitch was getting closer. The strapping was off his leg and he was walking almost normally. In a month, he'd be running again. *Yes, I will.* He gave himself a pep talk as he took the driver's seat. Since the accident, he'd only been in a car with Carys or Chris, not counting the one time with Pippa he'd erased from his mind. Despite Carys's self-confessed inexperience with driving, he'd felt safer with her at the wheel than he did with himself.

Taking the twisty road over the hill to Tobermory, he struggled to keep his eyes on the road. Mull had never looked so beautiful. Blue skies spanned above in bright February sunlight with only a few tattered clouds lingering. Glorious seas teased, appearing deceivingly warm and inviting. He would love to go back to the beach with Carys now. She wouldn't have to prop him up. He would carry her in, they'd swim in the tropical waters, and he'd kiss her under the sun and make love to her on the silver sands. He snorted. The water would be freezing and they'd probably be caught by every pap on the planet.

Ramming the Porsche into a parking place, he hopped out and clomped straight for the florist. He'd barely gone two steps when a voice spoke.

'Hello, Troy,' said Fenella Hansen.

'Oh, hi.' He dipped his head.

'I've been reading about you in the newspapers. I've never been a great football supporter but we count you as almost a local now, so everybody's interested in how you get on.'

He returned her smile. 'Yeah. Well, thanks for your help with the reading and stuff.'

'No problem. I didn't get a chance to thank you for the lovely Christmas present. So thoughtful. I thought you'd left the island already.'

'This is my last day.'

'Ah, I see. Well, I'll be following your progress from now on.' She glanced around. 'Is Carys going with you?'

'No. She's staying on. Her mum runs the florist shop, they've reunited.'

'Oh, yes. I heard about that. I didn't realise she was staying on though. Oh well, you take care and keep practising your work. It'll always come in handy.' She patted him on the arm. 'We need people like you out there championing the cause. Too many children suffer under the stigma; you're a great role model and football won't last forever. I'm sure your comeback will be excellent but remember, you have other options.'

'Thanks.' Troy ruffled his hair, frowning as he said his goodbyes. Were they really viable options? He'd never walked away from a tough situation and returning to football had to be the toughest of his life. His neck burned despite the chill. He wasn't a great role model, not for kids who were going through the same thing he had. Kids like Rowan. In fact, he'd turned down the chance to do something there. Now, he was going to say goodbye to Carys. This was a moment. He had to choose, either walk away from football or walk away from her. He pushed open the door and before he had a chance to second guess himself, he came face to face with her.

'Hi,' he said.

'Hi.' Carys stopped dead, her arms full of green foliage, and stared.

'I wanted to talk to you before I left.'

'Oh,' said Carys, 'I thought you'd already gone.'

'Hello.' Joanne came out of a back room and blinked between him and Carys. 'I'm not interrupting, am I?'

'Er, no,' he said, raking his hair.

'I think that means yes,' said Joanne. 'I'm fine here, Carys. Why don't you and Troy go for a walk?'

'Do you have time for that?' Carys asked.

'Sure.'

Joanne whisked the bundle of foliage away from Carys, effectively stripping her of further excuses, and Troy waited as she got her coat. She thrust her hands into her pockets and barely glanced at him as he held the door for her.

She looked around, almost like she was searching for an escape route. 'Let's go to the house,' she said, striding up the hill towards Joanne's house. This was definitely enough to prove his leg was back in action. The steepness of the slope pounded his thigh and he gritted his teeth. This pain was necessary. It was beneficial in his journey back to full strength but it was still a relief to see Joanne's house coming into view on the narrow lane.

Carys opened the door that led into the hallway directly from the lane and they stepped inside. 'Where are Ewan and Rowan?' Troy asked. Joanne worked on Saturdays but surely the others were around.

'They've gone to Iona to cycle,' said Carys. 'I almost went with them. They'll be away all day.'

Lucky she hadn't gone or he'd have missed her. He ran his fingers through his newly trimmed and styled hair, checking around the quaint hall with its slightly dated decor and maritime prints on the wall.

'You wanted to talk to me?'

'To apologise,' he said.

'For what?'

'All the stuff on the internet. I had you sign all the papers to keep me hidden from prying eyes but I should have poured all that energy into protecting you from this.'

Her eyes connected with his and he looked at her for a long moment.

'Nothing could have stopped that,' she said. 'I just didn't realise the dangers of working for you.'

He nodded. 'Yup, who'd have thought it.' Words failed but he couldn't pull his gaze from her. 'The dangers of the massage table.' And he wasn't lying. Every time she'd touched him, fireworks had erupted inside him. Her hands ignited his body. How often he'd had to send her away so he could calm down without her seeing what she did to him.

Carys gave a half-smile and he mirrored it. Smiling suited her best. She sucked her lip between her teeth, moving slowly forward, her pale eyes flashing. 'When you said...'

'That I loved you?'

She nodded. 'You were my boss. It was hard to process. You're not my boss anymore.'

He had no crutch, no strapping, nothing to get in the way and keep them apart. He stood tall, towering over her now he wasn't stooped. Every wild imagining he'd ever had came flooding back.

'I know, but does it change anything?'

'I'd just like...'

'What...?'

Her eyes flicked to his lips and back. 'To kiss you goodbye.'

'Ok,' he said. Carys swallowed and moved her head very slightly. He dipped down, sweeping his arms around her. Their lips met in a hot surge and everything was beautiful. No football, no complications, just Carys, her mouth hungry for his.

'Troy.' Carys breathed, taking hold of his jacket.

'What is it?' he said.

Her pupils burned into his like she was silently begging him for something.

'Carys... I need to go.'

'Stay, please,' she said. 'Kiss me some more, before you go.'

'Do you know what you did to me on the massage table? Every time? If we keep on kissing like this...'

'Exactly. That's what I want.'

She reached up and pulled him towards her again. They kissed slowly and deeply and their tongues played. Troy wrestled off his jacket and tossed it on the floor, then took hold of her coat zip.

'Are you sure you want to do this?'

'Yes. Very sure.'

He teased down her zip and slowly edged off her jacket. This was different from any previous encounter. He wasn't in a perfectly styled room with a four-poster bed and a woman who could give Barbie a run for her money.

He was with a woman he loved and wanted so badly. 'Carys, you're so gorgeous,' he growled into her neck, kissing it and running his hands over her t-shirt, following the soft curve of her chest. 'Everything about you is gorgeous, inside and out.' He captured her mouth again, slipping his hands inside her t-shirt, caressing her soft skin, kneading it with his hands. The reality of her was so much better than the dreams. He ground against her, groaning, keeping her close. She was his, all his.

He backed her gently into the living room and she lay back on the sofa. The tables were turned. She'd massaged him to the brink for months, now it was her turn. He was going to rock her world.

Chapter Twenty-Five

Carys

Carys could hardly breathe. She lay back gasping for air, her fingers knitted in Troy's hair. Troy moved off his knees from between her legs, gliding his hands over her sensitive skin. The touch made her whimper. He brought his mouth to her lips.

Who knew how much damage he could do with that mouth? Carys was in a state of overload. Her head was whirling, her body saturated with an excess of love and attention. He moved on top of her with a groan, lifting her legs around him like she weighed nothing.

'I've dreamed of this forever,' he said. 'I want you. I want us. Together.'

'Me too,' she panted, though she hadn't really recovered from what he'd just done. He wasn't only a smooth mover on the football pitch.

His hands stroked her and he kissed her, slipping closer, ever closer. He gently lifted her thigh and eased into her, still kissing her. She dug her nails into his shoulder. A few months ago, this shoulder had been broken. And so was he. She'd helped piece him back together. Now they were here, joined as one. Whole.

It was broad daylight, light streamed in the window, but Carys couldn't focus on anything in the room except the man above her.

'I love you,' he said, cupping her cheek as he rocked into her.

'Oh, Troy.' He was making her want to scream, cry and laugh all at once.

'I meant it and I still do. Oh, god.' He hung his head, rocking faster and groaning.

Carys slid her hands under his arms and down his spine, the spine she knew so well. This time she let her fingers glide all the way down, over his tight buttocks. She clasped them, her eyes closing as the tension built to a peak, then burst all around her.

Troy thrust hard, panting as he slumped onto her. She held him tight. Her breath rasped in short snatches as she came back to earth. The spinning slowed and her senses started to switch on. Touch was the first. Troy's back rose and fell swiftly.

I love you too. She wanted to say it but she couldn't. A tear pricked at the corner of her eye. Any minute now, he was going to leave. She'd stolen this moment but it couldn't last. He may claim to love her but he loved football more.

His expensive deodorant tingled in her nostrils, reminding her of the massage rooms. She'd dreamed of this and now they'd done it. Troy's breathing had slowed. Other than that, he was still, his head buried in her shoulder.

'Troy,' she said. 'Are you ok? You haven't hurt your leg or anything?'

He laughed and it tickled her neck. 'I've never felt better.'

'Good.' She caressed his back, prolonging the moment as long as she could.

Without any hurry, Troy carefully got up. Carys foraged around for something to cover herself. She was suddenly cold.

'Here.' Troy grabbed a folded fleece blanket covered in polar bear cartoons and draped it around her, then sat beside her, holding her. His fully naked body was beyond perfect, even with the scars. He knew how to make magic happen with it, as he did on the football pitch. 'I want you to be happy, Carys. But I don't know how to bring it about.'

'I don't think you can, Troy. You need to go back to football. I understand that.'

'I hate failing. And I feel like I've failed you.'

'You haven't. I just can't live your life.'

'Ok.' He squeezed her shoulder. 'Well, I hope whatever you do works out for you.'

'Yup.' She hoped so too, though she didn't know what that was. She was throwing away this chance even though she had nothing lined up. The dream she'd had for running the retreat with Troy had fluttered back into her make-believe world. 'And you,' she said. 'I hope you score hundreds more goals and win lots more matches.' She glanced into his eyes. 'Make sure you're doing it for yourself, not anyone else.'

'Of course I am. I don't care what anyone else thinks.'

She raised a sceptical eyebrow. 'If you say so.'

'I do.' He frowned and kissed her forehead. 'You're right. You always are. And I am doing it for myself. I need to do this.'

'Then you should go. Don't you have a ferry to catch?'

'Well, yes... But...' He looked at her. She gave a little shrug. He released her and got to his feet. 'Is the bathroom through here?'

'Yes.' Her head nodded like a puppet on a string.

He grabbed his clothes from around the room and whipped into the hall. Carys frowned at the door, unable to move. Wild thoughts rushed through her brain but she couldn't catch them or weave them into any sense. The loo flushed in the distance and seconds later he was back, fully dressed. After months of him taking ages to put on anything, this was like lightning. Carys pulled the blanket tightly around her, wishing it was him. It had come down to the final moment and he was going to choose his career over her – not that she expected anything else. It was stupid to have even entertained the idea of anything else.

'Carys.' Troy stood in the doorway. 'I wish it hadn't come to this.'

'You better go.' Why was he making it worse? Why had she? She should have sent him packing outside the shop.

'Ok.' After pulling on his coat, he stooped and picked up Carys's clothes, then placed them on the sofa and leaned over and kissed her cheek. 'I meant it. I love you.'

He gave her one last look before opening the door and striding out. Carys sat glued to the spot. He was gone.

She clung to the blanket, holding herself. Why wasn't he here, whispering in her ear and telling her he wasn't leaving after all? They were going to run Taigh Beinne as a health retreat and everything would be fine. Was she as bad as the paparazzi reports had suggested? Had this been nothing but a last-ditch attempt to get him to stay? How awful did that make her? She hadn't meant it to be like that but when did anything in her life work out the way she'd meant it? She clutched her face and welcomed the tears. Troy was gone. Like everyone else.

She was just Carys. Plain and simple. Friends came and went with the wind. So did guys. Even family. Her dreams would always be exactly that. Just dreams. She'd been stupid to think for one second he'd have shared them. His life was in a different category. He lived in his dream and used his skills to the optimum. What did it matter if he couldn't read or write? He could kick a ball and that made him something.

Carys wiped her eyes with her palms. Crying would get her nowhere. She'd learned that long ago too. Just because she didn't have any talents like Troy didn't mean she was worthless. Her mum had told her not to think like that and she had to try. She could accomplish little things on a small scale, but before she changed the world one mini-deed at a time, she needed to have a shower. Keeping the blanket tightly around her, she nipped to the bathroom. The delicious sensations from half an hour ago lingered as twinges in her body. It was too raw to think about.

She blanched. *Oh god, how stupid am I?* They hadn't even bothered to shut the curtains. The lights were off, so anyone passing on the lane hopefully wouldn't have noticed anything unless they'd stopped for a recce. 'Oh crap.' She hid her face in her hands. What if someone had spied them? This could be the next scoop. Naked pictures of them romping on Joanne's sofa. Was there no end to her idiocy?

Chapter Twenty-Six

Troy

Troy threw himself onto the bench and his head slumped into his palms. Everything was so familiar but alien at the same time. Surrounding him in the state-of-the-art gym were the training machines, monitors, and equipment he should have been strapped to for the last six months. Instead, he'd hidden away.

'Come on, Troy,' said his trainer, clapping his hands. Nate had the subtlety of a stampeding rhinoceros, and Troy winced at the sharp sound of his palms slapping together. This was the regime he needed now, not Carys's gentle massages and healing the mind, healing the body, woo-woo stuff. No matter how well it had worked.

'I've let everyone down,' he mumbled.

'Get a grip, Troy,' said Nate, his voice low and gravely. In his hand, his phone beeped, and he assessed the latest stats. 'Get back on your feet and get going. Your stats are coming up fine.'

Troy compulsively straightened the Garmin watch on his left arm – his electronic tag. He was back in prison under the constant supervision of his wardens; every move he made was recorded and fed into Nate's app. He was like the lab rat. They told him how high to jump and he did it, then they analysed it. He wasn't allowed to pee without someone knowing about it.

'Maybe,' said Troy, shaking his head. 'But I'm not fine, ok?'

'Come on, man. What's the problem?'

He wasn't ready but how could he admit it? 'I don't know.'

'And you'll never find out if you're sitting on this bench. Get up and get back on the machine.'

'It's my leg,' said Troy. A half-truth. The leg hurt but not as much as his brain.

'Everyone's checked it,' said Nate, the growl softening slightly. 'Your leg is fine. The break has healed great, as has the muscle damage. I know it's not popular opinion, but I think you were wise to keep off the training as long as you did. In that respect, you've done yourself a favour. You've healed fast. Now strengthening is the key.'

'I know this sounds crazy but it feels like it's going to break again if I push it too hard.'

'That's all in your head, Troy. We have the evidence to know that won't happen.'

Troy pushed his legs out in front of him and ran his palms down his thighs, across the smattering of soft hair. The scar on his left leg was there, plain as day, and wouldn't ever go away. Further down beneath his blue socks, his left ankle was strapped and would always be strapped for training and matches – Nate called it a precautionary move but it was part of the bigger deal for Troy. His body was falling apart. Every time he stood, the fear of hearing a snap and falling to the ground plagued his mind. On the treadmills, it was ten times worse. His first team-training session was later in the week and dread pecked at him like a vulture at a carcass. It would only take one person to crash into him and he could be back where he started.

'What if I make it worse?' He closed his eyes slowly, then opened them with a sigh. He sounded whiny and ridiculous. What had happened to the man who'd scored over sixty career goals? This wasn't how he'd imagined his comeback. He was meant to stroll back and everything would be a breeze. Walking on to the pitch should be feverish and exciting – not terrifying.

Nate threw out his arms. 'You'll have to try at some point. If you go AWOL again, it could be ten times as hard the next time you come back. Plus, it'll be harder finding a club that'll take you.'

'Yeah, I know.' Troy pulled in a long, filling breath and got to his feet. The ground was firm and his leg appeared normal, but inside his brain swayed and reeled like he was on a stormy ship. One false move and he'd be hobbling again, or confined to the wheelchair, and maybe forever this time. But playing this game was about taking risks.

Back on the treadmill, he watched as Nate keyed in the precise timing, resistance and speed. Like a robot, he started running. For the first few minutes, Nate stood by, analysing the monitors and the app.

'That's all fine,' he said, smiling through his grim undertone. 'I'll be back in twenty minutes. I've got some more checks to run, but I'll keep watching the monitor.'

Troy's feet pounded the belt. The rest of the room was eerily quiet. He was still the new guy in this team, but it felt like everyone was avoiding him. Perhaps his brain was being oversensitive. *Christ knows my body is.* His soul was cold and empty. Chatting to teammates and having some banter with the guys helped fill the chasm, though nothing could replace Carys.

He'd given himself to her, told her how he felt, poured everything into their last encounter. Then she'd told him to go and he'd done it. He had to. But somehow, he'd thought he could persuade her to come too. He'd failed.

A pain burned the back of his throat. He had to face the reality that this was the life he'd chosen, but the more he ran, the more he wondered if he'd done the right thing.

*

Troy kicked out, but his shot soared over the post, way off target. He bent down and rested his hands on his thighs.

'Not bad, mate,' said one of his new teammates. 'That's your first go in over six months.'

'Thanks,' Troy muttered. But the mountain he was climbing had grown several miles higher. Practice that day was a shitstorm. Troy returned to the locker room with his eyes downcast. How could he sort himself out? He was such an uncoordinated mess. The sickening sensation he used to get when faced with a form to fill out was here. He threw back his head and let rip a roar of anger.

'Hey, it's cool, man. Don't beat yourself up. The first is always the worst,' said a teammate.

'Exactly,' said another. 'It can only get better. It's a fuckin' miracle you can walk, never mind that you're back on the pitch.'

'Thanks, guys. It just feels shit.'

After a pep talk from the manager, Troy collected his kit and was about to leave when he noticed Chris sauntering in with his mobile pressed to his ear. From across the team room, he waved to Troy and put up his finger, alerting him to stay put, and mouthing, 'One minute.'

Troy dropped his kit and pulled out a chair. He massaged his thigh as he waited for Chris to finish his conversation.

'Troy,' he said. 'Sorry about that. Listen, a quick word.'

'Sure, what's up?'

'I wanted to check how you're feeling. Nate tells me your training isn't going too well.'

'Does he? He told me it was fine.' He rubbed his Garmin watch. This little gadget had all the answers.

'Physically, yes,' said Chris. 'But what about mentally?'

'What are you saying?'

'Come on, Troy.' Chris's grey hair and cheesy grin reminded him of Richard Branson. 'It's no shame to discuss mental health these days. I still think you should have accepted the counselling months ago. Nate thinks you've got some kind of mental block.'

'He didn't say any of this to me.'

'Listen, between you and me…' Chris leaned over and lowered his voice. 'Nate's torn between what he knows is right and what the club wants to hear. Disappearing to that island has caused a big debate. Some of the old schoolers think it was insane and you should have been back on the machines as soon as you were out of the hospital. Others think it was a brilliant move to concentrate on the healing before you started pushing again. But Nate's concern is that no matter how hard you push, you might never regain your original levels of fitness, irrespective of how you chose to heal.'

Troy furrowed his brow and threw up his hands. 'So, what's he said? That I'll be on the sidelines for the rest of the season? The rest of my career? I mean, what are we talking about?'

'All are possible. But Nate isn't sure whether it's a physical issue or something mentally stopping you.'

'Such as?' Though Troy knew perfectly well. He'd become a scaredy-cat, terrified to move in case he did more damage. And if he did more damage, his career would be over for sure this time.

'Your heart's not in it anymore.'

'What?' That was unexpected.

'Listen, you've had a life-threatening injury and a traumatic experience. I don't believe all the shit the paps come up with, but it looks like you met someone. How's that going?'

'It's not.'

Chris put his hand on Troy's shoulder. 'We all understood your need to get away after the accident. What I don't get is your need to come back.'

'Are you crazy? This is my life. This is what I do.'

'And you've done it brilliantly for over ten years. You're at an age now when lots of your peers are on the verge of retiring and moving on. You have other options.'

'Jesus Christ. I can't believe you're saying this. You actually think I'm finished, don't you? You agree with Daryl and all the others who're bitching behind my back?'

'I wouldn't lower myself to listening to anything Daryl says. I'm certain you could come back if you set your mind to it. But it won't be as quick as you want it to be and no one can guarantee you'll be as successful as you were before. Now, you can get out there and prove me wrong if you want. But I wondered when you were away on that island if maybe you'd had a taste of something different. There would be no shame in hanging up your boots and moving on to pastures new. You've had a top-class career and earned enough money to keep you going. With your charisma, we could easily secure you a future in other sectors.'

Troy stood, ignoring the woozy brain signal, warning him to go easy on his leg. If he was going to prove Chris wrong, he had to get rid of the talking demon and listen to the technology. If he was fine, he could damn well do this. He picked up his bag.

'What if I'm not done yet? I'm still a footballer.'

'You are, Troy.' Chris's expression softened and he smiled. 'You're a great footballer and you'll always be a great footballer. But your football career isn't infinite. One day it'll come to an end and I wouldn't like you to spend the next few years struggling to come back only to discover you'll never reach the pinnacle ever again.'

'But I never had the chance to say goodbye.' He'd never play that one last game and go out in a blaze of glory. 'If I chuck in the towel now, I'll always be the footballer who got beaten by an injury.'

'The only thing beating you right now is yourself. You have choices, Troy. And, as a friend, not your agent, I advise you to choose what makes you happy. When you get to my age, you'll realise life's too short for anything else.'

Chris's words flew around Troy's head as he got into the Porsche and sped towards his Glasgow mansion. Before he'd gone a few miles, he hit a traffic jam. He slapped the steering wheel and growled. His whole life was like this, a sudden burst of energy, then a long slow interlude. Getting back into football was going to be a gruelling process and one he'd have to face alone if he chose to face it at all. Maybe with Carys at his side, he could do it, but she'd chosen a different life. And who could blame her? He'd be away long hours, they'd hardly see each other. She'd found a home for the first time in her life and it would be cruel to rip her from it for his own selfish needs.

He leaned forward and settled his forehead on the steering wheel. What an addled mess. His stomach was in knots and he had no idea what to do or where to go next. If someone would just come along and tell him... Would he listen? Chris had just told him: choose what makes you happy.

Carys made him happy and football made him happy, but those two things didn't marry. *Does this reintroduction to football really make me happy?* No. He'd been miserable ever since leaving Carys. Would it really be so bad to say goodbye to football? He'd loved it so much for so long. But then… He also loved Carys. She was everything he needed and why not now? Chris was right. If he hung on trying, he would lose the most important person in his life for what might only be a couple of years more football.

'Jesus. I really am a stupid idiot,' he said. 'Why couldn't I see it?'

A car honked behind and Troy jumped and moved forward. That was the only way to go. Forward.

Chapter Twenty-Seven

Carys

The bright sky and the sparkling blue sea in the marina dazzled Carys. She held up her hand to shield her eyes as she peered across Tobermory bay from the window in the well-appointed flat. Her mum had said she could stay with her as long as she wanted but Carys liked her independence. Being close to her mum was good enough and if she got her own place, she could come in and out from night shifts without bothering anyone. She didn't like waking them up when both Ewan and Joanne had work and Rowan had school. Plus, she'd never had the means to get her own place before; even viewing flats was interesting.

'It has a shower room here,' said the landlord, opening a door.

Carys crossed the tiny living area and squinted through the door, not making eye contact with the landlord. Her mum had warned her about him: Calum Matheson. He was a local property tycoon and, apparently, notorious for his love of money and a good deal – as long as he was the main benefactor. So far, he'd seemed ok, though his eyes looked steely and Carys didn't want him to smooth talk her into taking something she didn't really want.

When she finally glanced at him, his expression was impassive. Carys vaguely remembered seeing him once before, at the market, asking Fenella for money. He was like the much-hated taxman of biblical fame and god knew he must have to put up with a lot. Carys had lived in flats in Glasgow that had been trashed by tenants. How anyone wanted to be a landlord when that sort of stuff went on was beyond her.

'I like it,' she said. The amount Troy had paid her would cover six months, job or not. Maybe she should take it and enjoy it. 'I'm worried about the six-month contract. I'm only doing temporary work at a local nursing home. I don't suppose you could make it three and then if I'm still needed, I could extend it?' Temporary work was all she could secure after Calvert Care let her go. Her dreams of writing self-care books and running a health retreat had died with Troy. She couldn't even face looking at her research now he was gone.

Calum's left eyebrow arced slightly but otherwise he remained pokerfaced. 'I don't mind helping people out in a pinch. Leave it with me.'

'Thanks.' Carys chewed her lip. Never in her life had she had such possibilities, some too ridiculous to be real. Part of her wanted to squirrel her Troy wages away and never touch them in case she needed them, but the other part was screaming at her to spend them.

'I'll get back to you when I work things out.' Calum ran his hand across his neatly cropped, dark hair.

'Great, thanks.'

He let her out and locked the door as she started down the steps. It was a far cry from Troy's mansions. The stairs, despite being on a much smaller scale, reminded her of that day about a hundred years ago when she'd met Jaylee coming out of Ronan's flat. What were they doing these days? Were they still together? She didn't care enough to find out.

The feelings she'd had for Ronan were nothing compared to the love she had for Troy, but she'd chosen to let him go. Was it the biggest mistake of her life? Troy's football career must come to an end someday. Couldn't she stomach the life for a few years? Or would it be unbearable? Troy's love for football would always mean it came first. Even if he retired, he would probably still do coaching or commentary. The media pressure might lessen but it would still be there. She could see him being hunted for *Strictly* or *I'm A Celebrity* and being away for months filming. Would living with those crumbs of Troy be better than not having him at all?

'Bye, and thanks,' she said to Calum.

'No problem.' He jumped into his 4X4 and drove off. Why couldn't Troy be like that? A normal guy with a normal job.

Carys crossed the road to the seaside. Parking bays filled with vehicles lined the edge. She shuffled along between the bumpers and the railings. Everything she was doing here should be right. She was building a life for herself in a way she'd never managed before, but it was all wrong. Without Troy, the island dream was nothing.

She reached the clock tower in the middle of the street and sat on the low rim at the bottom. Although she wanted to browse flats and consider her options, it felt like lip service because all she really wanted was to see Troy. She opened her phone and googled him. His name came up at the top of her search bar; it wasn't like this was a new thing.

She clicked on news and spotted a new article straight away.

Problems continue for Scotland International Troy Copeland.

Her heart sank at the words. What now? Hadn't he been through enough? She scanned through the article and words and phrases caught her attention: *After six months out with injury, Copeland's struggles continue; training sessions haven't gone to plan; Copeland fears his injury will return if too much stress is placed on it; teammates have voiced concerns about his fitness for the rest of the season; questions have been raised about a possible early retirement from the game.*

'Oh god, poor Troy,' she said. Of course, the media would have bigged it up, but Carys suspected an element of truth. The extent of Troy's injuries was no shock to her after tending them so long, and she knew Troy. If he decided to run before he could walk, he was going to fall, but there was no telling him. Did he blame her? Had she been negligent or not done enough to speed his recovery? Maybe his club would sue her.

She sucked her lower lip, trying not to dwell on the idea. She'd spent hours stalking him online. Pictures of him with Pippa Hayes, his ex-girlfriend, were abundant, and plenty of her with her new man – Troy's former teammate – also populated the search results. Carys could never aspire to that kind of glamour. She didn't mind putting on make-up and a nice dress, but that was as far as she got. Her stomach churned when the photos of her and Troy appeared. Nothing she did would get rid of them. It was out there for everyone to see. But people who knew her – really knew her – and cared about her weren't bothered by the pictures. They believed in her and knew she'd done nothing wrong.

Carys puffed up the steep hill towards Joanne's house. A few daffodils were popping out in the sheltered gardens along the street, giving off a chirpy spring vibe. Joanne was sitting at the table with Rowan, pointing to something in a book. She looked up as Carys came in and smiled. 'Everything ok?'

'Yeah, fine.'

'How was the flat?'

'I'm thinking about it. I liked it, but the contract might be an issue.'

Joanne rolled her eyes. 'Calum and his contracts.' She patted Rowan on the back and stood up. As she drew level with Carys, she said in a low voice, 'Calum can be a total arse when it comes to the small print. I'm not sure what goes on in his head. His mum and dad live on the island too. Nicest people you could ever meet. Calum carries all the grumpiness for them.'

Carys smiled. 'He was ok. I think he's just precious about his property.'

'He is.' Joanne clapped her on the back. 'Are you sure everything's ok? You seem a bit down.'

What could she say? She'd tried to keep 'Troy chat' to a minimum but her mum wasn't a fool.

'Carys.' Joanne tilted her head. 'Phone him, send him a message, reach out to him.'

'I can't.'

'You can. Just say hi. Have you seen the news about him?'

Carys nodded.

'Rowan's gutted. He loves Troy. Even more so since meeting him and getting to spend Christmas with him.'

'That seems so long ago,' said Carys.

'Such a pity Troy didn't feel up to doing the dyslexia conference, especially now the football doesn't seem to be going well. I know it's a silly thing but kids like Rowan would get such a boost having someone like that speaking up for them.'

Carys looked over at Rowan, hunched over his book. Yup, it would mean the world to him but Troy loved football too much.

'Call him, Carys,' said Joanne. 'He needs you.' Joanne returned to the table to help Rowan, and Carys slumped onto the sofa and pulled out her phone. Here not so long ago, Troy had taken her to another planet, lavishing her body with love like she'd never dreamed of. If she were to message him now, what the hell would she say? She'd sent him packing and he'd gone.

She thumbed out a message then deleted it, and again, until she wasn't sure what the hell she was trying to write.

Eventually, she was left with a bland text that barely scratched the surface of what was on her mind.

CARYS: Hi, I read the news about your recovery not going too well. Sorry to hear that. I hope you're ok. I still feel responsible for you and if anything I did or didn't do is causing problems with your comeback, then I'm sorry. If there's anything I can do, let me know. And if that means staying well away too, then I will.

She hit send, though she hated it the minute she did. It was awful. She should delete it. But too late. Underneath, the word *seen* displayed. Heat burned in her neck and she waited a few minutes, staring at the messages, hoping those three little dots would show he was replying. But nothing happened.

She needed to do something other than refreshing her phone screen every few seconds, so she took Joanne's car and travelled to Ardnish to deliver bouquets. Georgia and Archie were getting married that weekend. As she passed the house at Taigh Beinne, she tried not to look but it was impossible. Its prominent hillside position begged to be seen. The orchard was barren and sad. Round the back, the raised beds would be waiting. But no one would be there to fill them up. Not this year. Not unless Troy sold up and new people moved in quickly.

Georgia was at the walled garden chatting to another woman as Carys pulled up.

'Hi.' Carys jumped out of the car. 'I've got the bouquets.'

'Brilliant,' said Georgia. 'This is my friend, Holly. She's over for the wedding. We haven't seen each other for about a hundred years.'

'It feels like that, doesn't it?' said Holly. 'Can I help with anything?'

'Sure,' said Georgia. 'We can take the bouquets up to the main house.' She smiled at Carys. 'You're coming with Joanne, aren't you?'

'Yes.' She knew she'd been included on the invite but felt oddly detached from it. *Probably, because I can't stop thinking about Troy.*

'And Blair's building us an arch.' Georgia smirked at a Viking-like man holding up a timber structure.

'I still can't believe you're actually getting married,' said Holly.

'Have you not been engaged long?' asked Carys.

Georgia laughed. 'Just over a year. Archie proposed in the craziest way ever after we'd only known each other a couple of months, but I'll tell you another time; it's a long story. Blair knows it only too well and Holly probably doesn't want to hear it again either.'

'I don't mind,' said Blair. 'It's one of my favourites, you can tell me anytime.' He gave her a warm smile that contained some kind of private message and Carys suspected he'd had some role in helping them get together.

'Thanks,' said Georgia. 'But we'll let you get on with the arch, then you can get back to the lovely Rebekah. That's another story,' she said with a wink to Carys, walking to the car.

'It's such a beautiful place,' said Holly.

'It brings it home how lucky we are,' said Georgia.

Carys's phone vibrated and she stole a glance at it.

TROY: None of this is your fault. If anything, it's mine. I haven't decided what to do. I hope you're ok and everything on the island is good. The house is still mine and you can use it whenever you like. No need to ask. Even if you want to go sit in the garden with Joanne and the guys, then feel free. Troy X

Carys swallowed back a tear. She'd love to. Sitting in that garden on a warm afternoon, watching the sea while sipping a glass of bubbly would be like living in a dream, but none of these dreams worked without Troy. They were empty ideals. If she wanted Troy back in her life, she had to stop wishing, stop dreaming and go do something. Right now.

Chapter Twenty-Eight

Troy

Troy's phone hadn't stopped buzzing for days. It had got to the stage it was impossible to sift through the messages. Dyslexia or not, his brain couldn't cope with this bombardment. The world wasn't ready for the bomb he'd dropped the previous weekend. He was pulling out for the rest of the season.

He couldn't face anyone. Chris, Nate, the coaches, the team. No one. This was one step away from bringing the curtain down and it hurt like hell. It stabbed his chest like razor-sharp knives and blood pounded in his ears.

Before the accident he'd been a determined player and if he set his mind to something, he could achieve it. But had he been chasing the right goal over the last few months? The first thing he had to do was make a few business calls – not football, because he was learning, football wasn't the be-all and end-all of everything and, as bitter a pill as it was to swallow, he needed to do it, and soon, before the damn thing lodged in his throat and choked him.

Chris was right. Chasing happiness should be his number one priority right now. What Carys had told him had never rung so true. His return to football shouldn't be to please anyone but himself. Right now, it definitely wasn't doing that. He needed a new challenge and he wanted to face it head-on without regrets or doubts.

His parents and his sister needed to find out too. If he told his mum and dad, they would let Nina know. Troy sucked on his lip. No matter what he did, he never seemed to connect with his younger sister. She was always sweet and polite when they met but they'd never been close. He tried when he could, bought her a house and he sent her money, but she kept away and they rarely saw each other. After she'd visited him in the hospital, he'd barely heard from her. A voice message would be a start with her. He took a few minutes recording one and sent it.

But his parents should hear this first-hand. He put on his iPad and hit the FaceTime icon. As it connected, his heart bumped loudly against his ribcage. After the usual jiggling, his mum appeared, squinting into the screen. 'Good god, Troy. What is going on? I've been calling you.'

'Yeah, Mum, but everyone has been calling me. Plus all the paps. It's a nightmare.'

'Your dad's here too.'

'Hi,' said Troy.

'Son, I know what this means. Why didn't you tell us?'

'What does it mean?'

'You're retiring, aren't you?'

'Not necessarily.' Troy winced at the words. He'd signalled the final bell for his career but he hadn't signed on the dotted line. Not quite.

'Oh, Troy,' said his mum. 'Why didn't you tell us how bad the injury was? We thought it was under control.'

'And are the stories about you hiding on an island somewhere with some woman true?' his dad said.

'Yes. I didn't hide the extent of my injuries. I told everyone how bad they were but no one wanted to hear it. They just wanted to hear me saying I was getting better and making a quick return to football. And that's what I wanted too, but it isn't going to work like that.'

'So, how did hiding on an island help?' his dad continued. 'Shouldn't you have been training instead of… Well, whatever you were doing with that girl?'

'I was recovering. She was my carer and my friend.' *And the love of my life*. He kept that bit for himself in case his dad had a heart attack. 'She looked after me and got me through. Nothing like what the paps said. That was all rubbish. My surgeon told me not to overdo anything in the first six months, but the coaches weren't convinced. I couldn't handle anymore.'

'Why didn't you tell us you were there?' asked his mum. 'I thought you'd just gone for a fortnight.'

Troy smiled at her indignation. He had told her. But her interpretation had been what she wanted to hear. 'I went for a few months. I did tell you.'

'So, what will you do for money? I mean, I know you've made a lot already, but surely it won't last forever,' she said.

Was the worry for him or her? If he didn't keep supporting her in her lifestyle in Spain, they'd have to come back and get jobs until they were eligible for the state pension, not an appealing option for either of them.

'It's ok,' he said. 'I've got a lot of sound investments. None of us will starve.'

'But honestly, Troy,' said his dad. 'This may be temporary but the day is getting closer that you'll have to give up and what then? It's not like you have any other skills.'

And there was the blow, straight across the face like a blunt club. Troy the useless, Troy the thick. 'Yeah, I know. But I can read now and write a bit.'

'What do you mean?' said his mum.

'Didn't you know?' Troy asked. 'I went through school not being able to do either. I only learned recently. Carys helped me with that too.'

'Who? And what do you mean helped you?'

'I've been working with a tutor and now I'm a lot more confident.'

'Well, that's something,' said his dad.

'Why did you hide it?' said his mum.

'I didn't. You assumed I was thick. I'm dyslexic. It's not something I need to be ashamed of.'

His dad scoffed.

'What was that for?' said Troy.

'All these labels they hand out these days.'

'It's not a label, Dad. And if it is, then it shouldn't be a badge of shame. It should be an acknowledgement of the extra hard work a person is going to have to put into their life.'

His mum coughed and turned the tablet away from his dad. Troy was pretty sure his dad was pulling all kinds of unconvinced faces. 'Now you can read better, does that mean you'll go into commentary once you retire? You have a lovely speaking voice. People would like to hear it more.'

'No, I don't want to do that. I have a couple of ideas for life after football, but I'm not in a place to tell you yet.'

No amount of quizzing could get him to divulge his plans to them or to anyone.

'Please, will you tell Nina? She doesn't answer my calls.'

His mum frowned. 'She's a funny girl, away in her own world.'

'I'll send her a message,' his dad said. 'She hasn't been in touch for a while. I suppose we should check on her.'

A pang of sadness niggled him. His parents had never shown much interest in him other than his money-making potential, but the same apathy directed at his little sister struck him deeper.

'I'll call her myself,' he said. As soon as he ended the call, he tried her number but didn't get through. He spotted a reply to his earlier message.

NINA: Glad you're feeling better. Hope your new venture goes well. XX

And that was that. What else did he expect? This was the relationship he had with his family. Maybe in time, it would change, especially if he had fewer time commitments. For now, though, he had one last call to make before he'd set the wheels in motion. Then all he could do was wait. Instead of preparing for a cup final, he was preparing for something he'd never in his wildest imaginings believed he would do. He was going to show Carys how much she meant to him. The biggest decision of his life shouldn't have been about returning to football... But walking away from it.

He keyed in Joanne's number. This was it, the beginning of his new life.

Chapter Twenty-Nine

Carys

Carys and Rowan shimmied from side to side in the back seat, laughing as they sang along to Joanne's dreadful, yet annoyingly fun, playlist. "(Is This the Way To) Amarillo?" blasted out and they sha-la-la-ed down the loch side, heading away from the ferry terminal in Oban towards Glasgow some ninety miles south.

Rocking in the back seat passed the time and stopped Carys from thinking too much. At the beginning of the year, she'd imagined Troy going to the conference – because she'd been crazy and imagined Troy doing everything with her – now she would spend the time in the city with her eyes glued to the windows in case his Porsche drove by.

Worse than that, however, she couldn't in all conscience go back to Glasgow without calling in to visit her dad, Kat and the kids. The thought made her stomach squirm. Joanne understood but no way would she go anywhere near her ex-partner or the woman he'd dumped her for. Carys had to do it.

'Park around the corner,' said Carys. 'I'll run in and say hi, I won't be long.'

'Ok,' Ewan said. 'Do you want me to come with you? It looks a bit...'

'Rough?' said Carys. 'It is, but honestly, don't worry. Just wait for me.'

'We will,' said Joanne, her face pale.

Heart hammering, Carys jumped out and made her way to the rundown buildings. Once into the dull close, she mooched up to the door, her clenched fingers hovering. The clamour within told her everyone was home. It was the Easter holidays but they weren't exactly a family who did day trips or anything like that. She knocked. More noise, shouting, scuffling.

Kat wrenched the door open and goggled. 'Oh, it's you.'

'I came to say hi.'

She yelled over her shoulder, 'Lee, Carys is here.'

Carys hadn't reached the living room door before she came face to face with him. She couldn't remember the last time she'd seen him on his feet other than to go from the sofa to the loo or to bed. His belly bulged under his black t-shirt. 'You've got a nerve. Talk about disappointing.'

'How do you mean?'

'You were shacked up with a Celtic player, for Christ's sake.'

Carys struggled to keep her face even. If her dad objected to that, he would blow like Vesuvius when he discovered who she was living with. 'Yes, but he isn't with Celtic anymore, so you can relax.'

'Aye, he's good as finished, the little fucker. Serves him right. But he was with Celtic when you took up with him.'

'Really, Dad? I didn't know anything about it. When I took the job, I didn't even get given his name. And that's really nasty speaking about him like that. He's actually a good guy.' Her chest burned at the words. They were true. He'd always been good to her.

'Pa,' Lee muttered. 'I bet you thought he was good. I saw the pictures.'

Carys cringed. She couldn't go through this again.

'So, you're set up nicely in his mansion, are you?'

'No. I don't work for him anymore. I'm living on the Isle of Mull with… my mum.'

Kat's forehead creased first, then Lee screwed up his face and cracked his knuckles. Even the kids who'd been chattering in the living room or thumping around the bedrooms had gone quiet.

'Your mum?' he said. 'Do you mean that bitch? After all the years I protected you from her bloody interference. That's it, where does she live?' He muscled towards Carys.

She threw up her hands and put them against his thick chest. 'Stop. You aren't going to do anything to her. She is not a bitch. I know what you did to her. Both of you.' She glanced at Kat. 'You demonised her and we both suffered because of it. You've done enough. Now leave her alone. Let us be happy. She was always my mum and you had no right to separate us. I could have been happy with both of you, even if you weren't together. Like we can be now if you let us.'

Kat took hold of Lee's arm. 'Let her go. Let them both go. They can be miserable together.'

'Fine,' said Lee. 'If that's what you want. Kat's right. Go and live with her. You'll soon see what a mistake it was.'

Carys nodded. She briefly poked her head around the doors, saying hi to her half-siblings. They all looked grim. She would have hugged them goodbye but her dad had too fierce an expression in his eyes and Kat glared like she'd commit murder if Carys went too close to the kids.

Carys's shoulders slumped and she breathed the city air as her feet hit the street. She stood still for a few seconds, taking stock. The irony of Kat and her dad's words clanged around. They actually thought she'd be more miserable with Joanne than here?

Back in the car, Carys buckled up and Joanne pulled off. Ewan twisted around in his seat. 'Did it go ok?'

'Who knows?' said Carys with a shrug. 'My dad has some strange ideas.' She caught Joanne's eye in the rear-view mirror and the silent glance said it all.

Half an hour later, they pulled up at the SECC and spent as long waiting in the queue for the car park. After finally getting a space, they made their way along the riverside to the entrance and through the automatic doors into the central concourse. Joanne fingered the tickets, eyeing Carys as they jostled through the crowds to arena five. Carys wanted to assure her she was fine, but she wasn't convinced that was true. Her dad could be brutal but he was still her dad and her heart crumpled at the thought of him hating her now. She'd never meant to fail him but his ideas of what constituted success and failure were at loggerheads with hers.

The indoor arena was set up like a stage, with podiums and huge grandstand-style seating all around. Their seats were midway up the front section. Joanne sat next to Carys, clamping a programme to her lap. Carys had a funny feeling she didn't want her to see it. 'I hope this doesn't get too boring for Rowan,' she said. 'But some of it will be good for him to hear.'

'Can I see the programme?' said Carys, diving for it.

Joanne held it fast. 'What? Oh…'

Carys seized it and flicked through. Her eyes fell on the final speaker; a black-and-white photograph of a familiar face smiled back at her. A swirly blue and red pattern separated his picture from a brief blurb with the heading. *Keynote speaker, Troy Copeland. On overcoming undiagnosed dyslexia as an adult.*

'Did you know about this?' said Carys. 'I thought he'd pulled out?'

'What?' Joanne looked at the picture. 'Oh. I hope they haven't made a mistake. I'm sure I let them know he wasn't coming.'

'That's a pretty big mistake,' said Carys. 'They've printed all these programmes?'

'Oh dear,' said Joanne, though she didn't appear too worried. A slight smile was playing on her lips.

Carys narrowed her eyes. Something was going on. And if Troy was here? Was he? Could he be? What had instigated this U-turn? But there were four speakers to get through first. Carys's upper arms felt like they were being attacked by pins and her shoulders shook. Troy was here. The last time she'd seen him, she'd been naked in body and soul. All his and he'd been hers. What now? How could she face him? Even from this distance, she'd be visible. He would guess she was here. He knew Joanne was coming and it would logically follow.

Joanne turned to look at her, then swung her arm around Carys's shoulder. 'Don't worry, darling girl,' she said. 'Whatever happens, we've found each other.'

'I know, Mum, I know.'

Carys rested on Joanne and shed a few tears for her dad, Kat and her siblings. A few more for what she'd almost had with Troy. Then she wiped them away as Joanne kissed the top of her head and smiled through them. Joanne was right. She'd already achieved the impossible and found herself a mum at twenty-four – if that didn't count for something, she didn't know what did.

Chapter Thirty

Troy

Troy paced backstage, biting at his lips and running his palms down his jeans. This was more nerve-wracking than any football match he'd ever played. The stadium at Hampden Park held thousands more than this, but these people were going to see something completely new and way out of his comfort zone.

Press conferences were bad enough. He was notorious for hiding behind his baseball cap and spouting monosyllabic answers and wisecracks. Now he was dressed in his smartest jeans, a whiter than white shirt, and people were expecting him to string words together into coherent sentences. Jesus Christ, he must have been insane to think this was a good idea.

'So, Mr Copeland.' A woman approached him with a clipboard. 'You're up in ten minutes, assuming Charmaine sticks to her time. Now, because of the nature of your announcement, we're keeping the speakers and the foundation president on the stage until the end.'

'Great.' Whether it was actually great or an added pressure, Troy couldn't decide but it was too late to worry. Ten minutes. Just ten minutes. He had his notes laid out the way Fenella Hansen had shown him all those months ago. Each section was assigned a picture to remind him where to go next. If he took it slowly, he could do this. It was like putting one past the Juventus goalie in his last international. He could pull it out of the bag when he had to. He just had to keep his eyes on the prize.

Head down, he trudged onto the stage, but the warm applause fell like music on his ears. This wasn't the wild, expectant, hopeful, determined, and sometimes desperate chants of the football crowds he thrived on. Appreciative vibes flowed from the audience and he glanced up and smiled, responding to their welcome with a wave. He took the podium and waited for the applause to die out and the president to introduce him.

His moment had arrived. Never in a million years would he have pictured his life panning out like this and yet, here he was. He adjusted the collar of his crisp white shirt and breathed in and out very deliberately.

'Thank you,' said the president, 'for that wonderful welcome. I'm not going to waste any time telling you about the young man on the stage with me because his record speaks for itself. I'd like to say how delighted we are to have him here today, sharing for the first time publicly his struggles with undiagnosed dyslexia both as a child and an adult. So, without further ado, over to you, Troy.'

Troy nodded as a second round of applause started. 'Thank you,' he said, and the clapping subsided. 'It's an honour for me to be here today.' His voice was even and steady, much to his surprise, and it rang low and clear from the speakers. 'So, I'd like to start by saying, I've now been officially diagnosed with dyslexia and I was super surprised at how painless it was.' Spurred on by the laughs, he looked up. 'Yeah, the test itself was a formality really, something I wanted for myself.' He paused. 'I've just turned thirty-one and it's brought home a few truths. For over twenty years, I've lived with this. In my early years, as is true for most kids, it's hard to tell if there's an issue other than time. We all learn at our own pace; some pick up reading and writing quicker than others. But by mid-primary, the gaps start to show. That's when I first noticed it, but I didn't know it was an underlying condition. I was a kid, kids don't know any better.'

He took a deep breath and skimmed over the crowd. An all too familiar face drew his eyes like a homing beacon. He gave a brief smile, examined his notes and continued. 'I simply thought I was stupid.' The crowd murmured. 'And that was how I was made to feel. By other pupils, teachers and even sometimes my family. Recently, when I told my parents for the first time about my dyslexia, my dad said there wasn't any point in giving people labels. But I already had a label. I'd been labelled as thick and the class clown since I was in primary three.'

With a nod, he let the reaction sink in. 'Like I told my dad, there's nothing wrong with a label as long as it isn't a badge of shame. It should be an acknowledgement of the extra hard work a person is going to have to put into their life. Because life with dyslexia is hard. I didn't get the right label, so I spent my life hiding. Now, you might think becoming a professional footballer isn't a good way to hide, but I was one of the lucky ones. I had other skills and talents to get me through. But the shame was still with me. I changed from the class clown to the team clown, the bad boy who would do anything to get out of writing suggestions on the board. The one who insisted my agent fill out all the forms, pretending they were too trivial for me when, really, I just couldn't do it. I gained a reputation that didn't actually fit the real me.'

He paused and took a sip of water. 'My life literally turned into a car crash this time last year. Most of you will have heard the story. I was a passenger in an accident that could easily have been fatal. I was lucky to be alive, but I

241

didn't walk away unscathed. The accident has effectively ended my football career. The odd thing is, if I'd known and understood my dyslexia better, I might not have got into the position I found myself in. Because I saw myself as thick and stupid, I couldn't imagine another path. Football was all I could do. I've always been in denial about life after football and when that life was brought forward, I couldn't face it.'

Raising his eyes to Carys, he held her gaze for a second. The auditorium lights were low, and her expression was unclear, but her stare burned into his soul. He'd made peace with his decision and accepted the end of his career. Nothing was in the way now. She was everything.

'After my injury, I met a very special person,' he said, checking his notes, then looking straight back at her. 'And she's here now. Without her, I would never have accepted myself for who I am. She made me realise that it wasn't just my body that needed to heal. I sometimes laughed at her hippy ways, but she was right. She opened my eyes to my condition and got me help – help that should be available to everyone, without fear, without stigma. Her name is Carys McTeague.'

He zeroed in on her again. Carys lifted her hand to her lips and held it.

'Carys was my carer throughout my recovery and what I'm about to say next is all due to the incredible influence she had on me.'

Chapter Thirty-One

Carys

Carys held her breath behind her hand. Tears welled and soon they would spill out, no matter how much she tried to stop them. She dreaded what Troy was about to say but craved it too. Joanne took hold of her hand and squeezed it.

'I honestly never would have believed I'd be standing here now, talking to people about my struggles because I've been ashamed for a long time. Carys taught me to believe in myself. I always believed in my football skills, but she taught me to think out of the box, to see what I could achieve if I set my mind to it.' He lowered his head and smirked. 'You can imagine, I didn't welcome the idea with open arms. I'm stubborn and set in my ways. But then I remembered something she told me.' He looked at her and she froze. 'There are children out there in the same position as me. Children who don't want to speak up. Children who believe they're stupid when they're not. That's what I want to stop.' He glanced at the president, who nodded with a smile. 'It's my pleasure to announce that I'm taking on a new role as an ambassador for young people with dyslexia. With the uncertainty surrounding my career, it seems fitting that I have a life outside of football and this is something I understand and I'm passionate about.'

Carys stared at him and his gaze found hers. Her eyes misted over and she held her lips. Joanne gripped her hand. 'He's so lovely,' she said. 'This will make Rowan's day and so many other kids too.'

'I can't believe it,' said Carys, her voice hoarse. 'I never thought he'd do anything like this.'

'It's because of you,' said Joanne. 'Go and see him after.'

Carys shook her head.

'Yes. You have to.'

The president spoke again, detailing Troy's new role, and Troy leaned on the podium listening. He looked incredible in his smart shirt and dark jeans. As the audience clapped, he scanned around and smiled. When he caught Carys's eyes, he discreetly pointed with his thumb over his shoulder, passing it off as scratching his neck.

'You see,' said Joanne. 'That's him wanting to meet you. So go.'

The president gave his closing speech and Carys sat on the edge of her seat. When everyone rose to leave, she couldn't move.

Joanne took hold of her and pulled her to her feet, almost dragging her towards the exit. When they made it to the main concourse, the speakers were at a table swarmed by a crowd, and on one side, a throng of reporters with cameras and microphones were jostling around Troy. Cool as a cucumber, he wielded their questions with a smile, a far cry from the broody guy in the white hoody and the pulled-down baseball cap.

'Poor guy doesn't get a minute's peace,' said Ewan. 'Are you sure he'll want to see us?' he asked Joanne.

'Yes, he does. Well, not necessarily us, but definitely Carys.'

'Are you sure?' said Carys, though she knew. Her pulse raced.

Joanne cocked her head. 'Yes, because I know exactly how he feels about you. Why do you think you're here?'

'Because you asked me to come?'

'Because he asked me to bring you. He wanted you to hear this. And that's not all.'

'What do you mean?' Carys tried to play dumb. Her palms were sweating and her neck toasting.

'Keep moving forward,' said Joanne.

They inched their way through the crowd, jostling with hundreds of others until eventually they were close enough to Troy for him to see them.

He beamed and backed towards the stand, away from the reporters. Then he waved to Rowan and asked a few people to move out of the way. 'Hi, Rowan,' he said, putting his hands on his shoulders. 'This is a friend of mine,' he said. 'And meeting him helped me on my journey to coming clean about my dyslexia.'

Joanne smiled through her tears, and Ewan patted her arm. Troy beckoned Joanne and she joined them. The reporters started questioning them and a woman with a clipboard came and stood by them.

'I hope she's advising them what to say,' said Ewan. 'I don't want my private life spread across the tabloids. I mean, we all know what a racy life I have.'

'Shut up.' Carys grinned, smacking him on the arm, but her gaze had linked with Troy's. With a brief movement of his hand, he called her over. She didn't have a chance to hesitate as Ewan's large palm touched her back and propelled her forward. Troy moved to meet her and rested his hands on her shoulders.

'I'm sorry,' he said, leading her away from the crowd. 'For everything.'

'You don't have to be,' said Carys. 'It was me. I couldn't see what was right in front of me.'

'You did. You saw a man who loved you, but he thought he loved football more. I was wrong. I love you more than anything in the world. It just took me a long time to catch on. I thought I couldn't face the world without football, but really what I can't face is the world without you.'

Carys simultaneously wanted to laugh, to cry and to melt away into somewhere quieter than this. 'I feel the same,' she said. 'I want to be in your life, just not your crazy world. It scares me, but I'm more scared of losing you. I should have tried to reach you again, but I resigned myself to being on my own. I'm so used to people leaving and never getting too close.'

'I know,' he said. 'But you don't have to worry about that anymore because I'm coming back to Mull.'

'You are?'

'Yes.'

'But, Troy?'

'It's ok.' He sighed. 'I had to try. I know I was obsessed with proving to everyone I could do it but I had to prove it to myself too. I hold my hands up and admit it was a disaster. There might be a time for regrets, but it's not today. I have a new mission.'

'It's a great one,' said Carys.

He bent in. 'And it's not the only one.'

'What do you mean?'

'You and I are going to open that retreat.'

'We are?'

'If you want to.'

'Of course I do, but... why?'

'Because I want to. My agent told me to choose what makes me happy and I am. I choose you. I want to be part of your world and make it my world too.' He leaned even closer and Carys inhaled the expensive deodorant fresh from his skin on the warm gap where his shirt fell open.

She dipped forward so her forehead touched his chest. He kissed the top of her head and lights flashed all around. Looking up, she spotted cameras everywhere. Had everyone heard? Her heart pounded. She glanced at Troy.

A grin spread across his face and he leaned in and kissed her full on the lips. The shock was soon overcome with giggly surprise and she laughed onto his mouth as he kissed her. Probably the most ridiculous kiss ever and all caught on camera for the entire world to see, but it didn't matter.

'Winning the cup final has nothing on this,' Troy said, peeking up and beaming at the reporters.

A hundred questions fired at him and he shook his head. 'All in good time. Yes, this is Carys McTeague, the woman who inspired me to take my new path.'

'Are you together?' asked a reporter.

'And are you pleased that you've ended his career?' said another aggressively.

Carys raised her eyebrow, and as Troy went to speak, she put up her hand to stop him. 'Do you have any idea what it's like for someone who's suffered multiple compound fractures in a car accident? For someone to even walk again after that? Troy's career ended when that car went off the road. All I did was show him a different path. But we're here to talk about dyslexia and its impact on young people. If you want to ask about that, then do. Save the lies.'

Troy looked like he was trying not to laugh. The reporter shrugged but Carys supposed she'd write some rubbish anyway.

'You can put that on record though,' said Troy. 'I never thought I'd love anything or anyone more than football...' He glanced at Carys. 'Until I met you.'

The gaggle of questions started again and cameras flashed.

Margaret Amatt

Troy held up his hand. 'That's enough questions for now. You can address any other issues through the society.'

He swung his arm around Carys and they regrouped with Joanne, Ewan and Rowan. The paps lingered like a bad smell, but Troy put his back to them. 'Shall we go back to the house and order a takeaway?' said Troy.

'Your house?' said Rowan. 'Aren't we going to a hotel?'

'No,' said Joanne. 'It was a surprise.'

'Hang on,' said Carys. 'This was all planned?'

'Yes,' said Troy.

'But what if—'

'If you'd said no?' said Troy.

'Well, yes.'

'I would have paid for a hotel. I still will if you'd rather do that.'

They all stared at her. She half-rolled her eyes, then laughed. 'Of course not.'

Troy took her hand and led her to the Porsche. Joanne, Ewan and Rowan headed towards their own car with Rowan beaming from ear to ear. 'We're going to another of his mansions,' he said, loudly enough for them to hear.

'Somebody's excited,' said Troy.

'Are you sure about this?' Carys asked.

He stopped. 'Why wouldn't I be?'

'I don't know. I'm not used to people sticking around. I reunited with Mum and now you. I guess I just can't believe it'll work out.'

'I should never have left Mull. I should have stayed with you but my mind was so stuck on my career I couldn't see what was good for me.' He held her gaze. 'That's you. You're what's good for me. I walked away from the most important signing of my life. The one I should have signed last year. The one that makes sure you and me stick together.'

Carys let out a contented sigh. The unreachable stars had got a whole lot closer.

He shook his head. 'I made a mistake. I didn't want to let people down but in doing that I let us down.'

'Do we really have a future? You won't be tempted back to the bright lights?'

His soft laugh tickled her. 'All I want is you. I might need to go to occasional dyslexia events around the country, but when I do, you can come with me or stay with your mum, your family, our family.'

Carys nodded. 'It sounds too good to be true.'

'You deserve it. You deserve to be happy and if I can help with that, I will. I promise. You were my prop when I needed it and I'm ready to return the favour any way I can.'

Carys took both his hands. 'I love you, Troy. I have done for a long time.'

He dropped his gaze. 'Yeah, that whole employer thing was tricky, huh.'

'I didn't want to cross a line.'

'Me neither. But now it's ok. If we're going to cross lines, we can do it together. We can do everything and anything.'

'As long as we're together.'

'Exactly. And let's hope that's for a very very long time.' He dipped in and kissed her again. With no reporters or cameras flashing, Carys relaxed and felt the weight of the world drift off her shoulders. Dreams lay ahead but they weren't up in the air and out of reach. They were right here, waiting to be lived.

Epilogue

Troy

Carys's face was a picture every time she spied another article about them. Troy grinned as she stared wide-eyed at the iPad screen, sometimes grimacing, other times her lips curling up with a tinge of pink on her cheeks. From behind her on the balcony of their Mull mansion, the turquoise sea sprawled out, providing a glorious backdrop.

'They're still making stuff up about me,' said Carys

'Don't worry,' said Troy, propping his sketchbook on his knee and doodling. How weird was it doing this without having to hide it? 'It'll die out eventually.' The latest rush of interest had flared up because he'd finally made his statement about retiring from football once and for all. With July in full flow, they'd spent so much time imagining how the retreat would work when it opened the following summer, Troy had almost forgotten his past life. Almost. Football was in his soul and it would never go away. But new beginnings were exciting too. This was his home now and, in the spirit of community, he was coaching the kids' football team. It couldn't ever replace his life as a pro, but learning different skills was so demanding it didn't leave time for regrets.

Carys peered up and sighed. 'I just worry,' she said.

'Come here.' He laid aside his drawing. She put down the iPad and moved over to sit in his lap. He held her, running his hands over her, relishing every inch of her. 'Honestly, I'll become old news soon and everything will be fine. Even your dad quite likes me now, I think.'

Carys snorted. 'Only because your money bought them a new house. They don't really deserve it. He's never worked a day in his life.'

'I know. But he's your dad. And I know what he did for you when you were a child. Even if he's done nothing in between, he looked out for you when you needed him and that has to count for something.'

'Yup, that was his good deed for life.'

'And that good deed meant you grew up to be who you are. It meant you were thrown into my path and if you hadn't been, then god knows where I'd be. Maybe I'd never have walked again. Your care got me through.'

Troy saw in Carys's eyes the fear she still carried that one day, he'd up and leave. Nothing he said took it wholly away.

'Did you ever write to the people in the care home?' he asked.

'Yes. I forgot to say I had a lovely reply from Mrs Dowey. She's so excited that someone she knows is living with a famous footballer. Apparently, it's almost as exciting as when she met the queen in 1972.'

Troy chuckled into Carys's neck. 'You seriously are the most gorgeous person ever.'

The sun stayed high in the sky all day and the following day was equally as bright. Carys scuttled around outside, trimming bushes and making the front steps ooze with appeal. Troy couldn't help laughing; anyone would have thought royalty was coming. He did as Carys had instructed and dressed in his formal kilt and jacket. Gaping at himself in the mirror, he pulled a face as Carys sauntered in.

'I look like I'm going to a wedding,' he said. 'Are you sure I wouldn't be better in my normal clothes?'

'You look good in everything,' said Carys, sidling up and slipping her arms under his jacket.

'So do you.' He kissed her gently. 'But are you sure your hands aren't mucky? You've been in the garden so long.'

'Scrubbed.' She pulled them out and waggled her fingers. 'Now, I have to get dressed too.'

'I still don't get why I need the kilt,' said Troy.

'Because this retreat will be advertised globally and people from outside Scotland like to see Scottish men in kilts.'

'Do they?'

'God yes. Why do you think those tartan army nutters go around football matches in Europe wearing kilts?'

'Still not sure.'

'Because they think they'll pull lots of hot girls if they rock up in kilts. Men in kilts sell almost as well as women in bikinis.'

'So, are you wearing a bikini for the photoshoot?'

'Don't be ridiculous,' said Carys, slipping on a long white maxi dress. How alarmingly like a wedding dress could it look? They were going to be like a bride and groom. Troy frowned as he eyed her and the cogs in his brain mulled over a new plan.

'Ok,' he said. 'Let's do this.'

They strolled outside hand in hand as a pink van covered in bright floral decals pulled up the driveway. 'Georgia is a bit mad, isn't she?' Troy said.

Carys laughed. 'I like her and she's a really talented photographer. Her wedding was beautiful. She had on a short nineteen-fifties tea dress and she looked so lovely and so happy. You'd love the big house on the estate.'

'The vegetable place,' said Troy with a smirk. 'I remember.'

'She has a gallery in the grounds. It's a weird place, like an upturned boat, but she has some great photos and she's willing to display some of your doodles.'

'Seriously?' said Troy. 'You asked her that? You're so awesome.' He beamed at her, his mind racing towards his latest goal.

*

Carys

Georgia got out of the van and beamed a bright red, ear-to-ear smile. 'You two look fab,' she said, retrieving a large bag from her passenger seat. 'So, where do you want me to shoot you?'

Troy raised his eyebrow, but Carys pointed at the steps. 'Can we start here? It would look good to have us at the entrance.' She bit her lip and glanced at Troy. It was odd but tingly, saying 'us'. The dream was working out but seemed surreal and transient. What was to stop Troy from jumping ship at any moment?

'Are you ok?' he asked.

She nodded.

'Ok,' said Georgia. 'Let me fiddle about here for a moment until I get the best angle with the house in the background.'

'What is it?' Troy frowned at Carys.

'I don't know. Maybe I shouldn't be in the picture. It's your house.'

'Carys.' Troy took her hands. 'What's mine is yours. This dream is yours. I want to live it too, but I want to live it with you. There's no way I'm going to be in these pictures on my own. We're a team. A couple. I love you and I don't want to do any of this alone.'

She smiled, but her heart pumped a little too fast. She wanted to believe. *I really do.* 'Ok. Let's do it.'

'Right, can you stand at the top of the steps there?' said Georgia. 'I need to check the light's in the right place.'

Troy shuffled closer and put his arm about Carys.

'You're so tall,' said Georgia, squinting up at Troy.

'And I'm so short,' said Carys.

'Well, you're not much shorter than me,' said Georgia, 'but compared to Troy, yes. If you stood one step down… Let me see what that's like. It might look odd.'

Troy stepped down and Carys grinned. He was still just taller.

'I have an idea,' he said.

'Ok,' said Georgia. 'Go for it, show me.'

He returned to the top step and took both Carys's hands in his.

'How is this helping?' said Carys.

He didn't reply, but with one fluid movement, he got down on one knee. For a second Carys was so impressed by the mobility that, a few months earlier had seemed light years away, she almost didn't grasp what was happening. Until he increased the pressure on her hands and gazed into her eyes.

'Carys, the most special person I've ever had in my life.'

The camera clicked but Carys barely heard it. All her senses were focused on Troy.

'I'd like to seal the bond between us forever by asking you to be my wife.'

'Oh my god.' Carys's hands were pinned in Troy's, otherwise she'd have pinched herself. Had he really just proposed? Tears pushed their way up, threatening to spill over into a wash of happiness. She sniffed them back and raised her eyes to the heavens, letting gravity rein in the tears. 'Yes, Troy,' she said, looking back.

'Aw,' said Georgia, and the camera clicked again.

Troy smiled. 'And I'll never leave you. This is it, Carys. I swear, we'll be together as long as we're both alive. I don't want you ever to worry about that again.'

She tugged his hands. Before he stood, he turned to Georgia. 'I hope you got a picture of that. That's something I definitely don't mind photos of.'

With a watery smile, she put up her thumb. 'I got it.'

'You believe me?' he asked Carys, standing tall again. Carys bobbed her head.

'I do. I can hardly believe it's happened, but I believe *you*.' She pushed onto tiptoes and captured Troy's lips. So much had happened in the last year. It seemed just hours ago she'd been organising Zimmer-Zumba, now she was being proposed to by Troy Copeland and kissing him on the steps of their island retreat. Who on earth would have predicted that? Troy had kicked the curveball and suckered it straight in her tummy.

The camera clicked and she embraced the sound. These pictures weren't going anywhere but they would always be a reminder of what really was a striking result for them both.

The End

Share the Love!

If you enjoyed reading this book, then please share your reviews online.

Leaving reviews is a perfect way to support authors and helps books reach more readers.

So please review and share!

Let me know what you think.

Margaret

About the author

I'm a writer, mummy, wife and chocolate eater (in any order you care to choose). I live in highland Perthshire in a little house close to the woods where I often see red squirrels, deer and other such tremendously Scottish wildlife... Though not normally haggises or even men in kilts!

It's my absolute pleasure to be able to bring the Scottish Island Escapes series to you and I hope you love reading the stories as much as I enjoy writing them. Writing is an escapist joy for me and I adore disappearing into my imagination and returning with a new story to tell.

If you want to keep up with what's coming next or learn more about any of the books or the series, then be sure to visit my website. I look forward to seeing you there.

www.margaretamatt.com

Acknowledgements

Thanks goes to my adorable husband for supporting my dreams and putting up with my writing talk 24/7. Also to my son, whose interest in my writing always makes me smile. It's precious to know I've passed the bug to him – he's currently writing his own fantasy novel and instruction books on how to build Lego!

Throughout the writing process, I have gleaned help from many sources and met some fabulous people. I'd like to give a special mention to Stéphanie Ronckier, my beta reader extraordinaire. Stéphanie's continued support with my writing is invaluable and I love the fact that I need someone French to correct my grammar! Stéphanie, you rock. To my fellow authors, Evie Alexander and Lyndsey Gallagher – you girls are the best! I love it that you always have my back and are there to help when I need you.

Also, a huge thanks to my editor, Aimee Walker, at Aimee Walker Editorial Services for her excellent work on my novels and for answering all my mad questions. Thank you so much, Aimee!

More Books by Margaret Amatt

Scottish Island Escapes

Season 1
A Winter Haven
A Spring Retreat
A Summer Sanctuary
An Autumn Hideaway
A Christmas Bluff
Season 2
A Flight of Fancy
A Hidden Gem
A Striking Result
A Perfect Discovery
A Festive Surprise

Free Hugs & Old-Fashioned Kisses

Do you ever get one of those days when you just fancy snuggling up? Then this captivating short story is for you!
And what's more, it's free when you sign up to my newsletter.
Meet Livvi, a girl who just needs a hug. And Jakob, a guy who doesn't go about hugging random strangers. But what if he makes an exception, just this once?
Make yourself a hot chocolate, sign up to my newsletter and enjoy!
A short story only available to newsletter subscribers.

Sign up at
www.margaretamatt.com

A Winter Haven

She was the one that got away. Now she's back.

Career-driven Robyn Sherratt returns to her childhood home on the Scottish Isle of Mull, hoping to build bridges with her estranged family. She discovers her mother struggling to run the family hotel. When an old flame turns up, memories come back to bite, nibbling into Robyn's fragile heart.

Carl Hansen, known as The Fixer, abandoned city life for peace and tranquillity. Swapping his office for a log cabin, he mends people's broken treasures. He can fix anything, except himself. When forced to work on hotel renovations with Robyn, the girl he lost twelve years ago, his quiet life is sent spinning.

Carl would like nothing more than to piece together the shattered shards of Robyn's heart. But can she trust him? What can a broken man like him offer a successful woman like her?

A Spring Retreat

She's gritty, he's determined. Who will back down first?

When spirited islander Beth McGregor learns of plans to build a road through the family farm, she sets out to stop it. But she's thrown off course by the charming and handsome project manager. Sparks fly, sending Beth into a spiral of confusion. Guys are fine as friends. Nothing else.

Murray Henderson has finally found a place to retreat from the past with what seems like a straightforward job. But he hasn't reckoned on the stubbornness of the locals, especially the hot-headed and attractive Beth.

As they battle together over the proposed road, attraction blooms. Murray strives to discover the real Beth; what secrets lie behind the tough façade? Can a regular farm girl like her measure up to Murray's impeccable standards, and perhaps find something she didn't know she was looking for?

A Summer Sanctuary

She's about to discover the one place he wants to keep

secret

Five years ago, Island girl Kirsten McGregor broke the company rules. Now, she has the keys to the Hidden Mull tour bus and is ready to take on the task of running the business. But another tour has arrived. The competition is bad enough but when she recognises the rival tour operator, her plans are upended.

Former jet pilot Fraser Bell has made his share of mistakes. What better place to hide and regroup than the place he grew to love as a boy? With great enthusiasm, he launches into his new tour business, until old-flame Kirsten shows up and sends his world plummeting.

Kirsten may know all the island's secrets, but what she can't work out is Fraser. With tension simmering, Kirsten and Fraser's attraction increases. What if they both made a mistake before? Is one of them about to make an even bigger one now?

An Autumn Hideaway

She went looking for someone, but it wasn't him.

After a string of disappointments for chirpy city girl Autumn, discovering her notoriously unstable mother has run off again is the last straw. When Autumn learns her mother's last known whereabouts was a remote Scottish Island, she makes the rash decision to go searching for her.

Taciturn islander Richard has his reasons for choosing the remote Isle of Mull as home. He's on a deadline and doesn't need any complications or company. But everything changes after a chance encounter with Autumn.

Autumn chips away at Richard's reserve until his carefully constructed walls start to crumble. But Autumn's just a passing visitor and Richard has no plans to leave. Will they realise, before it's too late, that what they've been searching for isn't necessarily what's missing?

A Christmas Bluff

She's about to trespass all over his Christmas.

Artist and photographer Georgia Rose has spent two carefree years on the Isle of Mull and is looking forward to a quiet Christmas... Until she discovers her family is about to descend upon her, along with her past.

Aloof aristocrat Archie Crichton-Leith has let out his island mansion to a large party from the mainland. They're expecting a castle for Christmas, not an outdated old pile, and he's in trouble.

When Georgia turns up with an irresistible smile and an offer he can't refuse, he's wary, but he needs her help.

As Georgia weaves her festive charms around the house, they start to work on Archie too. And the spell extends both ways. But falling in love was never part of the deal. Can the magic outlast Christmas when he's been conned before and she has a secret that could ruin everything?

A Flight of Fancy

She's masquerading as her twin, pretending to be his

girlfriend, while really just being herself.

After years of being cooped up by her movie star family, Taylor Rousse is desperate to escape. Having a Hollywood actress as a twin is about all Taylor can say for herself, but when she's let down by her sister for the umpteenth time, she decides now is the time for action.

Pilot Magnus Hansen is heading back to his family home on the Isle of Mull for his brother's wedding and he's not looking forward to showing up single. The eldest of three brothers shouldn't be the last married – no matter how often he tells himself he's not the marrying type.

On his way, Magnus crashes into a former fling. She's a Hollywood star looking for an escape and they strike a deal: he's her ticket to a week of peace; she's his new date. Except Taylor isn't who he thinks she is. When she and Magnus start to fall for each other, their double deception threatens to blow up in their faces and shatter everything that might have been.

266

A Hidden Gem

She has a secret past. He has an uncertain future.

Together, can they unlock them both?

After being framed for embezzlement by her ex, career-driven Rebekah needs a break to nurse her broken heart and wounded soul. When her grandmother dies, leaving her a precious necklace and a mysterious note, she sets out to unravel a family secret that's been hidden for over sixty years.

Blair has lived all his life on the Isle of Mull. He's everybody's friend – with or without the benefits – but at night he goes home alone. When Rebekah arrives, he's instantly attracted to her, but she's way out of his league. He needs to keep a stopper on his feelings or risk losing her friendship.

As Rebekah's quest continues, she's rocked by unexpected feelings for her new friend. Can she trust her heart as much as she trusts Blair? And can he be more than just a friend? Perhaps the truth isn't the only thing waiting to be found.

A Striking Result

She's about to tackle everything he's trying to hide.

When unlucky-in-love Carys McTeague is offered the job of caring for an injured footballer, she goes for it even though it's far removed from the world she's used to.

Scottish football hero Troy Copeland is at the centre of a media storm after a serious accident left him with career-threatening injuries and his fiancée dumped him for a teammate. With a little persuasion from Carys, he flees to the remote Isle of Mull to escape and recuperate.

On Mull, Carys reconnects with someone unexpected from her past and starts to fall in love with the island – and Troy. But nothing lasts forever. Carys has been abandoned more than once and as soon as Troy's recovered, he'll leave like everyone else.

Troy's smitten by Carys but has a career to preserve. Will he realise he's been chasing the wrong goal before he loses the love of his life?

A Perfect Discovery

To find love, they need to dig deep.

Kind-hearted archaeologist Rhona Lamond returns home to the Isle of Mull after her precious research is stolen, feeling lost and frustrated. When an island project comes up, it tugs at Rhona's soul and she's desperate to take it on. But there's a major problem.

Property developer Calum Matheson has a longstanding feud with the Lamond family. After a plot of land he owns is discovered to be a site of historical importance, his plans are thrown into disarray and building work put on hold.

Calum doesn't think things can get any worse, until archaeologist Rhona turns up. Not only is she a Lamond, but she's all grown up, and even stubbornly unromantic Calum can't fail to notice her – or the effect she has on him.

Their attraction ignites but how can they overcome years of hate between their families? Both must decide what's more important, family or love.

A Festive Surprise

She can't abide Christmas. He's not sure what it's all

about. Together they're in for a festive surprise.

Ambitious software developer Holly may have a festive name but the connection ends there. She despises the holiday season and decides to flee to the remote island of Mull in a bid to escape from it.

Syrian refugee Farid has made a new home in Scotland but he's lonely. Understanding Nessie and Irn Bru is one thing, but when glittery reindeer and tinsel hit the shelves, he's completely bemused. Determined to understand a new culture, he asks his new neighbour to educate him on all things Christmas.

When Holly reluctantly agrees, he realises there's more to her hatred of mince pies and mulled wine than meets the eye. Farid makes it his mission to inject some joy into Hollys' life but falling for her is an unexpected gift that was never on his list.

As their attraction sparkles, can Christmas work its magic on Holly and Farid, or will their spark fizzle out with the end of December